REBEKAH L. PURDY

LEGEND OF ME by Rebekah L. Purdy
All rights reserved. Published in the United States of America by Month9Books, LLC.
No part of this book may be used or reproduced in any manner whatsoever without written permission of the publisher, except in the case of brief quotations embodied in critical articles and reviews.

EPub ISBN: 978-1-946700-89-6
Mobi ISBN: 978-1-946700-90-2
Trade Paperback ISBN: 978-1-946700-88-9

Published by Month9Books, Raleigh, NC 27609
Cover design by A M Design Studios

Month9Books

To Fran, Georgia, and Rachel without whom this book wouldn't have happened.

Prologue

Darkness spilled across the sky like wine on a tablecloth as silhouettes slithered over the grass toward Margaret Shepherdess. She shivered, pulling her cloak tighter. Her gaze shifted to the sheep dotting the hillside then to the tree line separating the woods from the pastures. A lamb darted away from the forest border; its bleating cries broke through the stillness as it ran across the open field, its legs nearly buckling beneath it.

Margaret jumped. Her fingers tightened around her wooden staff, heart thundering in her ears. She listened intently as her hand moved to the slingshot secured beneath her belt, but all she heard was the incessant croak of frogs

Thick clouds drifted overhead, blotting out of the moon. The whole pasture sank into shadow. The frogs went silent. A branch snapped in the forest and Margaret froze.

"Myron Stable Hand, if you're trying to scare me, it's not going to work." Margaret twisted around. Her eyes followed the edge of the woodland, but it was too dark to see anything. "Myron. You can come out now."

She took a hesitant step toward the trees. The odor of rotten meat clung to the air and she covered her mouth as acid seared the back of her throat. Perhaps it was a deer carcass.

A low guttural growl sounded, followed by a loud crash. Margaret stumbled back, trying to free her slingshot. *Wolves, it must be wolves.* No wonder the sheep ran to higher ground. Goose pimples prickled her skin as her pulse quickened. At last, lunar beams pierced the cloud cover. She screamed.

An elongated face, filled with teeth gnashed at the air in front of her. Dirty rags hung from an emaciated body and the stench of death filled her nostrils. Claws slashed Margaret's chest, ripping her flesh. Blood seeped through her dress as she scrambled to get away.

Margaret's shrieks pierced the night as the beast tore through her back. The angry chomp of fangs crunched down on her bones. She fell to the ground, unable to move. Her nails dug into the dirt, the pain increasing with every moment. Her frantic cries for help echoed as panic took hold, but no one came. Soon only the sound of gurgling came from her lips as she fought for breath.

The creature flipped her over with long gnarled fingers. Scarlet eyes burned like hellish fires. With a howl, the monster sank its dagger sharp teeth into her neck, shredding the soft tissue. When it pulled back, flesh hung from its mouth like strands of wet string.

Warm blood ran from Margaret's body in a crimson river. Tears trickled down her face. Her last vision was of the beast, hovering over her, and a strange ghostly figure of a woman standing behind it.

"The beast has come again," the woman whispered. *"He is almost here."*

Then all went dark.

Chapter One

"Gram, I'm home." I stepped into the dim light bathing the interior of our cabin in buttery yellows.

She stood stooped over the hearth, shoving something into the fire, muttering words beneath her breath I couldn't hear, but they sounded an awful lot like something from one of her "healing" books.

Her fingers glowed light blue with tiny sparks of magic.

Gram had talents most people only dreamt of. Most of which dealt with the ability to heal people. I hoped to one day follow in her footsteps. But so far, my own abilities were beyond my control. I'd been her apprentice since I was a child. I did well enough as a healer, but it was my visions that were more dominant. The problem was I couldn't always tell the difference between a regular dream and a premonition.

"Gram?"

She jumped and spun to face me. "Good heavens, Brielle, you 'bout gave me a scare."

I laughed, staring at her heavily wrinkled face. Her gray hair hung in a thick braid down her back and over a flowered dress worn with age.

She raised an eyebrow at me. "Did Rhyne Butcher walk you home again?"

I fidgeted with my basket as I set it on the table. *Here we go again.* "Yes."

"Some days I believe that boy is enamored with you. If you two weren't such close friends, I think he'd consider proposing at the festival, if only to get his father off his back."

Rhyne was my best friend. And to be honest, I'd never felt the sparks with him that other people talked about. There was only one man to garner those types of feelings, and I hadn't seen him in months.

Lately all anyone in the village had been talking about was the coming festival, and the marriage engagements that always accompanied it, but I was still hoping for a way to get out of going. Because all it would do was remind me how different I was from everyone else.

"You know how I feel about marriage," I said. "I have more important things to focus on." Although, that wasn't the complete truth, even I wasn't totally immune to the thought of falling in love.

She laughed. "Yes, you do. There's so much more to teach you about healing. If you're going to eventually take over for me, you must dedicate yourself to your studies." She watched me for a moment, then said, "There might come a time when you change your mind about romance. If that day comes, just remember what I taught you. You don't need a man to take care of you, Brielle. You're strong enough on your own."

I figured some of her push for me to stay single must have had something to do with whatever had happened between her and my grandfather—a subject she spoke little about, but when she did, the memory seemed painful.

Besides, she was right. My parents had died when I was a baby, too young to remember them. Me and Gram had lived on our own ever since. I saw no need to change that by getting married just because everyone else said I "should."

I went to the cabinet by the washbasin and pulled out two wooden bowls for dinner. "Sarah Weaver has shown a lot of interest in Rhyne lately."

She frowned. "That girl is a ninny. A spoiled child who could use a good whippin'. Lord knows what she expects anyone to see in her, least of all Rhyne. She falls in love with a new boy every week."

I snorted. "Ninny or not, her parents run this town. What Sarah wants, Sarah gets. And she wants Rhyne."

Fortunately, Rhyne looked to have his heart set on Gertie, not Sarah. If Sarah did manage to gain his attentions though, I wouldn't stand in his way. I'd tell him what I thought, then I'd be there as his friend, no matter what happened. Because who was I to say who he should or should not fall in love with?

I myself would likely end up an old maid, living alone in our cabin in the woods. Which would suit me just fine. Or at least that's what I told myself, but if a certain Wanderer named Raul asked to call on me, I wouldn't say no. Although, I was sure Gram would. She didn't let any suitors within a stone's throw of me.

Gram stirred the flames, and I noticed my blue dress sleeve charring on a log.

"Why are you burning my dress?" I shrieked. "You just made it for me."

"Well, you got stains all over the front of it."

"No, I didn't."

"Yes you did. No point in hanging on to an old rag. You want to be presentable, don't you?" She grabbed a couple of more chunks of wood and tossed them into the fire. "I've got to deliver this sleeping medicine to Michael Archer for his wife. You stay inside and don't be letting any strangers into the house."

"But I was supposed to meet up with Rhyne at the creek. He had to drop a cart of vegetables off for Peter Farmer."

"Fine, but go no farther than the creek. And bring that basket of fruit and vegetables so you can wash them off." She eyed me for a moment, then said, "And I meant what I said. Don't let any strangers in the house. In fact, don't talk to anyone you don't know."

"Any strangers I should be worried about?"

She looked at me for a few seconds, as though considering what to tell me. Or how much. "You'll be fine. Just remember what I said."

In one abrupt motion, Gram was out the door, her cloak pulled tight against her.

What'd got into her? Why was she burning our clothes and using magic to do so? And since when did I need to be reminded about strangers?

With a sigh, I grabbed my things and hurried out into the woods.

The cool stream kissed my ankles as I bent to scrub the vegetables, the water whispering as it slid over the rocks. The scent of honeysuckle reminded me summer was in full swing. I sighed in contentment as I tossed the fresh garden vegetables into my basket.

I swept my blond hair from my face and tucked it behind my ear. At least out here, I didn't have to keep it tied back.

The sound of a twig snapping disturbed the silence and made me go still. I shivered as my eyes darted back and forth over the woodland. The birds stopped chirping. Everything was quiet. Too quiet.

"Hello?" The hair on the back of my neck pickled, and I stepped out of the creek.

Two dead rabbits sailed through the air and fell at my feet. A shriek caught on my lips.

"Told you I'd find you." Rhyne leaned his bow against a nearby tree, and hung his game on a low branch.

I went straight to him, grabbed hold of his tunic, and gave him a good shake. "Rhyne Butcher, you are a pain in the arse!"

"And here I thought you'd have crept away to see if the Wanderers had come back to town," he said. "Like you normally do when they come around."

The Wanderers were a nomadic group that traveled to different towns performing shows, both acrobatic and otherwise, as well as selling trinkets from different, exotic lands. Some of them even told fortunes, for a price.

"I heard from Bartholomew Mason that a certain Roma man is amongst them. He mentioned seeing that 'Gypsy scoundrel's' carriage pull in late last night."

Heat flared across my cheeks. "Raul? He's here? I haven't seen him since this last spring."

"Trust me, I know. I've spent the last few months listening to you go on and on about how much you missed him. If I didn't know any better, I'd think you were half in love with my cousin." He gave me a pointed look. "Which, if I might add, would not be a good idea."

"You sound like Gram." She'd been warning me to stay away from Raul, as of late. When I was younger, she'd let me hang about his carriage all the time, but in the last year or so, she'd put her foot down, claiming I was too old to be meeting with him alone. She'd given me the talk about young men and their expectations, and how exactly it was that babies were conceived. To this day, her words still made me blush.

Rhyne chuckled. "Bri, it's not that I don't like him, he's my cousin after all. I'm just not sure he's the type of man you ought to go falling in love with. He's a Tinker and spends his time traveling about. He has no real home. What kind of life would that be for you?"

"Maybe you're right, but I just wish people would let me make up my own mind. He's kind to me, and I love being around him."

"Perhaps I can help you sneak down to meet him," Rhyne said.

I slapped his arm. "Stop teasing me. You know I'm not allowed to see him unless I'm properly chaperoned. And last I checked, Gram didn't think you fell into that category."

He clutched his chest. "Your gram adores me."

"Yes, but that's because she doesn't know how you act when she's not around." But the more I thought about it, the more I considered slipping to the other side of town to find out for sure whether Raul was truly back. What harm would it do if I stopped in to welcome him back? Nervous flutters tickled my belly. What if he'd forgotten about the night he'd held my hand when he'd walked me home or what if he didn't really want to see me? Maybe I ought to wait and let him come to me. I imagined his smile and dark brown eyes. My heart raced at the thought of him. He was the only boy who'd ever made me feel this way. I tried to ignore my sweaty palms and glanced at my friend instead. So much for not thinking about romance and love and marriage. I was just as bad as every other girl in the village.

"So, are you going to head over there?"

"I'm not sure if I should chance it. Gram was acting crazier than normal. You know, I found her burning some of my clothes?"

He quirked an eyebrow at me. "That's strange, even for her. I wonder what's got into her?" He smiled. "Ah, but don't feel bad. Da isn't letting me anywhere near the market—doesn't want Ma's family to talk with me. I think he's afraid I might run off with them and join their band of fire eaters."

Rhyne was almost as much of an outsider as I was. He was a "half-breed," or so a lot of people in town liked to call him. His mom was a Tinker, or at least she had been when she'd lived amongst the Wanderer Tribes. But she'd been banished at fourteen for refusing to marry the chief—who was three times her age.

Rhyne's dad, Bowman Butcher, met her and married her a year

later. However, Rhyne wasn't allowed to associate with the Wanderers when they came to Dark Pines. Bowman didn't want him getting pulled into all their magical, witchcraft type practices. And he didn't want to see him get hurt, the way his mother had. They knew they were outsiders, and they'd learned to keep their distance rather than risk being rejected, or in some instances persecuted.

Maybe that was why Rhyne and I were such good friends. We both knew what it was like to be different.

No one else knew it, but Rhyne secretly corresponded with his grandmother. I'd seen a few of the exchanged letters. He always burned them after reading them though, to keep his father and mother from finding out. And two summers ago, he'd even got to meet her in person.

I stared at his squared jawline. The late day sun shone on his golden colored hair. His ivy eyes seemed darker than normal.

"I got the courage up to stop by Gertie's to see if she could come out to the creek with us, but her ma said no. Even though I called on her all proper like. Not sure if her family will ever approve of me."

"They will."

He shrugged. "Yeah, maybe. I *am* charming."

I snorted. "And therein lies your problem."

"What's that supposed to mean?" He crossed his arms over his chest.

"Your conceit is enough to smother someone."

"Is that so?"

"I'm trying to be honest. I thought that's what friends did."

"Ah, speaking of honest … " He glanced around, like he was making sure we were alone so he could tell me a secret. "I heard some talk in the village today."

My gaze met his. "What kind of talk?"

"I overheard Lady Weaver say they found Walter Fisherman down by the dock, his innards strung about. Apparently they still haven't found his legs and arms."

"Great. The Beast again. You'd think the gossip mongers would be sick of spreading the same rumors over and over again."

He shrugged. "My bet is, Walter probably drank himself to death. But they did mention this was the second body found in five days."

For centuries, people had told tales of the "Beast" around campfires. Every time someone went missing or was found dead, the "monster" in the woods got blamed. But no one had ever actually seen this thing. So I believed it was the village elders' way of keeping the children in line. They claimed it came after the unholy. The sinners. So most of us were too scared to venture out after dark or make poor choices for fear their words might become true.

But what about my nightmares?

Chills raked over me.

The other night, I'd had a nightmare about the Beast. Had it been a vision of the Beast actually attacking someone?

And now Rhyne was saying someone's body had been found. Was it a coincidence? And last night I'd dreamed of Margaret Shepherdess being killed by the Beast ...

For a moment, I considered telling Rhyne about my gruesome nightmares. Of the headaches and nausea that followed these visions. About the ghostly lady who seemed to always watch from afar ... a woman who looked just like my dead cousin, Lucia.

With a sigh, I bit my lip. I didn't want to put a damper on the rest of my day. What I needed to do was try to forget about my dreams and visions and ghosts. So instead, I smiled and said, "See, this is why I adore you so much—you don't fall for Lady Weaver's antics."

Something or someone crashed in the trees next to us. We leapt apart and stared into the thicket. My heart catapulted into my throat as he reached for his bow. A buck and doe scampered out of the woods and stopped to get a drink at the creek.

Rhyne glanced at me, and I burst out laughing.

"What'd you think it was? The Beast?" I teased.

His lips twitched at the corners, and he tossed his bow aside while pulling me into the creek. "I'll show you beast."

With a giggle, I splashed him, getting his breeches and tunic wet. I grabbed the bottom of my drenched skirt and bounded through the woods, glancing over my shoulder as I rushed onto the main road and screeching as I saw Rhyne closing in.

I turned around and took a deep breath, ready to run faster, *faster*—and saw that I was about to collide with a black stallion coming toward me. I screamed and raised my arms to brace myself for the impact, but the rider pulled the reins, stopping the horse mere inches from me.

"Are you all right?" asked the rider with a deep, masculine voice.

The knight pulled his helmet from his head. My breath caught in my throat as he slid from his mount. Shaggy black hair fell across his forehead. His blue eyes the color of summer skies. He stood tall, his smile blinding.

"I-I'm sorry." I curtsied. "I'm afraid I didn't see you coming."

Any second now my heart would stop pounding. Right? Any second.

"No need to fret," he said. "I'm only glad I was able to pull up in time."

His soft tone sent a quivering across my skin that had nothing to do with me being dripping wet.

Rhyne came up behind me and rested his palm on my shoulder.

The knight glanced at his hand, then back at me. "My men and I are looking for the village of Dark Pines. I haven't been here since I was a boy, so my memory is not as clear I would like. Could you tell me if we're close?"

Rhyne cleared his throat. "It's just around the next bend."

The knight's gaze lingered on me as he stepped forward. "I'm sorry, where are my manners? Allow me to introduce myself." His grin widened. "My name is Lord Kenrick of Crowhurst."

In one smooth motion, he set his helmet on his saddle, then took my hand and raised it to his lips.

My skin blazed beneath his mouth, and my heart thudded like the beating of a thousand hooves in unison.

What's wrong with me?

I stood frozen in place, staring at him.

"Brielle, it's been too long since I've seen you." Lord Kenrick rushed across the stone bridge, moonlight at his back.

I laughed. "It's only been three nights."

"Three nights too many." He scooped me in his arms, his fingers tangling in my hair as he drew me closer.

My legs trembled and I shook my head to clear the mental picture. Of all the times for one of my stupid visions to hit me.

My eyes searched his, and I noticed the dazed look on his face as well. Hold on. Had he shared my vision? *No. Of course not.* Half the time I wasn't even sure what I was seeing *was* a vision. It was another magnitude of crazy to think that not only had it been a real vision, but that this knight had somehow *shared* that vision with me.

Rhyne stiffened behind me, his grip tightening on my shoulder. I swallowed hard.

"I'm Brielle Healer," I said at last.

Rhyne nudged me.

"And this is Rhyne Butcher," I added.

My face flushed when Kenrick released my hand. I took a step back and bumped into Rhyne.

"Pleased to meet you both." Kenrick gave a slight nod, his gaze still intent on my face. He raised an eyebrow. "You look so familiar to me. Is it possible we've met before? Perhaps in another town? Or at a ball?"

Tingles raced across my skin and my fingers itched to reach out to him. "No. I haven't been out of Dark Pines since I was a small child—"

"Speaking of Dark Pines," Rhyne interrupted, "what brings you here?"

Kenrick gave him a forced smile. "I'm hunting the Beast."

I frowned.

Visions of the Beast the last two nights.

A possible victim of the Beast this morning.

And now Kenrick, here to hunt the Beast.

I wanted to believe the Beast was a bunch of hogwash, but there could only be so many coincidences.

Rhyne shook his head. "Please forgive my bluntness, Lord Kenrick, but I'm afraid the legend of the Beast is nothing but a falsehood. A story meant to scare the young."

"I beg to differ. The Beast is real. I've been looking for it for a couple of years now." He stared at me, and his jaw clenched. "For decades my father and uncles have searched for its origin. And now my brothers, cousins, and I have taken up where they left off."

It wasn't that I didn't believe him, but if it were real, wouldn't someone have seen it or captured it by now? Yet he had dedicated his life to hunting it down. Which meant he must have real proof.

I opened my mouth to say as much, but then the sound of the bells echoed in the distance. These weren't the cheerful rings of celebration, but instead low drawn out drones. *Death tolls.*

I spun to face Rhyne.

His brow wrinkled in worry. "Come, we need to get to the village." He grabbed my hand.

"We can give you a ride." Kenrick gestured to his small retinue of soldiers sitting atop their steeds nearby.

"No, we'll meet you there," Rhyne said, his jaw firm, eyes wide.

I glanced at Kenrick and met his gaze. "Apologies, Lord Kenrick, we really must be going."

I took off on my own, with just a glance behind me to see Rhyne somewhat confused by my sudden departure. I guess he expected me to put up a fight. But then he came after me.

We raced into the woods, cutting across the small animal trail and through the rowan trees.

Rocks cut into the bottom of my feet and I cringed, wishing I'd remembered to put my shoes back on. But Rhyne jerked me down the short cut, straight to the main gate of Dark Pines.

I slowed as I caught sight of John Undertaker's cart and the white sheet draped over a lump in the back. It was obvious that it was a body. But whose? The wind picked up and the cloth came loose, billowing in the air. I went still as I gaped at the remains of Margaret Shepherdess.

Nausea clenched my stomach like a giant fist. Her arms and legs were missing, as was half of her torso, but the mask of terror she wore upon her face remained. Frozen. Vacant eyes. Forever staring at death.

She looked just as she had in my nightmare.

So much blood. I could almost smell the remnants of fear.

I buried my face against Rhyne. My breath came in gasps, tears trickled down my cheeks.

I wanted to believe it was a coincidence.

I wanted to believe my nightmare had been nothing more.

But here was the proof staring right at me. Could I tell Rhyne about it? *No. Absolutely not.* He'd insisted to Kenrick that the Beast wasn't real. If I started talking about visions that might confirm not only that the Beast was real, but that I sometimes saw the Beast making its kill … he'd think I was crazy.

At the sound of hoof beats, I peered around him to see Kenrick.

"It looks like I've come to the right place," he said, watching me intently. "Don't worry, milady, I'll protect you. And the good people of Dark Pines. You have my word."

But even as he said the words, I had a bad feeling that even a knight wouldn't be able to keep us safe from what was to come.

Chapter Two

L ord Kenrick's family crest glinted in the sun as he and his men
guided their horses toward the mayor's house. The crest depicted
a griffin with a serpent hanging from its mouth, surrounded by four
stars.

Where had I seen that before?

Had I seen it before?

"He's going to rouse up trouble," Rhyne said from beside me.
"Soon everyone will take to the woods. Don't think I'll get much
hunting done."

The undertaker's cart moved from the gate, and I stared after the
mangled corpse, unable to take my gaze from it. At last, I pulled away
from Rhyne.

"Do you think it was wolves?"

He glanced down at me. "I don't know. I've never seen an animal
tear someone up so badly."

Perry Dyer pointed to the departing cart. "Did you see her body?

All ripped apart. Looked like the Beast got her."

I shivered, and my skin puckered in gooseflesh. It was one thing to dream about someone being killed, quite another to actually see their dead body …

"I heard she was having an affair. Suppose she deserved it," someone else said.

Another villager said, "This makes the third person found dead this month. I tell you, the creature is marking the sinners."

What was wrong with these people? No one deserved to be torn to pieces. They acted as if they knew all along Margaret would meet an untimely death.

My hand fisted at my side. "You'd think finding her dead body like that would garner some sort of sympathy."

Rhyne took my arm, pulling me away from everyone. "Yes, well, we live amongst vultures."

We dodged out of the way as men on horseback rode past. Chickens scattered, sending up a flurry of feathers. Once the commotion died down, they went back to pecking the ground for food.

A familiar hunched figure caught my attention, and I saw Gram push through the crowd. Her eyes met mine as she drew closer, and she reached out a gnarled hand to grab my arm.

"The Beast," she murmured.

"That's what they're saying," I said.

She swallowed. "I have to get back to the cabin. There is much I must look into. Promise me you'll not talk with strangers. And that you'll not wander the woods alone."

"Gram—"

"Promise me, Brielle." Her grip tightened.

"I-I promise."

Rhyne quirked an eyebrow and I shrugged. "Don't worry, Loreen, I'll not let her venture off alone."

Gram gave him a forced smile, then let go of me. "I know you'll keep an eye on her. You're a good friend."

"Loreen Healer!" Anne Cook hurried toward us, her skirts hefted up. "My daughter was burned by the hearth. Do you have a salve?"

Gram nodded, clutching her cloak tighter about her shoulders. "Yes. Go on home. I'll be by with it soon."

Tears welled in Anne's eyes. "Thank you." She pressed some coin into Gram's hand, then left.

"I'd best head to the cottage so I can grab what I need to heal the child."

"I'll come with you," I said, hopeful for a chance to talk to her.

"Rhyne," a familiar voice called after us.

My eyes narrowed. Great. Pretty. Perfect. Sarah Weaver. Daughter of Lady Weaver and the town mayor. And the biggest pain in my arse.

I turned my head as she hurried over to Rhyne and leaned forward, her bosom nearly falling out of her dress, before glancing my way. "Oh, Brielle, I didn't notice you there."

Didn't notice me? I was standing right next to Rhyne.

My fist clenched as she batted her eyes. She shifted so even more of her cleavage was visible. "I don't want to keep you, but I wondered if you were going to the festival?"

"I planned on it," he said. "And you?"

She giggled, as if a dead body hadn't just passed through here. "Of course, although no one special has asked me yet."

Rhyne's face turned crimson. Did he like her after all? Maybe he wanted to ask her but didn't want to do it in front of me.

I glanced at Gram and she nodded.

"Listen, I'll see you later Rhy, I think Gram and I are going to head home."

Sarah smirked.

"Actually, it's getting dark. I should see Loreen and Brielle home safely." Rhyne tugged on my arm as if to get me moving.

Before we got too far, I heard Sarah say, "Nice shoes, Brielle." She pointed at me, then covered her mouth to snicker.

I glanced down at my bare feet and wet dress. Heat crept up the back of my neck, spreading across my face.

Gram's eyes widened, as if seeing me for the first time. "Why are you out like this in public? Hair down. Muddied gown. No slippers. I didn't raise no heathen."

"It's my fault. I chased her around in the creek." Rhyne gave me an apologetic look.

Gram glanced between the two of us. "You're getting older. You can't be running around like this. And you, Rhyne Butcher, know better."

"I swear we were just playing around in the woods. We never intended on coming into town. But we heard the bells."

"Just be more careful, both of you," she scolded.

"I'll take care of her," Rhyne said. He smiled at me. "We take care of each other."

"I know," she said. "But with Margaret's death … I need you two to do something for me."

"Anything," I said.

"Just give me a few minutes alone at the house to get that salve around and take care of some things. But don't stay gone too long. You know what tonight is."

Now it all made sense, and a rush of guilt came over me for not realizing sooner.

It was the anniversary of my Aunt Narcissa and Cousin Lucia's deaths. It'd been on my mind this morning, then in all the excitement of hearing about Raul and meeting Kenrick, I'd let the thoughts slip. Every year, Gram and I honored their memories with a small ceremony. I had scant recollections of them, I'd been so young when they'd passed away that most of the things I knew of them were because Gram told me. No wonder Margaret's death had pained Gram so much. And no wonder she wanted a moment alone. All this did was dredge up memories of our family.

When Gram disappeared into the woods, Rhyne turned to look

at me. "We better go back for your vegetables, anyway."

We made our way toward the creek. At last, we stepped onto the shore of the stream. I slid my feet into my slippers, then gathered the vegetables while Rhyne grabbed his bow and kills.

Once I finished, I glanced up to find him still waiting for me.

"You could've left, you know."

"Your Gram doesn't want you out here by yourself."

"Fine, I guess you can walk me home. But so you know, Rhyne Butcher, I'm quite capable of taking care of myself. I've been walking these woods alone since I was child."

He fell in beside me as we pushed through the brambles. We chatted about going fishing later in the week. Then our conversation turned to Margaret, something I didn't want to talk about, because when I closed my eyes, all I saw was her face. Pale. Scratched. Mouth opened as if to scream.

"You all right?" Rhyne tugged on my sleeve.

"Yes. Just a little spooked after seeing Margaret." I gave him a forced smile.

"I won't let anything happen to you, Bri," Rhyne said.

We hurried through the familiar shadow-drenched woods. The trees bowed beneath gusts of wind, their branches like deformed needles, the scent of pine heavy in the air. Lightning bugs lit our path as the gloom crept in. Some days the mile between the village and our home seemed long, but other times, like now, when Rhyne was with me, it seemed as if we lived right outside the gate.

As we rounded the curve in the rut-filled road, we took the small foot trail that veered to the right. Twigs snapped beneath my feet, while branches snagged at my dress. Deeper into the foliage we went, until at last we came to the clearing where Gram's cottage sat. Most of the villagers found it odd that we lived outside the town walls, but Gram worried people would take more notice of her and her healing abilities if we were inside. It was one thing to heal people when we could claim it was all the work of herbs and tender care, but the smallest rumor of something paranormal sent them into a fury. Just look at how they acted with the possibility of a beast being out there.

We stopped in front of our cottage, the thatched roof in desperate need of repair, the tiny porch sagging with age. Lantern light glowed from beneath the cracks in the shutters as smoke curled from the chimney like a coiled snake. The aroma of Gram's ham soup wafted out to us.

I turned to Rhyne. "Be careful going home."

He grinned, an arrogant gleam in his eye. "Trust me. Nothing's going to hurt me."

He sauntered into the woods and disappeared into the shadows. I turned to go in—but something stopped me.

The hair on the back of my neck prickled and I swallowed hard. Shivers raked through me as I scanned the woodland. Silhouettes uncurled from beneath the trees, stretching toward the cabin as if snaking toward me. Someone or something watched me.

Near the trail, a fog began to roll in. And from within it, a figure of a woman appeared, staring right at me. It seemed to float closer, then stopped. I took several deep breaths.

I'd never forget that face.

Lucia.

The fog passed over her. Through her. Like she was there and yet not there at the same time. A ghost.

My breath caught in my chest as she turned to me. Her mouth moved, but no sound came out.

Then, as if carried on the wind, the words she'd spoken reached my ears.

"Beware, the Beast will come."

Fear raced through my veins. I rushed into our home and bolted the door behind me, leaning against the wooden barrier, eyes closed, taking deep breaths.

"Get a hold of yourself, Brielle," I said.

My heart hammered against my ribs. As much as I'd hoped for

all of these coincidences to end up being just that, I had to face facts.

The problem?

I don't know what any of this means.

Night was in full swing by the time Gram got home. She set a bundle of nettles on the table, then hurried to grab two candles from the shelves. Staring up at the painting of Narcissa and Lucia hanging on the wall, she crossed herself, and one look at her eyes told me she was barely holding back tears.

I looked at the painting, too, half to give her another second to herself, half to compare Lucia's image to the face I'd seen earlier.

Long dark hair. Eyes the color of mahogany. Full lips that neither smiled nor frowned.

They were the same.

If Lucia's ghost was here, *why* was it here? Why had she come back? Simply to warn me about the Beast? But why now?

"Go on and get those rafts I put together," Gram said, pointing at two tiny makeshift boats sitting near the hearth.

When I had them in hand, I followed her outside and into the forest. We trekked through heavy brush, pinecones crunching beneath each footfall. The scent of dirt hung heavy in the air. The cool night breeze whispered against my cheek as we came to the bank of the river.

As we stood there, I contemplated telling Gram about Lucia's ghost. Would tonight be appropriate to bring up that I thought I'd seen her? The more I thought about it though, the more I realized I couldn't let it go, I needed to know what was out there.

"Gram?"

She peered at me with tired eyes. "Yes?"

"I-I think I might've seen Lucia's ghost … "

She took a staggered step back. For a moment, I thought I heard her utter the word "already." The look of shock quickly passed, and she patted my arm. "With it being the night of the anniversary of her death, it is no surprise that she might appear to you."

Gram took the two rafts from me, but said no more as she set them on the ground at our feet. Next, she produced the candles she'd brought from home. She cupped her hands around the first one, until a flame caught its wick. She then placed it on a raft and gave it to me to hold while she lit the next one.

When both candles twinkled with light, we walked to the edge of the river. "Let us remember our dear family, who were taken from this world too soon. May their memories be honored this night and may their spirits be at peace."

"We won't forget you," I said as I placed my raft on the gently flowing water and watched it bob downstream.

Gram stepped forward and did the same. When they were out of sight, I leaned over and hugged her. I could feel the tears tracing her wrinkled face as she pressed her cheek to mine.

"It doesn't get any easier," she said.

And she was right. We were the only surviving people left in our family. This was the first of many remembrance ceremonies we'd hold this year.

"We best get out of the woods for the night." Gram wiped her eyes and tugged me toward home.

In the distance, I heard something thrashing through the trees and knew she was right.

Chapter Three

S weat beaded on my brow and I wiped my forehead with my hand. "Hold still, Brielle Healer, unless you want a pin in your leg." Lady Weaver pulled the lavender silk tighter. She slid pins into the fabric to hold it in place then spun me around to face her. "Looks like you'll only need one more fitting after this." She eyed her work, adjusting the bust line. "You look charming in this color."

I smiled. "Thank you."

Although she was the worst gossip, she made the loveliest dresses, and I was grateful Gram managed to save enough coins for me to get something perfect for the festival. Now my only hope was that Raul would get a chance to see me in it.

Sarah glanced up at me from the counter where she was busy cutting material for a customer. Her lips tightened into a thin line as if her mother had sewn her mouth shut. She narrowed her eyes at me.

"Wait until you see my dress," she said. "Mother made me the best one in the village."

Of course she did, because Sarah's parents denied her nothing. She flaunted every tiny thing she had. It was only a matter of time before she dug her claws into some unsuspecting male. *What a shite.*

"Now, Sarah, mind your manners. There's no need to be a braggart." Lady Weaver set down her pincushion. "Go ahead and take it off in the back room. I'll fetch it in a moment."

I stepped down from the wooden platform and hid behind a partition. Trying to be careful of the sharp needles, I tugged the gown up and over my head, then folded it neatly and slipped into my plain brown dress. My fingers brushed against the large scar on my chest, right above my heart. Gram said I'd had it since I was child, although she never indicated how I obtained it, I only knew that it'd been a part of me for as long as I remembered. It was a good thing my dresses covered me so well. Not that I cared if anyone saw it, but it would lead to questions I couldn't answer.

"Mother, can I go to the creek with Rhyne Butcher today?" Sarah's voice carried.

My hands clenched. What if he took her to our spot? I scowled at the lavender dress.

Lady Weaver gasped. "Absolutely not. It's too dangerous."

"But Brielle is alone with Rhyne all the time."

"Brielle is not a proper lady. You know who her grandmother is. Be glad I don't let you run around like some bar wench. No. You will not go to the creek," she whispered, as if that'd keep me from hearing. "Besides, Rhyne Butcher is a half-breed. And no daughter of mine is going to be caught up alone with that boy. You know the Wanderers' reputations."

I stiffened. How dare they speak of us in such a manner? Just because we didn't have an abundance of money didn't mean I couldn't carry myself like a lady. My mother had been a noblewoman. And my father, well, he might not have been a lord, but he had been one of the richest merchants in the country. However, I didn't go around town shouting this to everyone. In fact, very few people were aware of my lineage. And she had no right to talk badly of Rhyne. He didn't deserve it.

Sometimes it was easy to forget where I came from, that Gram and I didn't always live in the cottage at the edge of Dark Pines. No. We'd only come here after Mother, Father, Aunt Narcissa, and my cousin Lucia died.

Tears burned my eyes and I wiped them away with the back of my hand. *Can't let them see me cry.* I sucked in a deep breath of air, smoothed down my dress, then marched into the main shop.

"Did you leave the gown behind the partition?" Lady Weaver asked.

"Yes. I didn't want to get it dirty—you know how unladylike I am. Kind of like a bar wench," I shouted.

Mary Dyer, one of the Weaver's friends, covered her mouth in surprise and hurried out of the shop as if she might catch something from me.

"Brielle, I didn't mean—" Lady Weaver tried to grab my arm, but I shook her off.

I snorted. "My arse. Good day, Lady Weaver."

Patrons stared at me as if they'd never heard the word *arse* before. Well, maybe not from a young lady. I pushed out onto the street and the door to the seamstress shop slammed shut behind me.

By tomorrow, I'd be the talk of the village. Me. My dirty mouth. And Gram.

Rhyne would make me feel better, but the butcher shop had a line of customers. The townsfolk were stocking up in case the Beast laid siege on us. The last thing I wanted was to get him into trouble. But I needed him.

I waved my hand, catching his attention from the doorway. He glanced at me, then leaned over to speak to his father. Bowman Butcher peered up at me and gestured for him to go. Rhyne took off his apron, washed his hands, and then hurried out to see me.

"So how did your fitting go?"

"Don't get me started on the fitting. That two-bit arse of a Weaver did nothing but speak ill about me and Gram. And you as well."

"That explains the gossip."

My head snapped up and my gaze caught his. "What gossip? How can there be gossip? I only left the shop but a moment ago."

He ran a hand through his tousled hair. "Mary Dyer said she was inside the store when a lady with a mouth like a tavern wench started yelling."

I groaned. "I hope word doesn't get back to Gram or she'll tan my hide for sure."

"Your secret is safe with me." He smirked as he rested a palm on my lower back to steer me around a pile of horse manure. "So, where do you want to go? Maybe a trip into the marketplace would make you feel better."

My gaze drifted to the marketplace. "Well, only if you want to?"

He grinned. "Come now, Bri, you know me better than that."

With a snort, I nudged him with my elbow. "All right then. But we can't stay too long. Gram might not care if I'm out with Wanderers, but if I'm out past sundown, she'll for sure punish me all the same. Remember what happened last time?"

Rhyne blanched. "Yes. But you have to admit … we did have a lot of fun."

"Easy for you to say. You're not the one who couldn't sit right for a week."

He laughed. "You know it was worth it."

We walked in silence for a bit, my mind wandering.

I chewed my lip and glanced at Rhyne. Should I ask him about Raul? He'd at least help me figure things out wouldn't he? My feelings that is. But I'd gone so long insisting that I didn't like *anyone* that he'd be right to give me a hard time now that things might have changed.

Of course, I didn't have to tell him everything. I could just ask him in a roundabout way …

With a deep breath, I decided to take a chance. "Rhy?"

"Hmmm?" He peered down at me.

"H-how did you know you liked Gertie?"

"I don't know. It just kind of happened. I started to notice small things about her. Like her smile and her laugh. Her eyes. Then when I lay in bed at night, I kept thinking about her. It's like I couldn't get her out of my mind. The more time we spent together, the more time I wanted with her. But why are you asking? Is there someone you're interested in?"

"Of course not. Who do you think you're talking to?" I refused to meet his gaze. Rhyne knew me too well. One look in my eyes and he'd know I was lying.

We hurried toward the marketplace. People bustled back and forth, carrying baskets, loading carts, bargaining for the perfect deal. My hand brushed against the leather purse belted at my side. I had a few coins left from doing Peter Farmer's laundry. Maybe I could find a few new books or parchments.

"Get yer fresh spices here." A bald vendor, wearing a dusty green tunic blocked my path, waving a jar of cinnamon in front of my face.

"No, thank you." I side-stepped him.

Other people offered up chickens, jewelry, knives, vegetables, rugs, and even maps. One after another, I declined. I sought something else. Then I saw *his* set-up. Rhyne had been right, the Wanderers were back. *Raul* was back.

"They're here." I grinned at Rhyne, quickening my step. It'd been months since we'd last seen them. He'd been here at the beginning of spring, and here it was nearly the end of summer. Excitement made my heart race as I stared ahead.

There, beneath the shade of the sycamore trees sat the colorful carriage, its wood panels painted in vibrant reds, blues, and greens, a great canopy erected in front of it. With a smile, I dipped beneath the green and white striped awning.

The scent of pipe smoke drifted in the air, while wind chimes made of shells and iron rings created eerie tunes. An array of feathers, jewels, and stones were spread over tables. Reed baskets filled with flower petals were positioned along the carriage. A collection of daggers, throwing knives, and scabbards sat on a wooden display next to a rainbow of silken scarves.

"I wondered when I might see you." A tanned hand moved in front of my face, holding a blue wildflower.

I smiled, shifting my gaze to Raul. Already my pulse thrummed in my ears. His sun-bronzed skin accentuated his dark hair, which hung about his shoulders with tiny beads braided at the sides. He wore green breeches tucked inside brown leather boots, with a white tunic unlaced revealing golden chains. Three silver hoops hung from his ears, his eyelids darkened by some sort of powder. Several new tattoos looped up his arms like artwork.

He grinned at me, his teeth like ivory against his tan skin.

"Raul." I curtsied, then took the flower he offered.

"You get lovelier every time I see you." He winked, ushering me inside his carriage.

"Don't even think about it, cousin." Rhyne caught my arm, pulling me back to his side.

"Ah, Rhyne Butcher. Dear cousin, I would never think about doing anything with your little Brielle. I just merely wanted to show her my goods."

"I'll bet you did." Rhyne snorted.

My cheeks flamed. Raul was exotic. Beautiful. Well-traveled. Dangerous. Forbidden. Everything Gram warned me to say away from. A scoundrel Gypsy, who'd been disowned by his family and banished by his tribe, just like his aunt, Rhyne's mother, or so Rhyne and the town gossips said. He traveled the world buying and selling unusual trinkets, and supposedly corrupting young ladies. Even though Gram told me not to visit him, her threats of punishment never stopped me.

Secretly, I thought she liked him, and the Wanderers in general. He always brought the best herbs with him, which she bought by the basketful for her serums and healing salves. It was hard to believe he was only five years older than me. He seemed so much more worldly and sure of himself.

"Have you got any new books?" I followed him, my palms slick with sweat. Did he remember the last time we were together? The night he'd walked me home? The way his fingers had entwined with mine, the promises he'd made to come back soon to see me?

He laughed, the sound warm and tantalizing. "Of course, you don't think I'd come to Dark Pines without something for you?"

Raul climbed up into the back of his carriage, where crimson and gold fabrics hung like curtains. He reached beneath one of the seats and pulled out a wooden box holding several books and scrolls. Some were sheepskin, while others were bound by thick leather. Most of them were ancient texts in Latin, Arabic, and Hebrew.

"Where did you find these?"

"It's a secret." He set the box in front of me and Rhyne, hopped out of the carriage, then winked.

With a giggle, I rolled my eyes. Sometimes he was insufferable. My hand trailed over a large, leather bound book. But it was the one next to it that caught my attention. The binding on it was worn more than the others, as if many people had handled it before. I pulled it free and flipped open to the middle. Blood rushed to my face. There, drawn on the center of the page, was a couple doing things that ought to be kept behind closed doors.

"Shite," Rhyne said, glowering at Raul.

Raul grabbed it from my hands and tossed it into the carriage. "You'll not be buying that one. Your gram would skin me alive."

I cleared my throat. "Um—I wasn't going to buy it. I didn't know … "

He laughed. "Of course you didn't. How about these? Greek mythology, histories of the church? They'll need translating, but I know how much you enjoy that kind of thing." He handed me a set of scrolls and a book made of sheepskin.

"Wha-what is that book called?" I gestured to the carriage. I knew it wasn't proper to bring up such things in mixed company, and in fact, Gram would be appalled. But I'd already seen the pictures, so it could hardly matter now if I knew the title.

"I don't think nice young ladies need to worry about such matters. Let's forget you saw that, shall we?" He quirked an eyebrow. "Unless of course, you plan on running away with me?" His hand cupped my elbow, his breath warm against the back of my neck. "However, I think your grandmother would have something to say about it. Actually, I believe she said she'd switch you if she caught you down here again."

I became all too aware of his closeness, the way the skin at my neck tingled like tiny, hot flames had been lit atop me. My eyes widened. "I'm nearly an adult."

"And you have plenty of time to figure out the wonders of the world. Perhaps even one day with me." His lips twitched.

"Are you trying to get me in trouble for bringing her here?" Rhyne tugged me away from him.

I laughed, digging into my purse for coins. "He's fine, Rhyne." My eyes shifted back to Raul again. "But with the way you flirt, it's no wonder rumors fly about when you're here."

His gaze softened as he raised a hand to his chest. "Ah, you shouldn't believe everything you hear, Brielle Healer. You wound me. But I shall forgive you, as I always do."

He took the coins from me and slipped them into a wooden box.

"How long will you be in Dark Pines?" Rhyne asked.

A breeze brushed against my cheek, bringing with it the musky scent of Raul.

Raul reached for my hand, raising it to his lips. "I think I might stay for the Festival of the Stars. If only to garner a dance from Brielle."

I tried to ignore the fluttering in my stomach. "Gram would die of rage." Why did I always react to him like this? *Because you're infatuated.* I could ask him to walk me home, Rhyne probably wouldn't mind too much, but if Gram found out she'd be furious. She didn't think anyone was good enough for me, especially a Tinker who spent most of his days traveling.

"Or put an evil curse on me." He released my hand. "Which reminds me, don't tell her you've been to see me."

"I'm not daft."

He cast me a long glance. "You best run along now or I might have to ask you to stay. We both know that wouldn't be a good idea."

"Raul," Rhyne growled. "I told you last time you were here that Brielle isn't like other girls. Now stop trying to flirt with her."

"He's only teasing, Rhyne." But a part of me wished he wasn't or maybe hoped he wasn't. "Besides, I'm quite capable of taking care of myself."

Rhyne gently pulled me aside. "Listen, I've got some things I need to take care of here. And not that I don't want you around, but I need to talk about some private matters with my family. Would you mind if I stuck around here for a while? Or if you want I could see you home first." His gaze shifted to Raul and some of the other Wanderers as if he was looking for someone.

"Of course I don't mind, I'll be all right. I'll see you soon," I said, then turned to Raul. "Thank you for the books."

He bowed. "You're welcome, milady. If I can ever, and I mean ever be of service to you, please don't hesitate to come by." When he stood erect, he gave me a wink.

I waved, and as I hurried away from his carriage, I saw him and Rhyne in deep conversation. What was going on? Why were they giving each other those knowing glances?

A part of me knew Raul was dangerous, but I didn't care. We'd met four summers ago, right before I turned twelve. Much to Gram's chagrin, he'd taken a liking to me and we developed a strange friendship. He brought me exotic gifts from his travels and in exchange, I'd spend hours talking with him. I was certain Gram knew I snuck down to see him, especially when I returned home with new books and jewelry not found in these parts. I'd been caught twice this last spring, which earned me several hours of stacking wood, but it was worth it.

Lost in thought, I wandered along the various stands until I ran into a very solid, very masculine chest. I raised my head to see Lord Kenrick, who reached out to steady me. "I'm sorry."

"Pardon me, Lady Brielle. I didn't mean to run into you. I fear my mind is elsewhere."

"Mine as well." I smiled, shifting my purchases beneath my arm. My heartbeat quickened as I watched at him.

He stared, intent on my face. We stood, silent, gawking for several moments, and I had no idea why. We barely knew each other.

His mouth turned up at the corners as he drew his hand back. "What brings you to the marketplace?" He glanced at my books.

"I needed some new reading material. Father Machai is running out of manuscripts for me to borrow."

"Ah, then you are friends with Father Machai?"

"I am. He tutored me for several years at the request of my grandmother. And he gives me access to the church's library." Unlike most of the villagers, Gram thought education important and wanted me to read and write and to speak other languages.

Kenrick grinned. "Then it is fate that has brought us together this day." He offered me his arm.

I accepted it. "What makes you believe fate intercedes, Lord Kenrick?"

We ducked into a shaded area next to the stables where the heavy smell of hay clung to the air, while horses whinnied from their stalls.

He leaned closer. "Because I have need of Father Machai's library, and for some reason he's taken a dislike to me."

I laughed. "What have you done to upset the poor priest?"

"I do not know. The moment I mentioned the Beast, he told me he couldn't help me."

"Why, Lord Kenrick, are you so certain that this Beast exists?

And what, pray tell, do you hope to find within the church?"

He raised a hand to shield his face from the sun. "I was told that my grandfather, rest his soul, was attacked by the Beast when my father was nine. For a long time, I thought they were just stories." He shifted his gaze to mine. "Until a few years ago, when I found my first body. It'd been torn, almost shredded, in the same manner as my grandfather. So I poured myself into research, and one day, while scouring books in a monastery I came across written accounts of the Beast. The attacks weren't restricted to one certain village, but rather occurred in several locations. Written testimonies spanned a couple centuries. The more research I did, the more proof I found."

"Pardon me if I find this highly unlikely. How could a creature such as this live for several centuries and avoid capture? It's too fantastical, even for me."

The wind picked up, tugging a scroll from my hand. I raced to catch it, but Lord Kenrick scooped it up and held it out to me. His hand brushed mine, sending jolts through my whole body. His skin was warm and the air sizzled between us as if I'd been sucked into a lightning storm. My fingers trembled as I took it from him.

"The tournament," he blurted out.

"Pardon me?"

He shook his head as if trying to chase a thought. "I—I remember where I saw you now. At a tournament, near Crawford."

Crawford? That was where my late aunt Narcissa and cousin Lucia's estate was. "Perhaps you've confused me with someone else. I really meant it when I told you I haven't been out of Dark Pines in years."

He smiled. "Maybe you just have one of those familiar faces."

I peered at him, unable to look away. I moistened my lips. What was wrong with me? Why did Kenrick elicit this type of reaction from me? It left me unsettled, almost confused.

"I'll talk to Father Machai," I said at last. "If you'd like, I can help with your research. Maybe translate the text for you."

"Perfect. Will tomorrow work?" His dark hair blew across his forehead and I had the sudden urge to swipe it away.

My hand rose of its own accord, as if it was natural for me to brush his hair aside. Startled, I dropped it back to my side. "Tomorrow would be splendid."

"I'll be at the church first thing in the morning." He bowed. "Thank you, Lady Brielle. I look forward to seeing you again."

I watched him walk away, his tall frame hard to miss amongst the shoppers. When he got to the corner, he turned and looked over his shoulder. Another smile formed on his lips.

Not wanting him to think me desperate, I averted my gaze and slipped into the crowd. Before I got too far, though, I spotted Raul racing after me like the devil was at his heels.

"Brielle Healer, wait." He waved his arms frantically.

People turned to stare at him, pointing and whispering as he drew closer to me. I was sure tomorrow we'd be the talk of the bloody town. But for today, I didn't care.

"What's wrong?" I asked when he stopped beside me, a serious look upon his face.

He caught my arm. "My grandmother just arrived in Dark Pines, and she told me I was to fetch you right away."

"Is she ill? Does she need a salve? Maybe I should send for Gram instead, you know she's more skilled in healing than I am."

"No, she doesn't need Loreen." He leaned closer and whispered, "She's here about your nightmares."

My throat tightened. I'd never mentioned my nightmares to him, so what could his grandmother possibly know about my horrific dreams?

Chapter Four

"Your grandmother is here, now?" I searched the crowd, wondering which person she was.

"Yes, she just got in and is waiting at my carriage. She didn't want to draw attention to herself."

"Very well, lead the way." After so many weeks of nightmares and visions, loath as I was to talk to strangers about this, I knew I couldn't ignore her. Because if she knew this much without me divulging information, she might have the answers I sought.

When we got to Raul's carriage, I saw an old, withered lady sitting next to a small fire, a dress made of various hues swept the ground as she rocked back and forth. Her long, gray-black hair was loose about her shoulders. Gold rings adorned her fingers, while large hoops swung from her lobes.

As if alerted of my presence, she raised her kind, brown eyes.

"You must be Brielle, the girl my grandsons told me about. Come, sit by the fire. Let us talk."

Raul tugged a blanket from one of his tables and laid it on the ground for us to sit on. I lowered myself and crossed my legs. Rhyne sat on one side of me, while Raul settled on the other, his knee pressed against mine.

A sensation ran up my leg at his touch. *Does he have any idea what his closeness does to me?* I turned to glance at him then quickly shifted my gaze forward again.

Smoke from the fire curled up in front of us, like long vines reaching to the stars.

"Now, why don't you tell me of your nightmares?"

I swallowed the lump in my throat.

"Go on, Bri, she won't lay judgment on you. She's here to help." Rhyne gave my hand a squeeze. The flames seemed to leap in front of us and I jumped. *How did that happen?*

His grandmother gave him a startled look. "Hmmm ... I think maybe there's more here going on than just her dreams. Is there something more we need to speak of, Rhyne?"

What did his grandmother mean by that?

Rhyne glanced at his cousin, who nodded his head no.

Raul chuckled. "Let's not get into that today. We're here for her."

My courage wavered, but I hoped she'd be able to figure out the horrible visions I'd been having. According to previous conversations with Rhyne, his grandmother was one of the strongest fortunetellers in his tribe or so his mother had told him. Maybe she could also explain the extreme headaches I got following them as well. So I spoke to her of my nightmares, of the death and severed limbs, and of the creature that stalked people in my sleep. But I left out the more recent images of Kenrick. When I finished, she reached for my free hand.

"Let me read you," she said. She closed her eyes and she rocked faster. The fire glowed more brilliantly and my hand pulsed, like all the blood had rushed to it. "I see a girl with tattoos upon her arms. There's a knight who hunts the darkness. Blood. Bones. So much magic. There's death and life. A curse. A ghostly woman, who could be friend, but could also be foe." Her lids shot open, and she stared right at me. "You will have to fight. And there will be pain. So much pain. But there will also be love." Her glance drifted first to Raul, then in the direction of town, as if the answer lay in wait there. "Your love can save you in the end. But you must trust in it and those closest to you. For darkness will come before the end."

Raul's grip on my other hand tightened, and this time, there was no denying it. The fire leapt higher, blazing brighter than it had before with Rhyne. Heat radiated from his fingers, thrumming up my arm. Feeling as if my hand were covered in flames, I released my hold. What was going on with him? His grandmother stared at him as well, as if in deep thought. I turned my head to find him watching me. So much emotion emanated from him, yet he remained silent.

For a moment, we inched closer, until I felt his breath on my cheek. If either one of us moved but an inch, our lips would touch. But as a horse rode by in the distance, I remembered where I was, and tore my gaze from his. Once more I looked to his grandmother. "A-and what of my nightmares?"

"You know they are not nightmares, Brielle. Trust your instincts. Let them guide you, and they will lead you on the right path," she said. With that, she slumped forward, as if all her energy had been sapped.

Raul released my hand and climbed to his feet. "Grandmother?"

She raised her head. "I will be fine. Now you boys, go on, see her home. I'll be here when you come back as there are things we need to discuss."

"Grandmother?"

"Be a good boy, Rhyne and do as I say."

Raul grabbed her a blanket, and I heard her whisper, "The magic is bound up around her. Someone knew what they were doing."

So many thoughts swirled in my mind. Who was the girl with the tattoos? And what did she mean by magic and a curse? Did the death she spoke of have to do with the attacks in the village?

As we ambled away, I swore I heard their grandmother's voice in my head. *"Go to the place it began and offer blood."*

I turned my head to find the Wanderer woman fast asleep, which meant I'd imagined it.

"I know you don't fully understand what she told you, but her words are encouraging, don't you think? That amongst death, there will be life and love … " Raul said, giving me a smile.

"Yes, it's very encouraging." I stared at him.

A few moments later, Raul delivered us back to where he'd found me earlier near the stables. "I'll see you around, dearest Brielle. Perhaps later this week you might be able to sneak away for a picnic."

He raised my palm to his lips, sending my pulse soaring into the sky. Raul was finally inviting me to spend time with him. Alone. How long had I dreamt of this moment? Of being more than just Loreen's granddaughter. He'd given me hope last spring when he'd walked me home. How many times had I replayed those scant moments in my mind, imagining his lips on mine? I cleared my throat, trying to seem casual.

"I'd loved to. Just send word to Rhyne as to when. And thank you for everything," I said, when he released my fingers. With a quick wave, I hurried away, Rhyne on my heels, leaving the marketplace behind, all the while rubbing my hand. It still tingled from where he'd touched it. I had a lot of things I needed to sort through, starting with the meaning behind Raul's grandmother's words.

When Raul was out of sight, I turned to Rhyne. "Rhyne, what was that back there? With the fire?"

He seemed to fidget, his gaze shifting away from mine as if he didn't want to talk about whatever it was that'd happened. "Don't worry, Brielle, I'm taking care of it. I promise; we can talk about it sometime, just not now." He gave my arm a pat and said, "Let's just get you home."

Rhyne and I were quiet as we made our way back through the

village. Although I was glad his grandmother had given me the reading, it left me more confused than ever.

Not able to stand the silence between us, I said, "I ran into Lord Kenrick today."

Rhyne jerked me to a stop. "What'd he want?"

"I've agreed to help him research his Beast. We're meeting at the church tomorrow to go through Father Machai's documents."

His face reddened, and his jaw twitched. "But you don't believe in the Beast. Besides, do you think that's a good idea? You barely know Lord Kenrick."

"Since when have you become concerned about who I spend time with?"

He sighed, kicking at a rock. "If you must know, I had planned on inviting you fishing tomorrow. Just the two of us. We haven't had a chance to talk much lately with your gram needing you to help make salves and Da having me in the shop."

"Really? You couldn't have been that worried about us going fishing, since Sarah was telling her mother she wanted to meet you at the creek."

He snorted. "She overheard me talking to Gertie Dyer about going on a picnic with me, and of course Sarah tried inviting herself along."

"Good, because you had me worried for a moment that you might actually fancy Sarah Weaver."

"Not in this lifetime."

We passed through the main gate and away from town. Dust spiraled in the air from the carts driving by. Trees cast eerie shadows in the late day sun, while birds chirped and whistled private melodies only they understood.

I nudged Rhyne in the side with my elbow. "You know, you don't have to walk me home every evening."

"I know, but I like to make sure you're safe."

Being with Rhyne felt familiar. There was a certain comfort

between us. We could talk about anything with one another. Our hopes. Our fears. The blasphemies of the villagers. Our love lives, or in my case the lack thereof. And now he knew my secrets. My nightmares.

I listened to the wind dance through the maples. For once, everything seemed perfect.

I bent down and picked a violet near our cottage, then glanced at Rhyne, who watched me. He rubbed his chin, as if in deep thought.

He cleared his throat then moved closer. "Bri?"

"Yeah?"

"Do you think I should ask Gertie to accompany me to the festival?"

Although I wasn't fond of Gertie's parents, she was nice enough. Most importantly, she made Rhyne happy. And she wasn't Sarah Weaver. "Yes."

"H-how do you think I should ask her? Show up at her house? Maybe take her for a walk and give her flowers? Or do you think I ought to get permission from her da first?"

I giggled, clutching his arm. "Listen to you, you sound so nervous. How about you wait until she walks by your shop tomorrow to deliver dyed cloth to the Weavers? You can catch her alone then."

His green eyes focused on me. "That's perfect. But what if she says no?"

"She won't. I mean, who could resist all that charm?" I teased.

"Indeed." He tugged on a strand of my hair. "I'm gonna borrow Da's cart. I want to make it proper for her."

"I'm so excited for you." I hugged him, still holding the books Raul had given me.

"Now all we need to do is find you someone." He winked at me. "Assuming you haven't already got someone in mind … "

With a smile, I glanced at the ground. "Rhyne, don't start that again. You know my place is here, with Gram." Although, my thoughts often drifted to Raul. But he was here for a short time, and soon he'd drive away in his carriage again.

"All right. But if that changes, you know you can talk to me." He chuckled. "And so you know, you best save me a dance at the festival." He playfully punched my arm. "I should probably head out so I can get home before dusk." He waved, and then sauntered down the rocky path, whistling as he disappeared into the pines.

When he was out of sight, Gram came outside, as clear a sign as anything that she'd been listening and waiting for Rhyne to leave. I would have rolled my eyes if I didn't love her for it.

I gave her a hug.

"What was that all about?" she asked.

"Rhyne has finally gotten the courage up to ask Gertie to the festival."

"Hmmm … She's nice enough." She mumbled something under her breath then held me at arm's length "The Wanderers are back at the marketplace."

"Oh?" I feigned innocence. *Shite.*

Gram snorted. "You've already been to see Raul, haven't you?"

"The Wanderers are not a bad people."

"No. Maybe not. But some of them, like Raul, are dangerous. Just you remember that."

I laughed. "You worry too much."

"And you don't worry enough. Rhyne better take heed as well. Bowman will not take kindly to being disobeyed," she muttered as she went back into the cabin. "For your disobedience, *again*, you can spend the night scrubbing the floor clean." She glanced at the stack of books in my hands, her face seemingly worried.

A howl sounded in the distance and I shivered. Why did I get the feeling she was hiding something from me? Something important?

Chapter Five

The clouds spread across the sky and I pulled my cloak tighter about my shoulders as I moved toward the church. Moss clung to its aged stone, while vines looped and crawled over the cross hanging above the doorway.

I walked up the steps to the heavy wooden doors.

"Lady Brielle," Lord Kenrick called from behind me.

I cast a quick glance over my shoulder, catching sight of his cloak snapping in the wind. He grinned, rushing to catch me.

"Milord." I curtsied.

"Please, call me Kenrick." He took my hand and brought it to his lips.

My pulse quickened. "Kenrick." His name fell from my lips like a whispered love poem. We stood, silent, staring, until the morning bell sounded. This seemed like an odd reaction to have for someone I'd barely meant. The only person who'd ever garnered this type of reaction from me was Raul.

Kenrick offered me his arm, then led me into the dimly lit church. "For a moment, I thought you wouldn't make it."

I smiled, clinging tight to him. "I'm a woman of my word. I promised to assist you and I will."

Candles flickered from the altar, casting shadows across the crucifix of Christ. Father Machai knelt before it, his head bowed in prayer. Not wanting to interrupt, I released Kenrick's arm and slid onto one of the many wooden pews. I bent my head and offered a prayer of my own. *Please protect us. Give us the knowledge to determine the cause of these deaths. Amen.*

When I opened my lids, I found Father Machai had risen.

"Brielle," the old man called. He hurried toward me, his brown robes rustling at his ankles. Kind eyes stared at me from a heavily wrinkled face as he took my hand in his. "What brings you here this day?"

"I wondered if you might grant us permission to use the church library?"

Father Machai frowned as he regarded Lord Kenrick. "Here I thought you'd read the library in its entirety." His brow furrowed and his grip tightened on my hand, but he refused to meet my eye.

"Father, we'd like to view the church's historic documents or parchments that might contain information on the supposed Beast in our woods."

He sighed. "Some things ought to be left well enough alone."

"I daresay, I doubt we'll find anything of great use, but I'd like to help Lord Kenrick in his research. If, for nothing more than, to prove the Beast is only a children's story."

"Very well. I know you'll not let me have a day of peace until I agree." Father Machai let my hand go then stepped back. He grabbed a candle and led us to the back of the church, then down a narrow hall to an ancient stone stairway.

The books were housed on the lower level, due to a recent fire that claimed part of the sanctuary. Villagers spent weeks aiding in the move and rebuilding. Cool, damp air embraced me as I followed Father Machai and Kenrick down the stairs. When we came to the bottom, the priest unlocked a wooden door and it swung open with a groan. We wound down another hall to the library.

Father Machai used his candle to light more waxy nubs around the room's perimeter, which did little to chase back the gloomy silhouettes that clung to the stone walls. I shivered, wishing I'd worn another layer of clothing.

"You know your way around well enough." Father Machai set a candle on the table in the room then handed me his ring of keys. "Make sure to lock up before you leave."

"Thank you, Father," Kenrick said. "I appreciate you opening your library for us."

Father Machai gave him a brief nod but nothing more, and I wondered why he acted so cold toward Kenrick.

"I'll be upstairs if you should need any help." He disappeared down the hall.

Kenrick hung his cloak over the back of a chair, then sauntered across the stone floor to the shelves lining the back wall.

"We'll want to search the histories of Dark Pines and any records of death over the last couple of centuries."

"The histories are along the west wall. Death records are kept in ledgers on the shelves beneath the tapestries. That is, if they were reported."

He cocked an eyebrow. "You really do know where everything is. I might have to employ your help for all my research."

My cheeks flushed. "Perhaps we can go through the stack of old letters as well. The priests kept many of their correspondences between the various churches."

Kenrick seemed surprised. "I never thought to search those types of documents."

I opened a wooden box with a cross burned into the top of it and gently removed several yellowed parchments, the wax seals long since broken. I sat at the table, spreading the documents in front of me, searching through the oldest. After sifting through several, I found one from the Fire Ridge Mountain Monastery. The date was smudged, the paper more brittle than the others.

Father Patrick,
Two fortnights ago, a dark-haired woman appeared at our church. She warned us of a great evil coming our way. I do not know if she was a witch or perhaps an angel sent from above. But I fear for our village. The forces of Satan are at work. A great demon comes at night, as the woman said it would. I have heard many a cry from poor souls caught in the woods after nightfall. Yet, we have no way to defeat it. We have called upon our great lord to protect us. However, we are still attacked. Perhaps because we are sinners. I pray that you might send forth your wisdom, dear brother. That you can aid us in our time of darkness …
I must hurry. It comes.
Father Gerard
Fire Ridge Monastery

My breath caught in my throat, not wanting to believe the rumors of a beast were true. I considered who this strange, prophetic woman might have been. A ghost? A witch? An angel? Was it the same one from my visions?

"You might want to read this," I called to Kenrick, who made his way around the table and sat beside me.

He scanned the parchment then shifted to me. "Amazing. I can't believe this has remained hidden for so long. It doesn't have a date, though."

"No. But it came from Fire Ridge, which is several days travel from here." I swiped loose strands of hair from my face, then scoured other letters.

He shifted in his chair, his arm grazing mine. My heart leapt as I attempted to keep my eyes averted. I was far too aware of his closeness to concentrate. His familiarity startled me.

In an effort to break contact, I gathered the letters and put them neatly back in the box then grabbed a ledger.

"Are there no other letters?" Kenrick leaned closer.

My fingers trembled as I pulled open the leather bound ledger. "No."

"Perhaps the priest who wrote it was killed, otherwise you'd think he'd update his brethren of the outcome of his dire situation."

"Maybe there is another box of letters stored in the library. I can look around for them." I leapt up and moved between shelves in search of another box, abandoning the ledger I'd just opened.

Kenrick bent over a book, the candlelight dancing on the table beside him. His dark hair seemed alight with bluish hues, his skin bronzed from being in the sun. Long, graceful fingers turned the page with utmost care. He was beautiful. Not in the same sense as Raul, but regardless my chest constricted. What hold did this man have over me? The need to be close to him, burned in my veins.

As if sensing my scrutiny, he raised hooded eyes. For a moment, I froze in place.

Kenrick sat upon his mount, armor glimmering in the sun.

"Do be careful," I said as I squinted up at him. "Prince Theodore is vicious with a lance."

He leaned down, his hand capturing mine. "Worry not, my love, I will not falter. I'm riding for you, after all." He took the lace kerchief from me and tucked it into the neck of his chest plate.

"Kenrick?"

He took his shield from his squire, then shifted to look at me once more. "I love you, milady, and soon everyone will know."

Flustered and confused, I blinked several times then pretended to study a shelf of books. Where were these visions coming from?

"Come, look at this," he said.

I hefted my skirts and hurried to the table. My brow knitted together as I stared at the page showing a crude drawing of a creature, humanesque in shape, but much taller. Its elongated claws looked like blades. The jaw was unhinged, revealing row upon row of teeth. Beneath the picture I found one word scrawled in Latin.

"Beast," I whispered. "Who drew this?"

"I don't know. It looks as though people have added accompanying text to the book over the years. Bits and pieces of history. And this drawing, stuck in the middle of it."

I reached out to trace the image. My heart beat frantically as it triggered visions of blood and bones, people running through woods trying to get away. Could it be the monster from my dreams? A sudden pain flashed behind my eyes, my head pounded.

"Are you all right?"

"Yes, sorry. I don't know what's come over me."

He pulled a chair next to his then gestured for me to have a seat, his face practically glowed with excitement. "This is what I've searched for. A description of what it is I hunt."

"How could a beast of this sort go undiscovered for so long? I mean, it can't very well be the same one terrorizing all the villages. Nothing lives that long."

"Don't you see? We've come across proof of its existence. Between this drawing, my family's tragedy, the letters I've found in nearby villages, and the correspondence we've discovered here, there's no denying it. This predator is real and has found a way to remain hidden." He turned the page, then his hand grasped mine. "Based on my previous research, its hunting patterns are all the same. But you're right, how could such a creature live for centuries. It's a puzzle, isn't it?"

"What if someone conjured a demon?" My thoughts drifted back to the letter and the mention of the woman. I'd opened my mouth to continue when the scrape of the door at the end of the hall sounded, followed by footsteps.

Kenrick released my hand and scooted his chair an appropriate distance from mine.

"Lord Kenrick, I hoped I'd find you here." Sarah curtsied, holding a basket in her hand. "I brought you lunch. I daresay, you must be hungry after being locked away in the innards of the church all day."

My eyes narrowed and I fisted the skirt of my dress in one hand. Why did she always interrupt everything? First with Rhyne, now with Kenrick. Was no man safe from her attentions? At last, Sarah glanced at me for the first time as if just noticing I sat beside him. Then she turned her focus back to the knight.

"You mentioned yesterday you'd be doing research. I'd be more than happy to help in this endeavor."

"I didn't realize you read Latin," I said.

He looked at her then back to me.

"I ... " Sarah sputtered. Her face turned crimson. "Not every text is in another language. I'm sure I can figure it out."

Kenrick opened his mouth, but before he said anything, I stood. "I better get home. Gram had a few chores she wanted done before nightfall."

"Won't you stay and have lunch with us?" Kenrick caught my arm as he, too, rose from his chair.

When Sarah's cheeks reddened, I bit my tongue to keep from grinning. How wonderful it'd be to ruin her day for once. However, villagers already had enough to say about Gram and me without adding to it, and it'd be best if people didn't know how much time I had spent with Kenrick. So against my better judgment, I let her have her way. For now.

"Perhaps another time." I gathered my cloak and tied it about my shoulders. "Good day."

As I hurried to the door, Lord Kenrick followed, stopping me when I reached the hallway. "There will be a town meeting tonight about the Beast. The mayor has sent word to everyone. I hope you'll be there. Perhaps we could manage a few minutes afterward to talk?"

"Yes, of course. Please don't forget to give Father Machai back his keys."

He gave me a slight bow and I hefted my skirts, rushing upstairs, unsure why he unsettled me with his every glance and touch.

As I emerged from the library, I saw Father Machai reading his scriptures. He glanced up.

"Father, do you believe in the Beast?"

He clasped his hands in front of him. "No. There have been many claims made through the years, but it is my belief these killings are that of wolves. Once they get the taste for human blood, it is difficult to deter them. Only last year a wild pack was caught tearing apart a hunter not too far from here."

I smiled. "Thank you, Father. You've put my mind at ease."

"That doesn't mean the woods are safe though. Not until the wolves are caught."

As I left the church, I wondered how the villagers would react at tonight's meeting. On the one hand, Lord Kenrick would present evidence to support his claims of the Beast. While, I hoped they'd remain rational, I knew what superstitions could do to even the most sensible of people. I'd heard of too many witch-hunts starting in a similar fashion. All it took was one person to point a finger and the accusations would begin. And with Gram's renowned healing skills, she'd likely be the one brought to the gallows.

Chapter Six

The winds howled, while the leaden sky threatened rain. I pulled my cloak tighter to my chest. Most vendors had already closed their stands; a few horses tethered in front of the tavern indicated the only life.

I walked to the butcher shop and lingered in the open doorway. Rhyne stood behind the counter, unaware of me. His face twisted in anger, eyes dark, he tossed a skinned lamb onto the wooden surface. *Thwack!* The large blade severed the leg from the animal.

I swallowed hard. Twice more he lifted the knife and hacked at the meat. Acid burned the back of my throat. A sneer pulled at his lips as he sawed away at the flesh. Then he laughed. A deep, frightening, guttural laugh.

For a moment, I just stood there. I'd never seen him like this.

"What's so funny?" I asked, unnerved by his outburst.

Rhyne's brow furrowed and the smile slipped from his lips. "Nothing."

Bowman came from the back room, carrying a hunk of pork, which he hung on a meat hook. He grinned when he saw me, then turned to Rhyne. "You might as well get cleaned up. I know you won't get any more work done today."

Rhyne hung up his apron then scrubbed at his hands. Once he finished, he walked to my side. When we were out of his father's earshot, he pulled me to a stop. "What's wrong? You've barely said two words since you came to find me."

"You never answered my question," I said. "Why were you laughing while you were hacking away at the meat?"

His face reddened. "Because, I imagined the lamb was Mary Dyer."

I gasped. "You *what*?"

He scuffed the road with his foot, his hands clenched into fists at his sides. "I was gonna ask Gertie to the dance today and she bloody interrupted, jerking her daughter away from me. She acted like I was some pariah, preying upon Gertie."

My shoulders tensed. "What a shite thing to do. Don't worry, you'll have another opportunity. I could always ask her for you, if you'd like."

"No, this is something I need to do myself."

"Well, if you need my help, I'm here for you." I gave his arm a squeeze.

"There is something you could do for me," he said.

"What's that?"

"You could do my hunting for me tonight so I can sneak off for a moonlight swim in the pond. Or maybe wrestle down the elusive pack of wolves everyone claims stalks our woods." He let out a low growl and gripped tight to my shoulder.

With a laugh, I jerked free and rushed down the road, Rhyne at my heels.

He easily caught hold of my waist, lifted me up, and spun me through the air. His eyes glittered like a predator. "See, you can never get away from me."

A loud clattering sounded from the road and Rhyne instantly put me down. I watched as a cart barreled right toward us, no driver to be seen. The horses veered to the right, and as they did, the wheel broke free from the frame and spiraled through the air like a great spoked weapon.

"Lady Brielle!" Lord Kenrick shouted from behind me. In one swift movement, he shoved me to the ground, out of harm's way.

Gravel dug into my body as he covered my head with his arms, shielding me from the accident. Screams erupted around us as the cart continued unmanned through the village until Henry Blacksmith, his father, and two other men, caught hold of the horses' reins, bringing them to a halt.

My pulse thundered in my ears as Kenrick lay atop me. His hand swiped my hair from my face, his gaze met mine.

"I'm sorry if I've hurt you. It's just I saw the cart—"

"No, I um, I—thank you," I whispered, my hand resting upon his. "But how did you get here? I thought you were going to do more research?"

"I left not too long after you, I wanted to talk with you more and didn't like the way we'd left things. Then I saw you … "

"Bri?' Rhyne stood over us.

Realizing we had an audience, Kenrick quickly climbed to his feet, then leaned down to help me up. I brushed the dirt from my dress and glanced across the street, where I saw Sarah standing with a smirk on her face.

"Are you hurt?" Kenrick asked.

I turned my attention to him. "No, I'm fine, thanks to your quick actions."

But as I glanced back at Sarah, I wondered if it was merely a coincidence. Or if perhaps she'd had something to do with this almost accident. Again, my head throbbed and I clutched it.

"Bri, are you well?" Rhyne, clasped hold of my arm, pulling me away from Kenrick.

"Yes. I've just got a headache."

"Well, you did just get smashed to the ground," Rhyne said, glancing at the knight.

"I'm sure that's it." But I didn't mention that it'd been there prior to the accident, when I had the strange visions of me and Kenrick. Were they connected? Maybe my visions meant that I was supposed to kill the Beast? Could that be why they'd come on so strongly? Were these premonitions a gift to aid me in the endeavor?

"Do you need me to escort you home?" Kenrick asked, his voice thick with worry.

"No, I'll make sure she's safe." Rhyne gave the sleeve of my arm a tug to get me moving.

Shaking Rhyne off, I turned to Kenrick. "I'll be fine. But thank you for your concern and for saving me."

"The pleasure was mine."

Flames from the bonfire licked and snapped in the darkness like a hungry dragon. People packed into the village square, where a wooden platform had been erected for the meeting, with torches secured to each corner.

Gram scowled, her grip on my arm tightening. "What the devil is the meeting for? Lady Weaver insisted everyone needed to attend."

"The Beast."

She snorted. "The only beast in these woods is Lady Weaver and her hen-like following."

Giggles erupted from my mouth. "And you call *me* a troublemaker."

We stood toward the back of the crowd, listening to the adults go on about how they always knew Dark Pines would be attacked. Even the kids who normally ran back and forth during village meetings seemed subdued. They stuck close to their parents, clinging to skirts and waists.

Rhyne strolled amongst a small group of blushing girls who seemed to hang on every word he said. He stopped in the middle of the road, his laughter carrying on the wind. Amazing that he had no clue what affect he had on them. Most of them would probably go home tonight and dream of him sweeping them off their feet or proposing. But I supposed that's what he got for flirting all the time. He stepped into the butcher shop and they all followed him. That, no doubt, would irritate Bowman to no end.

My skin prickled as if someone watched me. I glimpsed across the square and smiled. There, leaning against the side of the church, with his dark hair hanging loose about his shoulders, was Raul. He stared at me, and a slow grin spread across his face. He blew me a kiss.

Face on fire, I glanced away only to find Gram frowning. "What?" I asked innocently.

"I tell you that boy's trouble and all you do is encourage him."

"Oh hush. Don't pretend you don't like him. I know for a fact you get herbs from him."

"That's neither here nor there … "

In the distance, I watched Kenrick ascend the stairs onto the scaffold. His chainmail glittered in the firelight, making him look like an avenging angel.

Gram tensed next to me. "Shite," she muttered under her breath. "He's here so soon."

My head snapped to the side and I met her gaze. "What?"

Gram's eyes widened. "Nothing." She smoothed her dress down at her sides, and then turned to address me. "Have you spoken with Lord Kenrick?"

"Some."

She opened her mouth to say more, but instead she shifted her attention back to him.

"I would like to thank all of you for coming tonight." Kenrick clasped his hands together, staring out over the crowd. "In my research, I've come across many details of the Beast and tonight, I hope to further my knowledge by speaking to you, the citizens of Dark Pines. If we are to rid ourselves of the creature we must share our knowledge of it." He scanned the crowd. "I'd ask if you've had an encounter with the monster, please, step forward and share your story."

"I've seen the Beast with my own two eyes." Jacob Fisher pushed to the front of the mob and climbed the stairs to stand beside Kenrick.

I heaved a sigh of irritation. Sure he did, and likely at the bottom of a pint. How did Kenrick expect to get the truth when he listened to the drunkards and gossips? They wouldn't know the Beast if it came up and ripped off their arse cheeks.

"What occurred?"

Jacob shook his head. "Something big crashed through the brush toward the docks—and I heard the bleat of a nearby sheep. When I went to investigate, the animal had been torn apart. It left behind a trail of large tracks that disappeared into the nearby river."

"Your account sounds quite frightening," Kenrick said, patting Jacob on the arm as he finished his tale. "Anyone else?"

A few others raised their hands, one of whom was Bertrand Blacksmith who spent half his days chasing the ladies. The only angry creature he likely met up with was his wife with a rolling pin.

Not wanting to listen to him drone on, I stepped forward. "What makes you believe these aren't animal attacks? And how can we be so sure what you've seen is supernatural?"

Kenrick's eyes widened at the sound of my voice. His intense gaze met mine and he descended the scaffold steps, moving closer until we were standing nearly shoulder to shoulder.

"Because for centuries there have been too many sightings, too many similarities in the pattern of the attacks. The Beast always starts off by murdering one to two people within the first couple of years. Then by All Hallows of the fourth and fifth year, the killings increase."

I frowned. He hadn't mentioned this before. Maybe it was a clue or maybe not.

"I'd have to agree with Brielle Healer." Raul sauntered into the crowd. He flipped a coin in the air, its golden sheen glinting in the firelight as he caught it once more. "Packs of animals are known to attack humans in similar fashion. Wild dogs and wolves, both of which run about the woodland surrounding Dark Pines, have been known to slaughter cattle and deer." His eyes glowed in an unnatural way. "It would be foolish to let ourselves become victims of superstition."

Raul gave me a lazy smile then returned his focus to Kenrick. I went still, feeling the invisible challenge in the air. Did Raul know something? Or was the Wanderer merely playing the part of actor for the crowd?

Rhyne slipped from the crowd and joined me and Gram. Just then a piercing scream cut through the square. Kenrick whipped around, unsheathed his sword, and put himself between me and the direction of the shriek. People panicked and tried to push one another out of the way. They trampled closer to the buildings, their shouts and curses flowing from their mouths like water.

Sarah ran across the street, yelling, while her hands flailed this way and that. Kenrick sheathed his weapon and hurried toward her. She collapsed in his arms with a sob.

"The Beast. I-it attacked me." She held up her arm to reveal her torn dress sleeve and a single scratch that ran the length of her forearm.

Gasps went up around us, and the townsfolk moved in to get a closer look. Already, men murmured about hunting parties, while others spoke of getting home.

My teeth ground together and I stared at the wound. It was nothing like the descriptions I'd read, nor was it like Margaret's mutilated body.

"She's lying," I whispered.

Gram clutched my arm. "Yes, she is. And she's going to cause a witch hunt."

Rhyne looked at me, his glance darting back and forth over the townspeople, to his cousin. "How can you be sure she's faking it? She seems scared."

"If the accounts I've read about the Beast are real, then it never lets its victims live." I glanced at him, was he going to defend her?

Gram tugged me away from the meeting place. "Come, let's get home, child, before these fools take to the woods."

"I'll see you tomorrow," I said to Rhyne as Gram led me away.

Across the mob, I watched Raul. A scowl painted his face and he fingered the dagger at his side. As if sensing me watching him, he gave me a quick nod. What did he know?

Tonight had been a disaster and Sarah Weaver was to blame. She caused outright pandemonium, all to gain attention. Only time would tell what kind of trouble might ensue. Accidental killings in the woods? Widespread fear?

Chapter Seven

"I've been thinking," Gram said as she climbed down from her chair in the cottage, eyeing the newest bundle of herbs she'd hung from the rafters. "Perhaps it's time we left Dark Pines."

Startled, I turned to her. "What?"

"It's not safe here anymore. There are attacks in the woods, not to mention half the town sputters rumors about me being a witch. These are unsafe times for us."

"We can't up and leave. This is our home. We have just as much right to be here as anyone else," I said. "Besides, I thought you wanted me to finish my training here—you said this is the best place to find the herbs we need."

"There will be other villages that have a need of our skills. Besides, you don't know yet what you want to do for the rest of your life, and whether or not you'll even want to be a healer like me. Wouldn't you like to travel? To see other places? Lord knows you deserve a break from Sarah and all the troubles she causes."

My fingers clutched tight to the wooden bowl I was washing. "I don't want to leave. Please don't ask me to."

"I'm not saying this to frighten you," she said. "But you'll be an adult soon. You may not have a chance like this to explore new places, meet new people, do new things. Eventually, you'll find yourself out of options. And the choices you have left are already made for you."

I let go of the bowl and turned to her. "Exactly. I'm almost seventeen. I'm old enough now that I could stay on here by myself. My friends are here—Rhyne, Father Machai, Gertie, Raul—and we're already familiar with everyone."

She started to say something, but closed her mouth and shook her head.

"Gram, if you need to say something—"

"Is this really about wanting to stay in town?" She let that question hang there for a second, but she didn't wait for my response. "Or is this about Raul or that knight?"

I turned away from her, and only then, too late, realized what my hesitation told her. I was caught. There was no point denying it now.

"I like seeing Raul," I said. "Is that so wrong? And this knight … I'm merely trying to help him Gram."

"Raul's dangerous enough. Kenrick, he's a knight. But more than that. You know how dangerous things are getting. You know why he's here. To kill the beast. That's it. He won't let anything—or anyone—get in his way."

"But I wouldn't get in his way. With my visions, maybe I could even help him."

"No," she said, more forcefully than I think she intended because she took a deep breath before continuing. "He's a knight of the Crowhurst Order. He's hunted witches—and if he thinks our healing practices are suspect he will have no qualms about imprisoning us."

My teeth ground together. "I don't think he'd do that. You haven't even talked to him yet. He's kind. And smart." Why was I defending him? I barely knew him—but I didn't want to believe that he'd do something to harm us. At least she wasn't speaking ill of Raul again.

"He's been trained for one purpose," Gram said. "He's here to find evil and destroy it. And you know what people think is evil?"

I swallowed and closed my eyes. Of course, I knew the answer to her question. We'd dealt with this issue for years already. It was why we were so secretive in the first place. "People think anything they don't understand is evil."

She nodded her head in agreement. "If they knew what we could do … If Kenrick knew what *you* can do, especially that you don't have any control over it … "

She was right. I knew it. But she'd also taught me other things. She'd taught me not to be afraid of the unknown. She'd taught me that even if we lived in secret, we didn't have to live in fear. We were here to help people. Sometimes in ways they didn't realize they needed.

"Gram, you've always told me we should try and help where we could. How is our running going to do that?"

She sighed and smiled. She'd taught me too well.

"Stir the stew," she said. "I'll finish this lavender soap for Donald Carver's new wife." She gestured to the cast iron cauldron hanging in the hearth, then grabbed a knife to pry the soap from its mold.

I wiped my damp hands on my dress and walked across the room. The aroma of venison made my stomach growl. I picked up a wooden spoon and stirred the soup. The steam rolled off the pot, warming my skin. Someday, I imagined doing this in my own home and I smiled as I pictured Raul coming in from a day of selling trinkets, smelling of the woodland. How he'd hug me and tell me how good dinner tasted.

With a gasp, I dropped the spoon. I'd gone my whole life assuming I'd never feel anything like this for anyone. I wasn't about to just ignore these feelings. What Gram didn't know, Gram couldn't stop.

When we got to Dark Pines later that day, the town was aflutter with gossip; hatred and excitement buzzed in the air so thick I almost tasted it. People whispered how lucky Sarah was to survive the attack. Poor Sarah this and poor Sarah that.

Gram gripped my arm, tugging me out of the way of a patrol marching by. My gaze flickered over the square to the men on horseback, flooding the streets as others grouped together. Some held bows, while a few clutched pitchforks, picks, and axes. They were preparing to hunt. My eyes fell upon a large iron cage, with thick metal bars and shackles already attached at the base, set up on a cart. A prison for their prey.

Gram glared. "Sooner or later they'll see through her lies. For now, let's get on with our business and ignore it best we can."

Easy for her to say, she didn't loathe Sarah the way I did. With an angry sigh, I plowed through the gathering of townspeople.

"Hey, Bri." Rhyne came out of the butcher shop. "We still on for that picnic today?"

I glanced at Gram, who gave me a nod.

"If you think we can manage some privacy." I gestured to the gathering of villagers.

"Trust me, I know just the place. *I'll* see you later. At our spot near the creek." He grinned, then disappeared back inside.

"I've got some errands to run," Gram said. "Don't be home too late." I watched her hurry off in a flurry of skirts.

As I made a path through the crowd, a shoulder bumped into mine, and I glanced up to see Kenrick. I raised my hand, motioning for him to hold off until Gram was out of sight. I didn't want to face her wrath today. When her form was no longer within view, I fell in beside him.

"Milord." My breath caught in my throat. "Sorry about that, my gram is in a mood today."

"Have I already gained an enemy in Dark Pines then?"

"No—she's just really protective."

"I'll keep that in mind. Perhaps if I stopped by your home and talked with her, she'd feel differently."

"I'm not so sure about that." I laughed.

A slow smile crept across his lips, his hand clutching my arm. He cleared his throat. "My apologies for bumping into you. *Again.* It seems as though I'm always running into you."

"Yes. I'm beginning to think you're doing it on purpose." *Oh no. I sound like Sarah.* Heat crept up my neck, spreading to my face.

"And what would you say if I was?" He leaned closer, the scent of pine and cloves clung to him.

His scent. I closed my eyes, trying to place it. Where had I smelled it before?

I sat atop a steed, my arms wrapped around Kenrick's waist. My face rested against his shoulder, the aroma of pine and cloves tickling my nose. We dashed in between trees, until we came to a pasture filled with wildflowers.

"Shall we stop so I can pick you some flowers?" Kenrick turned to face me.

I giggled. "If you must."

He grinned. "I must."

The image faded as fast as it had come, leaving me dizzy and confused.

"Milady? Are you well?"

I swallowed hard, his hand still upon my arm. "Perhaps we could find a better way to meet."

"Will you come to the library with me again, to do research? And maybe afterward, you can take dinner with me or perhaps we could have a picnic soon."

"Are you sure that's a good idea? People like to talk, milord." Not to mention Gram had forbidden me from seeing him.

"I want to see you again. I … can't explain it, but it's like you've bewitched me." He gave me a smile that melted my heart. "The more time we spend together, the more time I want with you. I apologize if this sounds very forward of me."

"You don't have to apologize," I said. My skin felt on fire and my heart was thundering.

"I assure you," Kenrick said, "my intentions are not to put you in an awkward position. Perhaps I could purchase some food and bring it to your house to have dinner with you and your grandmother. Then it would be proper and we would not be left unattended."

"That would be nice." *Shite.* Of course, that would *never* work. If Gram wouldn't let me see Kenrick in public, she'd certainly never let me have dinner with him at our house. But maybe it was for the best.

"Now that we have settled that, I need to check in on Sarah Weaver. She had quite the scare last night."

Sarah. He had every right—every duty—to go check on her. But something didn't fit with her claim. "If this beast attack was real, don't you think it would've killed her?"

"I'm afraid I'm not following you."

"Sarah has a single scratch on her arm. All the other victims were torn to shreds."

"You think she's lying."

"I don't know if she's lying," I said. "But it doesn't make sense that she saw the beast and lived to tell us about it."

He nodded. "It is suspicious that she managed to escape. But we can't assume she would lie about something like this. What motivation would she have for falsehood?"

"It wouldn't be the first time she told a tall tale to get some attention. And the fools of this town will be in the woods killing anything that moves in the brush. Animals. Even neighbors."

"I don't want to believe she'd cause such a ruckus in the village."

"Then you don't know women very well. Good day, Lord Kenrick, I must be on my way."

Sarah needed a good switching. She had the whole village up in arms over the alleged monster. I only hoped Lord Kenrick came to his senses before something horrible happened.

Raul stood, leaning against a tree as I approached. His tunic sleeves were rolled up to reveal strong, bronzed arms. He'd already set a blanket along the bank of the creek amongst a scattering of wildflowers.

As if sensing my scrutiny, he turned to look at me. In a few strides, he was at my side.

"Ah, my little Brielle, you made it. I wasn't sure if Rhyne had got the chance to give you the message."

I swallowed hard, my pulse soaring out of control. "I'm glad you're here, I've wanted to get back to the marketplace to see you, but Gram has been watching me like a hawk."

"Well, we're here now. I hope you're hungry," he teased, reaching for my hand. "I've brought dried venison, bread, and fresh strawberries for lunch."

"It's perfect," I said, as he led me over to the blanket.

We sat down, facing one another, food spread out between us.

"So you'll never guess where I've just come from." He smiled, handing me a strawberry.

My blood sang in my ears as his fingers brushed mine. "The village?"

He chuckled, the sound intoxicated me. "I meant before my arrival in Dark Pines."

He always went to exotic places, countries and lands I only

dreamed about seeing. "Tell me."

"Bastiala. It's a small country along the sea. The waters are clear, sparkling bluer than the skies. And the sand is warm beneath your toes. When I sat upon the shore, I wished for nothing more than to share the sunset with you."

My breath caught in my throat. "It sounds beautiful."

He reached for my hand and clasped it in his. "It is. Perhaps one day I can show it to you."

"I-I'd like that." Shyness overtook me, and I glanced at our fingers, which were entwined. Maybe it was time for a change in subject. "Sarah is making quite the spectacle," I said as he released me and handed me a hunk of meat.

"So I noticed. Half the village is swarming the eastern portion of the forest. But fear not, soon they'll realize her folly."

I sighed, nibbling on the venison. "Why is she doing this?"

Raul's eyebrows shot up as he laughed. "I think she's jealous."

"Jealous? Of who?"

"You." He ate a slice of bread, then washed it down with water from the skin he carried. He wiped his hands on his breeches then slid closer to me. His palm slid over my arm.

My stomach fluttered as if someone released a jar of fireflies inside me. I caught my lip between my bottom teeth and raised my eyes until they met his.

"Bri," he whispered my name. "I've missed you. No matter what town or country I visited, I couldn't keep you from my thoughts. I lay awake at night, wondering what it'd be like to have you with me. To see your smiling face every day. So I hurried back here. To you."

He leaned closer, his hand cupping my face and I knew he was going to kiss me. What if I messed up or he thought I wasn't good at this? His knee pressed against mine, making me all too aware of the warmth radiating between us.

I lifted a hand to his firm chest. His heart beat erratically against my palm.

"Bri … " he said again.

The sound of horse hooves thundered through the pines and we leapt apart. *Shite.* What if it was Gram? She'd surely punish me.

Lord Kenrick came into the clearing; Sarah perched behind him, a smirk on her face.

"What are they doing here?" Raul glared as he climbed to his feet, temper flaring.

Kenrick climbed from his steed. "I hope we're not intruding." He glanced between Raul and me.

Right then, Rhyne came loping through the woods as well, with Gertie on his arm. Thank God. I grabbed tight to Raul's arm giving him an apologetic look. "No. Of course you're not interrupting." I gave a shaky smile, wondering if they'd seen how close together we'd been. "Raul, Rhyne, Gertie, and I were just about to have a picnic. You're more than welcome to join us."

Though deep inside, I regretted their interruption.

"Thank you. Sarah said she wanted to face her fears and come into the woods." Kenrick reached up to help her from the saddle.

My jaw clenched. He could've let her climb down on her own.

Sarah grinned at him then cradled her arm, playing up the injury. "Mother agreed I could go as long as Lord Kenrick accompanied me. So I made us a nice picnic."

Raul's hand squeezed mine. His nostrils flared like an angry stallion. Any moment now, I half expected to see him tackle our intruders.

"Sarah mentioned this was one of your favorite picnic spots." Kenrick smiled at me then spread a blanket out beside ours. "I can see why you like to come here. The stream, the flowers, lots of sunlight."

Had he come here because of me? He watched me, as Rhyne and Gertie plopped down on my blanket. With a smile, I tugged Raul to sit back down as well.

I turned to Rhyne. "Hope your shop wasn't too busy today."

"Not as bad as I thought it'd be. Luckily Da didn't need my help so I could get out of there on time." Rhyne cleared his throat and I caught his eye. He gave me an apologetic look, nodding toward Sarah and said, "Gertie has agreed to go to the festival with me."

The red haired girl blushed. "My mother was a little up in arms about it, but I told her there was no one else I'd rather go with."

"Oh, how wonderful. Do you have your gown picked out already?" I asked.

She popped a strawberry in her mouth and nodded. "Yes. Lady Weaver has made me a lovely green dress, of silk and lace."

"Sounds perfect."

"And what about you?" Gertie said. "Has anyone asked you?"

Sarah watched me carefully. I had half a mind to lie and say I had a couple invitations, but my conscience got the better of me.

I toyed with a blade of grass and felt Raul shift behind me so that his hand rested at the small of my back. "No. Not yet. Although, I doubt Gram will allow anyone to take me unchaperoned." I laughed.

A cloud rolled across the sky, blotting out the sun; the woods darkened like a cloak had been thrown over them.

Sarah gave a startled cry and raised a hand to her chest. "My, that gave me a start. Ever since last night, I've been so jumpy."

No way could I sit there and listen to her. I pushed to my feet, walking away from the creek to stand beneath an oak tree.

Raul joined me. He touched my shoulder and leaned forward to whisper in my ear. "I could see you home, if you'd like. Maybe we could stop off and pick some blackberries."

"But Gram's there. She thinks I'm with Rhyne," I said, watching my friend as he handed Gertie some food.

"Ah, I understand." He released his hold on me, sounding hurt.

"I—please don't think I'm embarrassed by you. I'm not. It's just, you know how she is. Gram doesn't fancy any males being around me—well, other than Rhyne, but he doesn't really count."

He chuckled. "Yes, I do. Fear not, I'm sure we'll find a way to meet up again."

Rhyne glanced at me then turned to Sarah. "So, what did this beast look like?"

"I-it had big teeth, with large horns protruding from its head. And it had fur, and scales." Her bottom lip trembled.

Kenrick, Gertie, and Rhyne gave her sympathetic looks, while Raul snorted.

"Why it sounds just like something out of a storybook." I envisioned the crude drawings of the beast I'd seen in the library—there wasn't a single similarity in her descriptions.

Sarah whimpered. "And just as frightening."

Kenrick patted her arm, and Rhyne nodded as if he believed every word. She wanted their attention and she got it. I pulled away from Raul and gathered my cloak. Sarah always had to have it all. The best dresses. The attention. Every male's adoration.

"I best get home. I don't want to get caught out here after dark," I said.

Raul started to gather his things as well. "I'll walk you."

"No—I'm fine. Besides, like I said, Gram's home and I'm sure you don't want to face her this night. And I'm positive Sarah will probably feel safer with you all here."

Kenrick frowned, peering over at me. I looked away.

"Bri, don't be foolish. It's not safe." Rhyne shoved to his feet, hauling Gertie up beside him. "We've got the cart parked further up the trail. We can take the lot of us home."

Kenrick stood as well. "He's right. You shouldn't wander the woodland alone. Let one of us see you home."

"I told you before, I don't believe in the beast."

"Let her go." Sarah brushed dirt from her skirts. "She knows these woods better than anyone else."

I seethed. More like she wanted to get rid of me. "Thank you, Sarah. I hope your knife wound heals, I'd hate for it to scar your beautiful skin."

She gasped. "You think I made it up?"

Instead of dignifying her with an answer, I spun on my heel and raced into the trees. Sticks snapped beneath my feet, my vision blurred with tears. Today should've been special. It was my first picnic with Raul, a chance to spend time alone with him. And we'd been on the verge of our first kiss. My first kiss. But, as always, Sarah ruined everything.

Brambles scratched my legs, snagging my skirt. Gnarled trees bent in gruesome forms, while thick shadows splayed out beneath them. A heavy gloom settled over the woodland as wisps of fog slithered like snakes against the ground. I shivered.

Don't think. I picked an animal trail to follow, stepping over dead branches and forest debris. Blood pounded in my ears and the hair on the back of my neck prickled. I twisted around to glance behind me.

Nothing there. Only the trees. Urgency gripped hold of me and I picked up my pace once more. As I scrambled through the thicket, an overwhelming scent of rotten meat made me gag. I covered my mouth with my hand and stopped running when a bright red piece of fabric caught my eye. With hesitant steps, I moved toward it.

"Oh God." I stumbled. There, sticking out from beneath a barberry bush was a severed arm, its finger pointed at me in accusation. My breath came in gasps as I scanned the rest of the clearing.

My foot nudged against something and I looked down in horror to find the head of Liam Gatekeeper staring up at me.

I screamed, backing away as fast as I could. All around me were pieces of his body, scattered like breadcrumbs. I shielded my eyes with my hands, until I bumped into something else.

With another scream, I whipped around only to find myself faced with an oak tree covered in dried blood and deep claw marks. My vision darkened and I prayed I wouldn't faint, that I wouldn't be stuck in the woods. Because somewhere out here, a monster lurked. If I didn't believe it before, I did now. The Beast was real.

Chapter Eight

The snap of a twig drew my attention. There, moving in and out of the tree line was a dark haired figure. As if sensing my scrutiny, she turned and a gasp lodged in my throat.

Lucia. My dead cousin's ghost.

"He's here ..." Her voice wailed, carried on the wind.

My eyes darted about. Who was here? The Beast?

"Who do you mean?"

She slowly looked up and behind me. *"He will kill you ..."*

Kill me?

My legs wobbled beneath me, but I forced myself to stay put. Lucia's ghost had come to see me again, to warn me. Was that why I'd seen her before? Had she been trying to warn me then, too?

"Brielle!" Raul's voice echoed in the woods around me.

At the sound of his voice, Lucia's ghost began to fade.

"Don't go yet," I said. "Please—"

A crash sounded next to me, and Raul burst into the clearing, panic etched into his face. He took one look at the body, then scooped me into his arms, shielding me from the gruesome scene.

"Shh … it's all right. I'm here now. I won't let anything hurt you."

I clung tight to him, burying my head against his chest, as tears trailed down my face. He stroked my hair, gently, speaking soothing words. "Nothing will ever harm you, I promise."

When I looked again, Lucia's ghost was completely gone. Now it was just us and a dead body.

"It's Liam." My words came out in a choked sob.

His arms tightened around me, as if that alone could shield me from the world. For the moment, maybe it could.

A horse whinnied and I lifted my head to see Kenrick riding toward us with Sarah behind him, clinging tight. After loosening her arms from around his waist, he leapt off his horse, his jaw tight, as he scanned the surroundings. His mouth turned down when he noticed the body. What was left of it.

Then his gaze met mine. Within two strides he was next to me. He gave my arm a gentle tug, pulling me from Raul. He clutched my face in his hands as if searching me for wounds.

"Are you hurt?"

I shook my head, trying to ignore Raul's rigid posture. His dark glance bored into Kenrick like a loosed arrowed.

Kenrick held me at arm's length, brow furrowed. "Did you see anything?"

"No," I whispered. "Just the body." I left out the part about the ghost, not wanting to sound crazier than I already did. "There's so much blood. Oh, God there's so much blood."

Kenrick's fingers dug into my arms and he gave me a shake. "Try to remain calm."

"She's just found the shredded remains of a body, how do you expect her to react?" Raul's chest puffed out, fists clenched at his side. His face darkened. Fiery heat seemed to radiate off him as if he'd been dipped in flames.

Just then, Rhyne and Gertie came into the clearing as well. "Oh shite." Rhyne quickly grasped hold of Gertie, shielding her from the sight. "Bri, are you all right?"

"Y-yes, I'll be fine."

"Come on, Gertie, let's get out of here. You don't need to see this." He led her back the way they'd come, casting one last worried look at me.

Kenrick glanced between me and Raul. "Take Brielle home. I'll be back with soldiers to collect the body and carry it back to town." He released me. But his hand grazed mine, his fingers giving a gentle squeeze. "Be safe."

When he turned away, Raul gathered me to his side once more. "Come on, let me see you home."

When we arrived, a sense of relief washed over me. I caught the familiar scent of our fire and the welcoming glow of candles in the windowsills, and the urge to get inside consumed me.

"You shouldn't come inside," I said. "Gram will—"

"I promised I would see you home. Not simply to your door."

Still holding my hand, he whipped the door open. The aroma of pheasant and potatoes spiraled in the air. Gram sat at the table with Father Machai, a brown package on the table between them.

Gram glanced at us then leapt to her feet. She circled me, stopping only when she came to stand in front of me. "What's happened?"

"I-I found a body." My hands trembled. I swallowed hard, trying not to cry. "It was Liam Gatekeeper."

She opened her arms and I rushed into them. As I nestled into her shoulder, she stroked my hair. "Hush now. Everything will be fine."

"There was blood everywhere."

"You're home safe now, there's nothing to worry about."

I hiccupped then rubbed the wetness from my lashes.

Father Machai's chair slid back as he too stood. "This is grave news. Has anyone gone to notify Liam's family?"

"No. Lord Kenrick said he'd retrieve the body."

Gram glanced at Father Machai, exchanging a silent communication.

"I will attend Liam's family. And I think it'd be best if Raul accompanies me to the village when I leave," Father Machai said. "I don't think it's safe to be out alone."

"Sure. I'd appreciate the ride." Raul's arms crossed his chest and worry lines furrowed his brow as he stared at me.

"Why don't you two make sure Father Machai's cart is ready to go while we finish our conversation?" Gram's voice had an odd tone, as if she knew something she wasn't willing to tell me.

I followed Raul outside to where the cart was parked near the tree line.

"I'm sorry our picnic didn't turn out. I'd planned on us being able to spend time with one another." He twined his fingers through mine. "I wanted it to be perfect, so you'd know my intentions toward you are sincere."

"It *was* perfect. Well until I found the body." My thumb grazed his knuckles. Emotions swam through me. I knew Gram wanted me to stay away from him. And I was sure after he left tonight, she'd have some words for me. But something drew me to him. Something I couldn't explain.

We stopped next to the cart, the leaves dancing as a breeze came through. Raul drew me against him until our bodies pressed together. My hands rested against the muscled contours of his chest. I felt safe with him, like he alone could keep the monsters away. He bent down, his lips brushing against my cheek.

I took a deep breath, gripping hold of his tunic to pull him closer.

He traced my jaw, his touch sending delicious chills through my body.

He leaned closer, his mouth a breath away from mine. My heart skittered against my ribs. More than anything, I wanted him to kiss me, for him to make me forget everything else. The body. The ghost. The strange whisperings. I didn't want them to be my final thoughts of the day.

This time he leaned down and there was no doubt in my mind what he wanted.

His lips captured mine, sending a shock down to my toes. I wrapped my arms around him, my lids drifting shut, and lost myself in him. He tasted of strawberries, his mouth soft against mine. Raul's fingers tangled in my hair and he deepened the kiss, his tongue darting between my lips, grazing mine.

My pulse raced, my skin flushing as if someone held a flame to me. I'd waited sixteen years for this moment. I stood there letting the explosions of light flash behind my lids. Everything felt right, as if this moment had been written ages ago. I'd dreamed of being kissed for far too long, and it was everything I'd dreamt it'd be.

Just then the door banged open, and we leapt apart as Father Machai made his way outside while Gram stood with her arms crossed.

"I'll see you soon, my little Brielle. We definitely need to talk." Raul gave me a crooked grin.

Did he feel it too? The connection?

Breathless, I said, "Promise?"

"Yes. Nothing can keep me away, not even your gram." With one last squeeze of my hand, he backed away.

"Come on inside now, Brielle," Gram called from the doorway. "I think you owe me an explanation as to why you were alone with Raul."

Shite. I was in for it now. With a sigh, I turned toward the cabin and went indoors.

Blood seeped into the wood. Everything around me was drenched in deep crimson. Heavy footsteps pounded the ground behind me, my pulse quickened. I needed to get out of the forest. Moonlight filtered through the treetops, like a ghostly beacon. The bushes rustled and I spun to face them. Something was there. Closing in on me. My skin prickled with the awareness that I was being watched. With a yelp, I turned to run, only to find myself in a pile of bones. Skulls stared back at me with empty sockets. Leg bones, arm bones, and spines, all stained with blood.

I screamed. There crouched in front of me was Robert Stablehand. He held his arm in front of his face to defend himself. But the creature was too swift. Claws swooped down upon his flesh and he cried in agony. Yet the Beast didn't stop. Several times its dagger-like nails tore at his skin. I couldn't see the monster, only its claws. But I knew it was there.

"Help me!" Robert screamed.

As I reached for him, he disappeared beneath the pile of skeletons.

His face was replaced by my cousin Lucia's.

"The beast is here … "she whispered.

"No!" I shouted.

Something cool touched my head, shocking me fully awake. Gram was wiping my forehead with a cool cloth.

I kicked my blankets off and sat up. My head ached, and I felt as if I might vomit.

"I-I saw Robert Stablehand in my dream," I said, throat thick with emotion. "The Beast killed him. And I saw Lucia."

"Hush now. You're running a fever, child. You've had a rough day." She frowned, dipping the cloth into a basin of cool water.

She offered me a cup of elderberry wine, and I took it from her. The cold liquid slid down my throat. If only I could chase away the remnants of the nightmare so easily.

The thunderous sound of horse hooves reverberated outside. Loud voices echoed in the night, and within moments, frantic knocks pounded at our door.

I leapt from my bed and rushed to open it.

Kenrick stood on our stoop, his dark hair disheveled as he gawked at me.

"Thank God, you're all right," he said. "We followed the Beast's tracks this way. At first I thought it might've attacked you and your grandmother."

I sucked in a ragged breath. "The creature? It was here?"

"We tracked it to the other side of the clearing, then lost it."

What if it had stalked me? Was that why Lucia's ghost had appeared to me next to Liam's body? Was she trying to warn me that the Beast was near? My stomach clenched. Maybe it knew I'd found Liam's body and wanted me next.

Kenrick's gaze trailed over me, a reminder that I wore only my thin shift. My skin blazed when he glimpsed the scar above my heart. Embarrassed, I raised my hand up to cover it.

He reached for me, clutching me close to him.

Gram gave a strong, loud cough, and Kenrick pulled away from me.

"I apologize," he said. "A knight should have better manners." He lowered his head in supplication.

Gram tossed a blanket over my shoulders, and then tugged me back, putting herself between us. "We're quite all right, Lord Kenrick.

My granddaughter suffered a shock earlier and has been with fever most of the night."

He bowed. "I apologize for calling on you at this late hour." He clasped my hand. "Feel better soon. I am riding through this area tonight to search for signs of the Beast. I'll make sure to ride by your house often, to make sure you're safe."

Gram smiled. "Oh, that isn't necessary, milord. We'll be safe enough."

"Please." His eyes never left mine. "I'd feel better knowing Brielle is well guarded."

Gram pursed her lips, but finally she said, "Very well, Lord Kenrick. One can never have too much protection, after all." She turned around and went back into the house. "Come back to bed, Brielle," she called behind her.

I caught Kenrick's eyes. There was a fire in them. "Goodnight, Kenrick."

He bowed but never took his eyes from mine. "Goodnight, Brielle."

Chapter Nine

The village was in complete pandemonium.

The line into the butcher's wound around the side of the building. For the second time this week, the panicked masses bought food as if they thought they might never eat again. People shouted at one another, some accused each other of cutting in line. Little acts of aggression that signaled the violence waiting to break free.

Those not purchasing meals waited at the blacksmith's to procure better weapons. Another hunting party circled outside the mayor's house, much in the same fashion as they had the previous day.

Rhyne caught my eye and waved me toward the counter.

"Hey, no cutting," Samuel Boat Hand hollered at me.

"She ain't cutting. She's here to see me." Rhyne came to the doorway and pulled me inside.

A couple men chuckled, others grumbled.

"How are you?" Rhyne's voice lowered. "I've been worried."

"I'm better today. Just can't wait for this to be over."

Rhyne raised an eyebrow, his gaze scanning the line. "You and me both."

"At least you're keeping busy." I laughed. "Nothing like a little crisis to drum up the customers."

"I'd rather be fishing with you or having a picnic with Gertie," he teased, nudging me with his elbow.

"Me too."

"So did you get in trouble for having Raul see you home?"

I grimaced. "A little. Gram wanted to know where you were. I told her that we'd bumped into Raul in the woods and he'd joined us, along with Sarah and Kenrick, and that after we found the body in the woods, you took Gertie home, while Raul saw me home."

"Guess we need to be more careful, eh?"

"We need more pork," Bowman shouted from behind the counter.

Rhyne frowned. "Sorry. I've got get back to work. I'll talk to you later."

"See you." I smiled, as he leapt over the counter, his bloodied apron flapping like a sheet caught in the wind.

Once in place, he gave me a wink, and I hurried from the crowded shop. I crossed the busy street, trying to dodge horse carts as I made my way toward the church.

"Lady Brielle," Kenrick called from the side of the road.

I went to him, unable to hide my smile. The rest of the village was falling into chaos, but he could still find a bright spot. "Good day, milord."

"I'm surprised to see you up and about today. Should you be out of bed?"

I was still feeling out of sorts, mostly fatigued in a way that wouldn't seem to go away. But then, after the events of yesterday, I hadn't expected to sleep well anyway.

"I'm headed to the church for more research. Perhaps you'd like to come with me?"

"I wish I could join you. Unfortunately, I have a creature to hunt. Last night yielded nothing but tracks and trails."

"Maybe some other time." My voice faltered and I peered up at him. "I wanted to apologize for my gram last night. She was kind of abrupt."

"No need to apologize, she's looking after you. I suppose I'd do the same if I was in her place." He smiled. "I should be off."

I forced a smile in an attempt to hide my disappointment. "Good luck today."

I turned to go, but he caught my arm. The warmth of his fingers seeped through the fabric of my sleeve. I inhaled deeply, taking in his scent. Pine and rosemary.

"The festival is coming up," he said softly. "Do you plan to attend?"

"Yes. And you?"

His hand slid down my arm, until his fingers gently gripped mine. I tilted my face and stared up at him. My heart pounded in my ears, and each beat threatened to explode through my body.

"Yes, I will be there. Perhaps you would allow me a dance or two?"

"Of course." As long as Gram wasn't in view.

He grinned at me. "Good, because I'd like to see more of you."

Sarah came toward us, flapping her arms back and forth like an excited chicken beating its wings. "Lord Kenrick."

Swallowing hard, I took a step back and curtsied. "I-I'll see you, milord."

Before I could leave, he leaned closer to me. "We'll talk more later, Lady Brielle."

Somehow I doubted it, because Sarah was on the prowl. *And he thinks* he's *hunting.* The eagerness on her face was undeniable. She planned on landing Lord Kenrick and wouldn't stop until she succeeded. The only good thing that'd come from this was at least now she'd let Rhyne be.

I hurried to the church, cursing the day Sarah Weaver was born.

A brisk wind swept down the nape of my neck as I slipped through the doors. The sanctuary was empty, save for some candles burning near the altar, however voices drifted from the hallway near the back of the room.

"Perhaps you'd like me to stay on and help you rid your village of the Beast," a voice said.

"I thank you for your concern, Brother Reynaldo. But I assure you, things are under control. I pray every night to our Lord. He'll watch over us," Father Machai said. "Our town has taken precautions and has hunting parties out as we speak."

I pressed myself against the wall and inched closer.

"Several deaths does not sound like things are under control. Do not make the same mistakes other villages and churches have. Do not underestimate the power of this creature." A robust frame passed the doorway to the hall. I caught sight of a bald head, a roll of fat folded up near his neck. "If you don't believe me, look at the ruins of the church outside the western woods. There is still evidence of the monster's wrath upon the stone walls."

I froze in place. This had happened in Dark Pines before? Why didn't I know of this? My mind raced as I tried to remember where the ruins were; maybe it'd be a good idea to investigate them myself. Possibly they contained more answers.

"For now, I will forego your offer of help," Father Machai said. "But I promise, should I need you, I'll send word to Fire Ridge. Now, perhaps I can offer you some bread and cheese before I head out."

"Of course, Father," the man said.

I backed closer to the main entrance and took a seat in one of the pews so they wouldn't know I'd eavesdropped.

The oversized priest emerged first. Cold seeped up my spine when I met his dark, beady eyes. My stomach knotted. Darkness seemed to halo him. His black beard was trimmed into point at his chin, his fat, sausage-like lips curved up at the corners. His gaze swept over me, making me pull my cloak tighter. "Good day, milady."

My fingers gripped the fabric as I stood. "Father." Something about this man frightened me.

After long minutes, his scrutiny of me ended. "Thank you again for your hospitality," he said to Father Machai. "I'll see myself out."

This man knew something. I could feel it in my bones. He spoke with such assurance, as if he alone knew how to defeat the Beast—that he knew where to find it. And it was my curiosity that led me out the door, trailing after him.

He pulled his hood up over his head and trudged through the busy thoroughfare, but instead of stopping in town, he pushed to the outskirts. He glanced behind him, and I quickly ducked behind a cart.

Did he know I trailed him? I took a deep breath and dared to peek around the side of my hiding place. He was moving again, his large body wobbling like a broken wheel. A moment later, I saw him standing in the tree line, peering into the shadows.

Then *she* stepped out. Lucia. Or rather, her ghost. What was she doing here now? Was it possible she was appearing to Reynaldo as well?

Reynaldo leaned forward as if to speak to her, then dropped to his knees as if in prayer.

What did they say? Could he even see her? I swallowed hard and pushed closer, tugging my own hood up over my head. I walked alongside a couple soldiers who were heading down the rut filled road. When we passed the spot where Reynaldo was, I slowed my pace and came back around, pushing myself against the tree.

It was then that I heard the voices.

"Father Machai refuses our help with the Beast," Reynaldo said. "What should I do?"

"The Beast will keep attacking, and soon they'll be forced to run. He'll come for her. Mark my words. He always does."

The whisper came out like the hiss of the wind, and the air grew suddenly colder.

"Tell me," Reynaldo said. "Where can we hope to stop this madness?"

"*Fire Ridge. They will come. And when they do, you must be ready.*"

"Then I shall go there and wait," Reynaldo said. I heard the sound of his heavy footsteps leaving the woods. Then and only then did I poke my head around the tree to survey the forest.

Fog swept in like eerie fingers, reaching toward me, and I saw the retreating form of the woman. She seemed to evaporate before my very eyes, disappearing into the mist, as though her form lost all substance and returned to the afterlife.

If I'd been doubtful about the purpose of Lucia's ghost, I wasn't any longer. She'd been brief when she'd passed her warning to Reynaldo, but it had been clear. There were people working with the Beast, and it was up to Reynaldo to be ready when they came to Fire Ridge.

Relief flooded me when I got back to the church. The shroud of darkness I'd felt in the woods had dissipated. I could breathe again.

Father Machai came from the corridor; a warm smile enveloping his face when he saw me.

"Do I even need to ask why you're here?" he teased. He took out his ring of keys and handed them to me. "There is ink, parchment, and quills in the library, should you need it. No one will bother you today, what with all the lunacy surrounding the Beast."

"Thank you." Now, more than ever, I needed to find out more about the Beast.

"If you'll excuse me," he said, "I have to step out for a bit. Daniel Barber has requested I call upon his brother to read him his last rites." He clutched a worn bible to his chest and skirted past me.

Silence settled over the stone building as I made my way down to the library, trying to forget about Father Reynaldo and the ghostly woman. I carried a small candle to light the way. The flame flickered, casting eerie crimson shadows, which pooled near the floor like puddles of blood. A chill writhed beneath my skin and I shuddered.

Stay calm. I'm in a house of God, not the bowels of hell.

But my fingers trembled as I pushed open the door to the library. I clambered inside and lit as many candles as I could find, yet they did little to chase away the bleakness.

Once my cloak was off, I searched through several rolled parchments until I found a wooden tube containing Father Machai's maps. As carefully as possible, I slid the largest one out then returned the rest.

My skirts swished against my ankles as I moved across the room, then set the map on the worktable, holding it in place with a small book at each corner. My teeth grazed my bottom lip as I picked up a quill and dipped it into the inkwell. From memory, I marked X's along the villages with known attacks, places Kenrick had found mention of in letters. Fire Ridge Mountain, Dark Pines, Candle Shore, and Moxley Way. When I put down the quill, I realized the pattern made a horseshoe shape. But I was no closer to understanding anything beyond what I already knew.

There had to be more clues. More texts. I wondered if there would be any information about the local church ruins and what'd happened to it. With my mind running wild, I scoured the shelves, searching through titles for anything remotely close to the Beast or creature. But I found nothing until I noticed a much thinner book hidden at the back of a shelf, behind the rest of the parchments and leather bound volumes.

My hand closed around the sheepskin cover and flipped it open. I gasped.

The attacks continue. Two more bodies have been found. The Beast draws ever closer to our fortification. We have sent for reinforcements.

My palms grew slick with sweat as I made my way to the table to sit. I pulled a candle closer and leaned over the book to read on. A total of twenty attacks from the village of Moorhaven had been recorded. The unknown author described the mutilated bodies in great detail. Limbs torn from them. Heads missing. Strange claw marks.

"It can't be," I whispered. I traced the date at the bottom of the page. 1299. Three hundred years ago.

The dank air became heavier. From outside, the low howl of wind beat against the church like an angry mob and I closed my eyes. Visions of Liam and Margaret clawed at me. Blood. Bones. Screams. So many victims.

Waves of nausea washed over me, and I gripped tight to the table to steady myself. I took several deep breaths, then opened my eyes once more and continued to read.

Our savior has come. A knight to slay our beast.

A rough drawing revealed a tiny picture of a man in full armor sitting upon his steed. A crest containing a griffin holding a serpent in its mouth surrounded by four stars was etched in the corner of the page. I examined it closer. Kenrick's crest.

With careful strokes, I scribbled the new information on the parchment Father Machai had left for me. The timelines of the attacks showed that the beast struck every thirty-five to forty years.

But why?

I tapped my fingers on the table, then glanced back at the small book. I turned the page and found several pages torn from the book. Only one remained.

We are free at last. The good knight has slain the Beast, just as the dark haired lady said he would. The curse is broken.

I went still. If the knight had slain the Beast, then what stalked our woods? My skin prickled and erupted in patches of gooseflesh.

Could the beast come back to life? Or were there several of them? A new one for a new generation?

And what of Kenrick's crest? How was he involved in the curse?

"You're still here."

I jumped, then turned to find Kenrick leaning against the wall behind me.

"So it would appear." I gestured for him to come in.

He sauntered across the room, his shaggy hair sticking up in messy tufts. "Have you found anything?" He bent over the map, tracing the X's I'd marked.

"Yes. I located a book hidden on the shelves. It delves into the attacks in Moorhaven." I paused, then decided if I wanted answers, I had to ask questions. "The documents show that someone with your family crest has hunted the Beast before."

He nodded. "Of course they do. Because we have. Every generation in my family is trained for this purpose."

A simple enough answer. But one thing didn't fit. "The documents show that the Beast only appears every thirty-five to forty years. What does your family do until the Beast appears?"

"We never know when it will return," he said. "From the moment we are born, thus begins our watch." He stroked his chin as if in deep thought then shifted his gaze to me. "According to these markings, it looks like the creature is circling round."

I gasped. The symbol wasn't a horseshoe after all. And he was right, if I plotted Moorhaven next, it made a complete circle. At the center of the circle was the town of Crawford. My late Aunt Narcissa had owned an estate there. The place where both she and my cousin were murdered. Maybe there was a connection.

Kenrick lowered himself into the chair next to mine, scrutinizing my notes. He picked up the sheepskin book and flipped through it. He stopped momentarily to rub his temples.

"Are you well?" I asked.

He glanced my way, his eyes unfocused. "Yes, sorry. It seems I'm not feeling very well. It's odd, ever since I got here, I've been having symptoms of sickness. I wake up some nights from strange dreams, feeling as if I've lost time and don't know where I am."

"Perhaps you should have my grandmother call on you," I said.

He turned his attentions back to the book. "Thank you for your offer, but I'll be fine."

He continued to thumb through the transcript. When he got to the page with the knight on it, I asked, "Is this your family crest?"

"Yes." He grinned. "Likely one of my ancestors fought the Beast before me."

"And won." My finger pointed to the text regarding the monster's death.

He frowned. "Then there must be more than one."

"My thoughts exactly. But if you read the next line, it mentions a curse. Have you come across any other details in regards to that?"

"No. Perhaps it's another clue. The only good news is, at least we know the creatures can be killed. But with how many casualties, I don't know."

"You'll succeed."

He tilted his head and watched me closely. Nervous, I reached for a parchment and a quill. The need to stay focused on research hummed in my ears, but Kenrick caught my hand and raised my fingers to his lips.

The beat of my heart drowned everything out. My gaze met his. The air around us seemed to ignite.

He lowered my hand but did not release it. My skin blazed, and I could still feel where his mouth touched.

"I'm glad to have met you, Brielle Healer. You are intelligent. Quick witted." His thumb traced my palm. "And in all my nineteen years, I've never come across anyone as beautiful as you."

I swallowed and pulled my hand back. "Do you whisper such niceties to Sarah Weaver as well?"

He sat straighter, then leaned closer so our eyes were level. "No. I am being a gentleman to her because of her parents. I examined her arm more closely, and you were right. She lied about the Beast attack."

"Will you let her know that you're aware of her falsehood?"

"No, I'd rather she realize her own mistake. And she will, in time."

"And what of her … other intentions?"

Kenrick looked at me until I met his gaze. "She has eyes for me. I am not a fool. But she is of no consequence to me."

The hallway door slammed and echoed in the library. Startled, I leapt to my feet.

"Stay here." Kenrick unsheathed his sword and hurried from the room, then moments later returned, his brows knit. "I didn't find anyone. Maybe a draft caught the door."

"I'm sure that's all it was." Hands shaking, I gathered my notes, then put the books away, except for the one I'd found hidden, which I tucked safely into my leather purse. When everything was cleaned up, I pulled on my cloak.

Kenrick watched me from across the room. "It's getting late. Let me see you home safely."

"Are you sure it's not an inconvenience?"

"You, Lady Brielle, will *never* be an inconvenience."

In two long strides, he stood at my side, offering me his arm. As we left the church together, the shadowy hands of dusk clutched the sky. Soon it'd be dark.

Kenrick led me toward the mayor's house where his horse stood tethered out front. Before we reached there, though, a strange sensation ran through my body, almost as if someone had brushed strands of thread across my skin. My arms puckered with gooseflesh. From above me, I heard the undeniable sound of a loud crack.

Raul peeled from the side of the building and raced into the square. "Brielle! Look out!" He shoved Kenrick and me to the side right as a large chunk of rock fell from a nearby structure.

The stone hit the ground and burst into several pieces in the place I'd just been standing. My legs quaked as I realized how close I'd come to being harmed. As I scanned the square, I noticed a woman, half-hidden against the edge of the stables, slip away into the night.

This was now the second time I'd been caught in a nearly fatal accident. And if the last few days had taught me anything, it was not to ignore what seemed like coincidence.

"Raul, how can I ever thank you?"

"No need for gratitude, my little Brielle, I'm just glad I was in the right place, at the right time." He helped me to my feet and held me at arm's length. "Are you injured?"

From behind him, I saw Rhyne step forward. "Does Bowman know you're wandering about tonight?" I said to Rhyne.

He frowned. "No. And it'd be best if we could keep it that way."

"Why are you with Raul?"

He shrugged. "He's helping me sort some things out. So if you're looking for me, and can't find me, I'll likely be with the Wanderers in the western woods."

"I think Brielle has had a trying night. Perhaps we should let her get home," Raul said. His gaze shifted between me and Kenrick, his eyes glowing like they'd been lit by flames. "Does Loreen know you're with Lord Kenrick tonight?"

"I—um, no ... " I stepped closer to him. "What is wrong with your eyes?"

"My eyes?"

"They're glowing," I whispered under my breath.

He turned his head from me. "Nothing. It's likely just a play of the light."

"Raul, we need to return to camp now." Rhyne tugged him away from me.

I blinked, and when I looked again, Raul's eyes had turned back to their normal mahogany color. Maybe it was a play of the light, but somehow, I believed not. What was Raul hiding from me? And why was he all of a sudden so interested in having Rhyne come out to the Wanderer camp?

Rhyne and Raul moved further away from me as Kenrick joined us.

"I owe you a life debt," Kenrick said, his palm resting against the small of my back. "It happened so fast, I didn't have time to even react."

Raul gave a slight bow and glanced toward the stables. "My honor. Now, I must get back to my carriage. Be safe."

I watched him and Rhyne disappear in the same direction I'd seen the woman go. Had they seen her, too?

"Are you all right?" Kenrick touched my shoulder.

"Yes," I said. "Thank you. I'm a little shaken up, that's all."

"Well then, let's get you home."

I was going to object, knowing Gram would not be pleased. But he gave me no chance to argue. In one swift motion, Kenrick lifted me atop his horse, then climbed into the saddle behind me. He reached around and gathered the reins, making me all too aware of his presence.

Kenrick dug his heels into the flanks of the horse and led it into a slow trot. Kenrick's left arm encircled my waist as if to belt me into place.

"You can lean back, I've got you," he whispered, his breath tickling my neck.

I sank into his chest, and his chin rested against my hair as he steered the horse through the main gate. A contented sigh escaped my lips. I loved the feel of his arms, the way I fit perfectly against him. If I turned my head just right, I could hear the sound of his heart, and I marveled at the way it beat in time with mine.

Again, I wondered what pull he had over me. He seemed so familiar, yet shouldn't.

As we moved through the woodland, the trees danced as a brisk wind rattled through their branches, the gloominess of night settling at their trunks. The birds quieted, while the frogs took up their song.

I swallowed hard. "Do you think you'll catch the beast?"

"It's only a matter of time. With your research and my prowess, we're unstoppable."

I giggled. "We make a great pair, don't we?"

"Yes." His voice deepened.

Kenrick urged the horse down another trail until we came in sight of the cabin. Candles glittered like tiny eyes in the windows. Gram was home.

Kenrick dismounted first then turned to help me down. His hands caught me just under my arms and I slid down. When my feet hit the ground, he didn't release me. Instead, I fell forward against his chest. I sucked in a deep breath. He was so close. He tipped up my chin so that I looked at him, and his fingers traced the contours of my face with feather-like gentleness.

"I can't stop thinking of you," he whispered. "You haunt my every thought. It's as if you've cast a spell over me."

I memorized his every feature, as his strong arms pulled me nearer. The tenderness splayed across his face. The way his fingers trailed along my skin.

"I know no spells," I said softly.

He smiled at me. "No? Then tell me why I dream of you every night? Why my every waking moment is spent wondering about you? Why I feel as though we've met before?"

My hand rested against him, every part of me drawn to him.

His thumb swept across my lips as if to steal a kiss. "Swear to me you'll save me a dance at the festival."

We leaned forward, his forehead resting against mine. "I promise."

As the promise escaped my lips, an image of Raul flashed in my mind. I couldn't do this. In the end, Kenrick would leave like everyone else who came through Dark Pines.

He was here for one purpose. To find and kill the Beast. He wouldn't let me get in the way of that, and when his purpose was done, he'd be gone as quickly as he'd come. Tears burned my eyes, my stomach clenched. Kenrick's hand fell back to his side and already I missed his touch. Yet, I felt a sadness that lingered within, as if perhaps our chance to be together had come and gone. Yes, he would leave one day soon. Assuming he survived his encounter with the Beast.

At the sound of footsteps coming to the front door, we stepped apart just as Gram opened the door.

"I bid you good evening, Lady Brielle." He bowed, then climbed atop his mount once more.

Gram came outside to stand beside me. When he was out of earshot, she turned to look at me.

"Not tonight, Gram," I said.

"I can't help it," she said. "When I see you with him, I worry for you."

"He brought me home. That's all." I shrugged. "Remember, you're the one who said I needed an escort."

She took one of my hands in hers. I wanted to go inside, but her touch and the way she looked at me contained such sincerity that I couldn't turn away from her.

"I know this doesn't make sense to you," she said. "But I worry you're rushing headlong into something you're not ready for."

"What would I not be ready for?"

She shrugged. "To let go of your youth. Your innocence. It seems like several lifetimes ago, but I was once your age. This is a time you'll never get back. And you'll regret not savoring it while it lasted."

I saw the sense in her words, but we both knew this wasn't simply about my youth and my innocence. "Gram, why do you hate Kenrick so much?"

After a moment, she said, "I don't hate him. But I have questions about him. I fear he is not fully what he seems."

"He's a knight. What else would he be?"

"Perhaps a knight. And perhaps something more. Those Beast attacks didn't start getting bad until he came riding into Dark Pines."

I went still. "So you're saying he might be responsible for them?"

"No, nothing like that. I believe his purpose is to find and kill the Beast. But I also believe there is more going on here than we realize."

Chapter Ten

I was on my way back to the cottage after dropping off medicine for Jakob Fieldhand past Champston Bridge. My gaze flitted over the thicket. Already shadows and gloom consumed everything. Twigs crunched beneath my feet as I made my way to the rut filled road.

Even though I'd come this way dozens of times there was something unsettling about it today. My pulse thundered in my ears as I scanned the ground for blood and bones. What if the Beast lay in wait for me? Would I be able to defend myself? Goosebumps broke out over my skin. If I wanted to keep my wits about me, I needed to shut off my mind.

Overhead, clouds gathered in the sky like a retinue of soldiers ready to do battle, and raindrops pelted my head, running down my hair and into my face, while the wind whipped this way and that.

Cold droplets seeped through the skirt of my dress, setting my teeth chattering, and I picked up my pace, eager to get home. Fog floated about the tall grass, inching across the road ahead of me.

As I made my way onto the bridge, the boards creaked beneath my footfalls, almost like the whine of a child. I grasped hold of the rail when my feet slid across the wet wood.

My mouth went dry and I came to a halt and stared at what looked like the figure of a dark haired woman standing in the center of the wooden structure. I didn't know if this was a friend, foe, or hallucination. Mist swirled around her like a billowing cloak. Her body seemed to carry an unnatural glow.

The rush of water grew louder as I took several steps backward. My head snapped up and I watched in horror as the river rose at an alarming rate, spraying up from beneath my feet between the crevices in the boards. I fell to the side, my hands wrapped around the railing in an effort to hold on.

I heard a high-pitched scream as the wooden beams beneath me started to sway. *Oh God.*

"Brielle!" someone yelled from the shoreline.

My eyes came to rest on Kenrick, who jumped from his horse and raced toward the bridge. The cold river rushed against my knees, but still I attempted to move forward.

"No! Go back, it's too dangerous," I shouted over the roar of wind and water.

But he didn't listen; instead he waded through the thigh deep water that'd already overtaken the bridge. "Hold on, I'm coming."

"Kenrick, go back." My grip loosened, and I slid further down.

"I won't leave you."

My legs came out from under me as the rapids slammed into me. I sank beneath the currents, water washing over my head. Darkness surrounded me as I rammed into the other side of the bridge, where I wedged my foot against the boards, and pushed my head above water, sputtering.

Kenrick swam toward me. After a moment, he caught my arm and tugged me closer to him. We fought against the current, which grew stronger by the moment.

I kicked my legs beneath me in an attempt to propel myself forward to the riverbank faster, but my heavy garments made it nearly impossible to maneuver. With numb fingers, I untied my cloak from my shoulders and let it wash away.

A loud crack reverberated from behind us. "Brielle, move."

Kenrick managed to shove me out of the way, right as the bridge broke free and came barreling down the river behind us. But he wasn't quick enough to get himself out of harm's way.

I screeched as I watched the structure ram into him. One moment he was there, the next, he disappeared beneath the surface.

"Kenrick!" Panic coursed through me as I grabbed for the long reeds of grass along the shoreline and pulled myself from the raging river, climbing to my feet. My chest burned as I attempted to catch my breath. I cupped my hands around my mouth. "Kenrick?"

I dropped my satchel to the ground and rushed down the bank, searching for him. Tears blurred my vision as I scoured the murky, debris-filled waters. My chest tightened.

Then, I saw him, his body caught up on a downed tree further up. "Hold on, I'm coming."

I struggled to run in my soaking wet dress, slipping in mud and on wet grass. When I reached the place where the tree was, I held tight to the trunk. One wrong move and I could get pinned beneath the tree and drown. I inched my way forward, which seemed to take hours.

"Kenrick," I called, but he didn't answer. My throat constricted and I prayed I'd be strong enough to get him to shore, and that he'd be alive when we got there.

When he was within reach, I looped one arm around him from the back and yanked his body toward me. I stumbled, nearly falling, but I caught hold of the tree with my free hand. As I struggled back toward the bank, the waters slowed like someone had put a dam in to stop the flow. At last, we reached the shore and I climbed onto the embankment, dragging Kenrick up.

I noticed the bloody gash across his forehead and fell to my knees beside him. "Please, Kenrick, wake up. You've got to be okay."

My head bent closer to his as I listened to hear his breathing. "Please. Don't leave me," I sobbed. "You can't leave me."

He sputtered, and his lids flew open. His blue eyes were wild as he glanced around. When he saw me, he tugged me into his arms.

"Brielle, you saved me."

"I thought I'd lost you." Tears streamed down my cheeks as I hugged him. "You went underwater and I couldn't find you." What was my attachment to him? Why did I care so much? He had no right to garner these types of reactions from me. He had become a friend over the course of time he'd spent in Dark Pines, but it seemed like I'd known him much longer. Like we had indeed met somewhere before. Yet, even I knew it to be impossible and quickly brushed the thoughts and feelings aside.

"Shh … I'm all right now." He smoothed the hair back from my face, his gaze intent on mine.

It was a miracle he hadn't been wearing his armor tonight, or he could've died in the river.

All around us, dusk set in. Already the air had grown cooler. We needed to find shelter for the night because there was no way we could travel down to the eastern bridge before darkness enveloped everything. And there were far too many dangerous things about in the woods.

He cringed as he sat up, his arms still encircling me. "I'm a little dizzy, but I think I can walk, if you help me stand."

I nodded and pushed to my feet, then reached down and offered him my hands. With a grunt, he pulled himself erect. Blood streamed down his face, and he wiped it away with his hand, leaving a crimson smudge behind.

A horse whinnied behind us, and I turned to see Kenrick's mount nearby. "Let me bandage your head, then I'll help you onto your horse. There's an abandoned barn just up the road where we can find shelter. It's the closest place."

Once I finished cleaning and bandaging his cut, he caught my hand in his. "Thank you."

"You're welcome. Now, we must hurry and get in out of this rain before we catch our deaths."

I didn't want to mention just how close we'd already come to that. My mind flicked back to the figure I'd seen on the bridge. Had she caused it to collapse? Was she the one responsible for the rise in the river? Or maybe she'd been here to warn me.

Either way, I knew her appearance wasn't a coincidence. The more I thought about her, the more I realized we needed to get in out of the dark. And off the road.

Kenrick managed to climb atop his horse, then help me onto the saddle behind him.

"The barn is just around the curve."

The horse took off at a slow trot and I wrapped my arms around his waist; the heat from his body warmed me through my cold, wet clothes.

He guided the horse into the tall grass until we came to the dilapidated barn. Part of the roof was missing, while several boards had been stripped from the outside.

Kenrick slid from his mount. "Wait here a moment. I'm going to check and make sure there are no wild animals or bandits inside."

He drew his sword then crept toward the leaning building. Long minutes went by as I sat, my arms wrapped around my chest as I shivered, listening to the rain hit the side of the shelter.

Soon he poked his head out. "It's all clear. You can come in now." He sheathed his sword then came around to help me down. His hands grasped my waist as he set me on the ground.

Once we were in the barn, I set to work, unsaddling the horse and rummaging through the pouches. I found dried venison and cheese, as well as two woolen blankets, and a skin of water. There was also a small sack of oats for the horse.

Kenrick gathered an armload of broken boards, beams, and posts, then shoved bits of dry hay beneath. He produced flint from one of the saddlebags and kneeled down to get a fire going.

Tiny sparks sprayed across the hay, and Kenrick leaned forward to blow on it. After a moment, flames sprang to life, igniting first the straw, then a couple pieces of wood. The flames danced in the darkness, creating a ring of light around our makeshift camp. Already the heat caressed my chilled body.

I knew I needed to get out of my dress and hang it to dry, even with no spare clothing to change into. My shift beneath would cover me enough.

"Can you turn your back for a moment?" I flushed. "I-I need to remove some of my wet garments."

Kenrick glanced at me across the fire. Our gazes locked. Damp, dark hair swept across the white bandage around his forehead, and his white tunic clung to a sculpted chest. With a nod, he spun so that his back faced me.

As quick as I could, I untied the back of my dress then proceeded to fight to get the sodden garment over my head. When I finally freed myself from it, I draped it over one of the horse stalls. Next, I bent down and took off my boots and stockings. Barefoot, I crept back to the fire in only my shift and sat down.

"You can look now," I said.

He spun around and glanced at me. I heard the intake of a deep breath, then watched as he grabbed a blanket from the ground. He moved to my side and draped it about my shoulders.

He smiled. "I never thought I'd be stranded out in the wilderness with you."

I reached next to me and grabbed our food as Kenrick plopped down and slid he boots off. I averted my eyes while he stripped out of his wet shirt and put on the dry one he'd pulled from one of pouches on his horse's saddle.

We ate in silence; the only sounds were from the snap of the embers and the rain hitting the side of the barn. I snuggled into my blanket and watched Kenrick across the flames.

"My brothers would make fun of me if they knew a lady had to save me today." He grinned.

I laughed. "Well then, we best keep this a secret, Lord Kenrick. So tell me, how many brothers do you have?"

As he tucked into the venison he told me about his three older brothers, Leonardo, Bartholomew, and Daedric, who were still in search of the Beast, and his father who'd recently retired to head up the Knights of Crowhurst.

In the distance, howls echoed through the night. Chills snaked up my back and I moved closer to the fire. Noticing my unease, Kenrick picked up his blanket and came to sit next to me.

"Don't worry, I won't let anything harm you this night

We sat in a boat, Kenrick rowing toward a distant island.

"Where are you taking me?" I asked, dragging my fingers across the water's surface.

Kenrick laughed. "You really don't like surprises do you?"

My lips twitched. "No."

The sun illuminated him as he sat tall, eyes blazing like blue flames. He was perfect. The way his face lit up when he smiled or told a joke. To the kindness he showed me and Gram.

The bottom of the boat hit the sandy lake floor as we made it to shore.

"This, my love, is where I live." He pointed to the castle, where roses and vines climbed against stone walls. "This is home to the Knights of the Crowhurst Order." He climbed from the boat, then hefted me into his arms and set me on land.

"Kenrick, it's beautiful." I spun, staring at sparkling waters that surrounded the island. Everywhere I looked there was life. Thick green trees, long blades of grass, birds singing and gliding on the wind. It was like a private paradise.

"Someday, I plan to bring you here to stay," he whispered as he caught my chin in his hands. When he leaned down as if to kiss me, a boisterous

voice interrupted us.

"Ahh, little brother, you've finally brought the lass home to meet us!"

I twisted to face a tall, dark-haired man, who looked almost exactly like Kenrick. Dark locks hung to his shoulders, but instead of blue eyes, he had green. He stood a couple inches taller, his shoulders a bit wider.

"Brielle, I want you to meet my brother Daedric … "

"Brielle, are you well?" Kenrick asked from beside me as the image drifted away.

"Um—I, yes, thank you. Sorry, I must have drifted off for a moment."

Was it a coincidence that I had these flashes? Or was I seeing the future? Things like this never happened before he came and I wondered if he triggered the visions, but I stopped short of asking. Gram would have warned me to keep these odd hallucinations to myself. Not to mention the fact that the Beast attacks seemed to have worsened with his arrival. Did he have something to do with them? These were not thoughts I wanted to entertain tonight, especially since I was stranded out here with him.

"I think I'm overly tired. Perhaps we should bed down for the night. We'll have a long trek to the other bridge tomorrow."

Today had been filled with mysterious happenings. The lady I'd seen on the bridge, the rapid rise in the river, and the strange vision of Kenrick. I needed to figure out what was happening. The sooner, the better, because I sensed my life and many others depended on it.

Chapter Eleven

Gram had barely talked to me since I'd come home from being stranded with Kenrick the previous night. That is other than to interrogate me on what happened and warn me about the rumors, which might surface because of it. Then she'd punished me by making me cut wood.

I hated it when she was mad, but it's not like I could change anything. Nor would I. Kenrick had needed me, so gaining a bad reputation or not, I would still have stayed on with him.

Thomas Horse Trainer cringed as I bound his ankle with bandages. "The swelling is going down, but the cut was deep. You need to stay off your feet for a few days."

"Then who will care for the horses?" He glared at his foot. "They can't train themselves."

"The horses will survive. And you'll be back to work sooner if you let the medicine work to rid you of the infection." I closed the jar of salve and slipped it into my bag. He'd taken a fall off a wild stallion, injuring himself when he struck a large rock.

He snorted. "You sound just like Loreen."

Gram chuckled as she stood. "Then I've taught her well." She patted his shoulder. "Now you listen to Brielle and keep your leg elevated. Your son can handle things until you're up and around."

We said our goodbyes and paused at the door of his home while two carts filled with manure rolled by.

"Will you stay angry with me all day?" I peered at Gram.

She sighed. "Hard to tell. Will you start doing as you're told?"

Before I could answer, Matthew Woodsman skidded to a halt alongside us, his expression filled with fear. "Did you hear? They just found Robert Stablehand's body in the woods."

My legs turned to lead. "W-what happened?" I caught his arm.

"Mayor says the Beast got him." He made the sign of the cross. "Wasn't much left of his body. An arm, his head ... nothing else."

The village spun before me as nausea gurgled in my stomach and Gram looped her arm through mine to steady me.

"Thanks for the news, Matthew." She excused us then guided me toward the corner of the trading post. "Are you all right, child?"

My lip quivered. "Gram, I dreamt of his death, of his attack." I buried my head in my hands. "The vision was a premonition. I could've stopped it. We could've warned him."

She gripped my chin and jerked my head so I faced her. "Hush now. Do not speak of your visions." Gram's eyes darted around as if she suspected someone listened to our conversation. "If the wrong person heard about your ability, they'd condemn you as a witch."

Her lips pursed, the wrinkles on her face deepened as if she'd aged fifty years right in front of me.

"That isn't how you raised me." I ripped myself from her grasp.

"Yes, well, we didn't have a Knight of the Crowhurst Order in our village before. Kenrick answers to the church, Brielle. Best you remember that. If he finds out what you can do, he'll surely forsake you to burn."

"Truly. You think he would do me harm?"

Gram clasped my arm once more. "Come. Let's not fight. Today should be happy."

I frowned at her. "Happy how?"

"You have clearly forgotten we are to pick up your gown from Lady Weaver." She smiled, dangling her leather pouch of coins in front of me.

"How come you always change the subject when we're speaking of serious matters or of Kenrick and Raul?"

"I do no such thing. Now, come along or would you rather not see your gown?"

There was no use in arguing with her because as far as she was concerned the matter was over. That's what Gram always did. With a sigh, I stared ahead. "The dress is ready?" I asked at last.

"Lady Weaver sent word yesterday." Gram led me toward the Weaver's.

A small crowd gathered outside the shop. A few rolls of fabric were unraveled at the entrance, stained with boot prints. A glass vase lay shattered on the wooden walkway.

We pushed our way through, squeezing inside the store, where we found two chairs toppled over and the table on its side, one leg missing. Finished dresses still hung up about the room. All except one. Mine.

Tattered pieces of the lavender gown were strewn about. The lacy sleeves lay at my feet, the silken remains torn apart like the recent wave of dead bodies.

Lady Weaver hurried to greet us. "I'm sorry. The shop was broken into last night." She paused. "Brielle's dress has been destroyed."

A few weeks ago, I'd have been thrilled to have an excuse not to go to the festival. But now I had a reason to go. Raul would be there. And Kenrick.

My gaze shifted to the counter where Sarah stood, a smirk on her lips. I went still. My teeth grated together like a blade on a sharpening stone.

"You." I seethed. "You did this."

Lady Weaver looked startled and turned her head to see where I pointed.

Sarah shrugged. "I don't know what you're talking about."

"Liar! You can't stand the fact that I had something pretty to wear."

She glowered. "Why should I care what a poor commoner like yourself has to wear? I'd never be jealous of you."

I dropped my basket and ran at her. "Then why is mine the only dress destroyed?"

Gram gripped hold of my waist, jerking me backward before I tore out Sarah's perfect curls.

"Brielle, love, wait outside for a moment." Her hardened tone left no room for disagreement

Crying, I rushed from the shop. It wasn't fair. She'd ruined everything.

"You need to mind your daughter." Gram's loud voice carried to the street. "She's nothing but a lying, jealous, witch's tit."

"How dare you?" Lady Weaver gasped.

"Oh, I dare much more," Gram hollered. "Bunch of pompous arses. You might run this town, but you don't run me."

Across the street, I noticed Kenrick, but it was Rhyne who hurried to my side.

"What's going on?" He took one look at me and the gathered crowd.

"Sarah ruined my dress." I bowed my head, staring at my feet.

Rhyne pulled me to his chest, his hand stroking my hair. "I ought to teach her a lesson. One she won't forget." His rage rolled off him like a herd of cattle stampeding.

"I have nothing to wear. Maybe I should just stay home and forget going to the festival."

He cupped my chin in his hand, forcing me to look at him. "No. If you don't go, then she wins. The Bri I know would show up wearing a saddle and a pair of breeches just to spite everyone. And you'd still be the prettiest girl there."

I laughed, in spite of everything. "I'd definitely draw attention. Although, I don't think Gram would allow me to wear the saddle."

She stormed out of the shop, her cheeks crimson with anger. "Don't worry. You'll have a dress, and mark my words, it'll be perfect."

"Gram?"

She gave me a quick smile. "Rhyne, be a good boy and keep Brielle company for a bit. I've got some things I need to take care of."

"Sure. I just need to let Da know I'm taking a break." He released me and headed into the butcher's.

Gram patted my hand then rushed off in the direction of the market place.

I stood there with my shoulders slumped. Nothing like sharing our personal lives with the whole town. I sighed.

Once Gram was gone, Kenrick walked up beside me. "Is everything all right?"

My smile wavered. "I-I'm fine."

He glared at the storefront. "She's nothing but a foolish child."

"Perhaps. But she knows well enough how to bring people down."

"In time folks will see her for what she is."

"Lord Kenrick." Rhyne grabbed my arm, pulling me away from him.

Kenrick's jaw twitched. "Rhyne."

They stood, staring each other. I glanced between them. Why was Rhyne being so protective?

"We should probably go now." Rhyne placed my hand through the crook of his arm. "Da said you can use his rowboat."

I nodded. "I'm ready to leave when you are. Good day, Lord Kenrick. Thank you for your concern."

"Milady." He bowed, then made his way over to his tethered horse.

I walked away with Rhyne, dodging between carts, people, and horses. When I peeked back over my shoulder, Kenrick sat upon his steed, watching me.

When we got to the woods, I glanced at Rhyne. His face reddened as he cleared his throat. "I've got to tell you something."

"What is it?"

"I-I finally kissed Gertie last night." My eyes met his.

"And, how was it?"

"Perfect. I can't explain it really. It was like my whole insides were on fire. I've never felt like that before" he said. "That probably sounds stupid."

"No. Not stupid at all. So, do you love her?"

He smiled, his eyes lighting up. "Yes, but her ma hates me. The only reason she's been allowed to be around me is because her da and mine are such close friends."

I clutched his hand. "And will you propose to her?"

He squeezed my fingers. "Perhaps. But you are sworn to secrecy. I still have to ask her da for permission."

"Of course, your secret is safe with me."

"And what of you? Seems you have drawn the attentions of my cousin Raul."

I sighed. He was my best friend, and we'd always been honest with one another. "Raul kissed me. I can't tell you how perfect it was. It was like he branded me, as if no one else in the world existed for me."

"What of your gram?"

"That is where the problem lies. Gram doesn't approve of him. She's been trying to discourage me from any interactions since he arrived back in Dark Pines. But I'm attracted to him and I feel drawn to him. But Gram has been acting strange about a lot of things lately. She's been very adamant about me staying away from Lord Kenrick as well." I drummed my nails against his sleeve.

He stared at me. "Lord Kenrick has been keeping close tabs on you, but he will leave soon. I know you think highly of him, but there's something off about him." He ran a hand through his hair.

"I'll be fine. But I appreciate your concern."

"Do you think it's a coincidence that the Beast attacks seemed to escalate with his arrival?" Rhyne scuffed his foot against the ground.

He sounded just like Gram. I shook my head. "I hope so. I mean I think there's something going on in Dark Pines. There have been too many accidents and attacks as of late. But to place the blame all on Kenrick, I'm not sure that's fair."

"Perhaps not, but I'll keep a closer eye on him, while he's in town, if you'd like."

"Thank you." I reached across the way and hugged him. "This is why I adore you so much. You understand me like no one else."

He took a step back. "I suppose I ought to head back to the shop or Da will have my head. Enjoy your day, Brielle. Make sure to take the rowboat out and enjoy the sun. Don't give Sarah another thought."

I saw Raul waiting beside a tree and glanced at Rhyne.

"Did you arrange this?"

He smiled. "Yes. Da said we're too busy for me to be gallivanting all over the woods today. Luckily, Raul was buying meat in the store. I told him you two could use the rowboat on the pond today."

"Thank you," I whispered.

Once Rhyne left, Raul sauntered toward me.

"My little Brielle, I'm sorry about Sarah." His fingers touched my cheek.

"It's all right."

"No, it's not. And if I had it my way, I'd see that she was punished for what she did to you." He glowered.

My hand covered his and I inhaled his scent. Why couldn't I just stay like this forever? Here, alone with Raul?

"Come, let's go to the pond. Rhyne said we could stay here as long as we'd like." He released me then led me down the trail.

The canopies thickened overhead like giant green bonnets blotting out the sun, while pinecones crunched beneath our feet as we made our way along the well-worn path to the Butcher's pond. The scent of earth mixed with pine tickled my nose. I smiled.

A bee buzzed around my head and I swatted it away, stepping over a downed tree in the process. I watched Raul's back. The contours of his muscles were evident as he held back branches for me. Tiny beams of sunlight snuck through the trees, embracing him like a sun god. Everything about him spoke of strength and beauty.

At last, we stepped into the clearing and onto the shore of the pond. Water bugs and birds darted over the surface. Ripples fanned out, creating waves. We pushed our way to the lone dock where the rowboat was tied.

Raul climbed into the boat first, then reached to help me in. The vessel swayed, and for a moment, I thought we might tip over into the cool water, but Raul held it steady, waiting for me to take a seat.

Once in, I plopped down on the back bench as he untied the rope and shoved away from the dock. He fastened the oars in place then faced me.

"Look over there." He pointed behind me.

I turned my head to see three swans swimming across the emerald colored waters. "They're beautiful."

As he rowed, I dragged my hand over the side, distorting our reflections as we went. After a few minutes, he maneuvered us to the center of the body of water and hoisted the oars into the boat.

Sweat glistened on his brow and he wiped it away with the back of his hand. Raul clasped hold of my arm and tugged me next to him then proceeded to pull us both down. We lay side by side in the bottom of the boat, staring at the sky. I was all too aware of his leg pressed against mine. How close we were. I focused on the sky, trying to ignore the loud clatter of my heart thudding against my chest.

Wisps of clouds floated by, while birds sang cheerful tunes. The rowboat rocked back and forth, lulling me into peaceful thoughts.

"Bri?" Raul touched my arm.

I cocked my head to look at him. He propped himself on his elbow and watched me.

He gazed at me as if I was the most precious piece of artwork he'd ever seen. And I liked it. "Yeah?"

"Are you happy? Being here with me?"

I took a staggered breath, feeling his knee slide against mine. "I'm always happy when I'm with you."

He brushed strands of hair from my face. "I'm glad. You don't know how long I've waited to spend time with you. And the other night, when we kissed, I felt something, Brielle. I know your grandmother told you to stay away from me, but I don't think I can stay away from you. You make me feel so much—like I can be anything I want to be. You make me want to be better. To prove to people I'm more than just some Gypsy trader."

I tilted my head as he shifted. "You're already perfect, Raul. You don't know how badly I miss you when you're gone. How I dream about running off on one of your adventures with you. Far from Dark Pines."

"Brielle ... " He leaned closer, his thumb stroking my lips. "I care more about you then I want to admit. I always swore I would never have any attachments. But you're proving to be someone I can't be away from. Believe me, I've tried."

"Then don't keep away. I don't care what anyone says or does. I want to be with you." Deep down, I knew my feelings for him went beyond caring. But I wasn't sure if now was the time to blurt them out. Not when there were so many things going on.

"Soon, we'll find a way to be together. For now, we must settle for times like this."

He bent closer until his lips crushed mine. In that single gesture, he made promises that he wouldn't voice aloud. My skin burned beneath his touch, he started a fire in me that couldn't be put out. I deepened the kiss, my fingers tangling in his hair, drawing him closer. Why couldn't I get enough of him?

He pulled me against him, sending the boat swaying back and forth. After a second he leaned back, his breathing labored.

"Bri, I think it's best if we head back to shore." He grinned. "Not that I'm opposed to staying out here a while longer, but the last thing we need is for the wrong person to happen upon us like this."

My eyes widened and I sat up, attempting to smooth down my hair. He was right.

Raul resituated himself then refastened the oars and rotated us around to paddle us back toward the dock. When we got into the shallows, he hopped from the boat, the water coming up to his thighs. He reached back in for me and lifted me up, his hands around my waist.

"Thank you for this. I needed it today."

"There is one thing I want you to know."

"What's that?"

"That you're the only girl I think of, and I'll always watch out for you. Promise me you'll be careful, my little Brielle. I don't want you to get hurt."

"I-I don't understand." Did he mean he'd hurt me?

As if recognizing my confusion he said, "Lord Kenrick has seemed particularly interested in you as of late. And I can't help but feel there is something strange about him."

I blushed. How many of my interactions with the knight had he witnessed? "I'll be fine. You're not the first one to warn me of Kenrick. I'm still not sure what to make of him."

Once he tied the boat off to the dock, Raul offered me his hand.

My pulse soared and sparks of fiery hot bolts seared my blood to near boiling point. I was all too aware of his closeness, of the heat radiating off our skin. My mind flipped back to our kiss and I felt the blush creep up my spine to my face. I cleared my throat. "I should probably head home now. Gram will likely be there soon."

"Let me walk you," Raul said right as Bowman and Rhyne came down the path in their cart.

Bowman's eyes narrowed as he stared at our clasped hands. "What are you doing on my property?" He directed his comment at Raul.

"I gave him permission, Da."

"Did you also give him permission to bring Brielle out here, alone and unchaperoned."

"Bowman, please, it's not what you think," I said. "You know me better than that."

"You don't know the way a man thinks, lass."

"Da, they weren't doing nothing but taking the rowboat out fishing. Brielle does the same thing with me."

Bowman glanced at Raul then back to me. "If you want, lass, we can give you a ride home. Your gram will be worried about you by now."

I felt Raul stiffen next to me. My fists clenched at my sides as anger swelled inside on his behalf because of the way Bowman glowered at him, like he was no better than the dirt beneath his feet. Of course, I knew how much Bowman disliked the Wanderers, and I was sure Rhyne would get a good thrashing when he got home for arranging this. "No, I'll be fine. Raul will see me safely to the cabin. Thank you."

After sitting for a moment longer, Bowman slapped the reins against the horses. The cart creaked as it rolled toward the woods. When they disappeared, I turned to Raul, and his eyes blazed.

"I'm sorry he acted like that," I said.

He glanced down at me, the hostility melting away. "It's all right."

My brow furrowed and I reached for his hand. "No, it's not. If he knew the real you, he wouldn't say such things. You're so kind, gentle, nice ... well maybe a *little* threatening."

He stared at our entwined hands. Slowly, he raised my fingers to his lips. "You're why I come back to Dark Pines. You see beyond what others do. Like I said, the other night, when we kissed, I felt so much. You don't know how long I've waited for that moment."

My skin scorched where his mouth touched, as if he'd marked me. Tiny flutters tickled my belly. There was something mesmerizing about him. He exuded danger and heat, the forbidden, but I wasn't scared of him. If anything, it made me want to spend more time with him because underneath that exterior, I knew there was something gentler. Something worth unearthing.

"As have I," I whispered. "And so you know, I will always see you."

He smiled as he lowered my hand. "I know. Now, let me see you home before Loreen decides to come hunt you down."

He slid his cloak from his shoulders and draped it over mine. With that, he guided me into the woods and toward home. There was no denying the connection between us. Soon, I'd have to make a decision. I'd have to figure out what it was I really wanted.

Chapter Twelve

The front door of the cottage burst open, and Gram walked in, toting her basket. She set it on the table, her mood dark.

"I'm sorry for what Sarah did. That girl, she'll get what's coming to her. You just wait and see." She hobbled over to the large pine trunk at the foot of her bed.

"She isn't worth our worries, Gram. If she wants to be miserable and jealous, I say let her. Besides, maybe it'd be best if I didn't go to the festival."

"You know that's not possible. Mayor Weaver would find a way to make a spectacle of us. Besides, you should never let someone like Sarah make you feel unworthy. You should go and have fun, enjoy the celebration. You don't want to have any regrets."

She sighed and set her cane down on the floor. When she tugged open the trunk, Gram finally smiled at me. She rustled through the contents, until at last, she held up a light blue gown, woven with silk and lace. "This was your mother's wedding gown. It's a little outdated, but we can make some adjustments. It will be perfect." She carried it over to me.

I gasped. It was beautiful. Something a princess would wear. Pearls shone along the hem of the high waistline, while spirals of light blue lace danced across the white silk of the sleeves and skirts.

"I love it." My fingers trembled as I traced the looping, lace-like leaves. "Don't change a thing."

"Maybe this was a blessing in disguise." Gram laid the gown on her bed, smoothing it out. "When Sarah sees you in this, she'll wish she let you wear that lavender dress her mother made."

A lump lodged in my throat and I stood to hug Gram. "Thank you. I was worried I wouldn't have anything."

She patted my back. "I'd never let that happen. You deserve the stars, Brielle, and if it were in my power, you'd have them."

Her gaze shifted to the painting of Aunt Narcissa and Cousin Lucia, which hung beside her bed. Narcissa had been Gram's only daughter. Gram never talked much about their deaths, other than to say she never wanted to set foot back in the Crawford Estate again.

"Are you all right, Gram?"

She gave me a wobbly smile. "Fine dear. You go on and get yourself ready to bed down."

"Gram, we can talk if you'd like. I'm old enough now to hear these things."

She wrung her hands together. "The truth is, I think our family is the target of these Beast attacks and killings."

I froze in place. "What do you mean?"

"I-I was the one to find your aunt and cousin's bodies. They'd been torn beyond recognition. The only thing that made me sure it was them was the jewelry we found on their fingers. It's why we moved from Crawford. But now, the attacks have started again, and they seem to draw closer to our cottage. It's as if we're cursed."

"Why haven't you mentioned this before?"

"Because I didn't want to frighten you."

I wet my lips. Now was the time for me to come clean too. "Gram, I-I think I've seen Lucia's ghost in the woods *again*. She showed up when I found Liam's body, then I saw her again the night the bridge washed out."

My hands trembled and I clutched them together.

Gram gripped hold of the table as if to steady herself. "Perhaps it's an omen. We both know ghosts dwell in our world. Since Lucia was murdered, possibly by the Beast, it would explain why she shows herself near the attacks. I beg you not to mention this to anyone else, do you understand?"

"Yes." With a sigh, I agreed, wondering if she knew more than she was letting on. Even though I knew she was protecting me, I couldn't help but feel that she was keeping secrets. And somehow, it involved what'd happened to our relatives. Plus there was the research she was doing.

"And you should also know, this isn't the first time Kenrick has been to Dark Pines," Gram whispered.

"What do you mean?"

"He came through here with his family when he was younger. That is when we had our first attack. It just seems odd that twice now he's come to our village and both times the Beast started to prey on our people."

I stared at Gram. Could it be true? I'd spent time with Kenrick. There was no way he'd hurt someone. His job was to save us. Wasn't it?

But then another thing dawned on me, hadn't he brought up the town of Crawford before? The place my aunt and cousin were murdered? Had he been there then? Even if he was, he would've been a child.

It didn't seem possible that he could have had anything to do with their deaths.

I didn't want to believe it. I wouldn't believe it. But even as I tried to push these thoughts away, they still lingered at the back of my mind.

"No, please!" a voice screamed in terror.

Something crunched beneath my feet. I glanced down to see a scattering of bones. A low growl vibrated behind me. My hands trembled. I didn't dare turn around for fear of what I might find.

"Please. Help me."

Oh, dear God. I knew that voice. I whipped around to find Peter Farmer holding his arm, his hand missing. Blood soaked the ground at his feet, his eyes widened with fear. So much blood.

"Peter!" I moved toward him. This wasn't happening. I needed to save him.

Claws swiped the air in front of me, raking across his chest. Blood spurted from the wound, his agonizing shrieks for help echoing in my mind. Something warm sprayed my face.

Shaking, I raised a hand to touch it. Panic coursed through me as I stared at the crimson fluid painting my fingers.

"Leave him alone, he's done nothing to deserve this." I ran toward him, but tripped, falling into the shadows.

"Nooooo ... "

"No. Please, stop!" I screamed.

"Brielle. Child, you must wake up."

My lids fluttered open to find Gram shaking me. Sweat soaked my shift and my skin burned with the remnants of fever.

Tears streamed down my face as I stared about the room. Two candles flickered on the table, droplets of wax pooling on the wood. Gram released my arms and grabbed a wet cloth to wipe my forehead.

"It's Peter Farmer, Gram. We have to save him."

"Shh ... just settle down. We can warn him in the morning."

116

"No." I leapt from bed, my shift tangling about my legs. "It'll be too late by then."

With a sigh, Gram dropped the cloth into the basin of water and wiped her hands on her apron. "Fine. But you must follow my lead and not mention these visions." She walked across the room, where she retrieved a cloak. "Get dressed while I ready the horse."

My pulse nearly deafened me as I tugged on a brown dress, fastened my cloak around my shoulders, and then slid my feet into a pair of knee-high leather boots.

What if we are too late?

Gram came back inside and grabbed her medicine bag. "If anyone asks, we are answering an emergency at the Farmer house. Under no circumstances do you indicate otherwise. You understand?"

"Yes."

We hurried outside. I climbed atop the horse first then reached down to help Gram up. Once situated, I dug my heels into the horse's fleshy sides and we dashed through the night. The woodland lay swathed in bleakness. Tendrils of fog trailed along the moonlit path, like ghostly serpents. Every clump of foliage took on the appearance of monsters, while the wind wailed through the trees as if crying out to me, begging me to turn back. I wanted to plug my ears, to ignore my surroundings, but I needed to stay focused on the darkened forest before me.

After long minutes in the woods, we rode out into a field of high grass on the outskirts of Peter Farmer's property. His thatched house sat upon a hill overlooking the valley.

I tugged on the horse's reins, bringing us to a stop, then I hopped down and raced across the yard.

"Slow down, Bri. You don't want to give the man a scare, rushing in like this."

I pounded on his door. "Peter. Open up. It's Brielle Healer." When he didn't answer, I struck the door harder until my hand pained me.

"I'll check around the back." Gram's face contorted in worry as she hurried to the side of the house.

Taking a deep breath, I twisted the doorknob and the wooden barrier swung open. In the darkness, I noticed the light shimmer of coals in his fireplace.

"Peter?" I walked carefully through the room. But he wasn't there. The bed lay empty, the blankets undisturbed, indicating he never came home to sleep.

"Brielle, what are you doing in there?" Gram scowled, jerking me outside. "You can't just barge into a person's dwelling like that."

My throat tightened. "He's not here."

She shut the front door then led me back to the horse. "We'll ride into the village. Perhaps Peter is at the tavern. You know the menfolk like themselves a good drink and naughty ladies."

We climbed back onto our steed and raced toward Dark Pines.

Please let us be in time.

There was no point in my visions if I couldn't stop the attacks from happening.

The village streets were nearly empty when we arrived, save for the drunks and ladies of the night wandering around the Iron Wheel Tavern.

"You stay put," Gram said as she slid from the saddle. "This isn't a place you need to be seen at this hour."

"But Gram … "

"No. You'll not be stepping foot amongst those scoundrels. Why, Lady Weaver would have a day with it." She straightened her skirts. "If anyone asks, you're escorting me to deliver medicines."

She patted my leg and hurried toward the entrance. Streams of music and raucous laughter poured out the door as she went inside, the scent of pipe smoke drifted out, heavy in the air.

The sound of hoof beats roused my attention. I turned in the saddle to see Kenrick riding my way, wearing full chainmail, his sword belted at his side.

"Lady Brielle, what brings you to Dark Pines at this hour? Is everything all right?"

My lip quivered. *Keep it together.* "Gram received an emergency call. I couldn't bear to let her go alone, not with the attacks."

He frowned. "You worry me, being in that cottage far from town."

"I assure you, we're quite safe." But were we? The creature's footprints had been found near our property.

Our gazes locked. His concern touched me and I wanted nothing more than to tell him the truth. Perhaps my visions would aid in his discovering the Beast's whereabouts. I opened my mouth, then shut it again when I noticed Gram hurrying across the street.

When she saw me, she shook her head no. My heart fell. Peter wasn't here. Where had he disappeared to?

"Lord Kenrick." Gram curtsied then came to stand next to our horse. "We best be heading home now."

"Loreen Healer." He nodded and nudged his horse so it came up alongside ours. "You may want to consider staying with someone in the village until the Beast's found. It'd be safer."

Gram pulled herself onto the saddle in front of me. "I'll think about it. Perhaps I can speak to the Butchers after festival."

Kenrick offered a quick smile. "I think that would be a splendid idea. If we can get everyone safe behind the village gates, protection will be easier, as will hunting for the creature."

He led us through the blackness of the night, his horse keeping pace with ours. When we came to a stop outside the cottage, he hurried from his mount to help us down.

First, he caught Gram and set her on the ground then turned to me. His hands rested on my waist as he lifted me from the horse. My feet touched the grass, but neither of us moved back.

I swallowed hard. "Thank you, for seeing us home."

He released my waist and brought my hand to his lips. "My pleasure."

"Come along, Brielle. You get inside where it's safe while I unsaddle the horse." Gram stood on the stoop, hands on her hips.

"Lord Kenrick, I think it's about time you move along, don't you?"

Kenrick bowed, his eyes resting on Gram. "Of course, I don't want Brielle to catch cold."

"Good night." Kenrick nodded at me then pulled himself back onto his mount.

I stood there for a long moment, watching him ride away, wariness consuming my mind.

Chapter Thirteen

A knock echoed through the cottage the next day. I set down my embroidery and stood to answer the door, trying to ignore my headache. Ever since last night my head had pounded like someone had taken an axe to it, and not even Gram's elixirs had helped. I squinted as I opened the door.

"Morning. Is your grandmother here?" Catherine Basketweaver asked. She rubbed her arms against the cold wind sneaking in behind her. Her robust frame filled the entry, her brown hair knotted atop her head like a giant hunk of sausage.

I moved aside to let her pass.

Gram dried her hands on her apron, then joined us. "What can I do for you, Catherine?"

"My son, John, has come down with fever. He's been bedridden for two days." She wrung her hands together. "I wondered if you might have time to check in on him."

Gram nodded. "I'll stop by once I finish the wash."

"Thank you. I don't know what Dark Pines would do without you."

I knew. They'd perish. But of course, no one remembered that until one of their own was ill. Any other time they spoke badly of Gram behind her back.

Catherine turned to go then stopped. "Not to be a gossip, but did you hear about the newest killings?"

My chest tightened, and I had half a mind to plug my ears against the news.

Please don't let it be Peter.

"No, we haven't." Gram rested her fingers on my shoulder as if to lend me support.

"Marcus found Samuel Herder and Peter Farmer in the fields. Tore to pieces they were, just like the rest they've found."

I blinked back tears. I was supposed to save Peter. This wasn't fair. To give me the gift of a vision, yet not give me a chance to use it for good.

Gram patted my shoulder then said, "Well, I appreciate you coming by with the news. I'll be over soon to check on John." She ushered Catherine out the door.

When she left, I squeezed my eyes shut. "I don't understand why my premonitions aren't giving me enough time to do anything about the attacks."

"This isn't your fault. We went to his home last night." Her hand patted my back. "He must've stayed in the fields late."

"I just feel so helpless," I said, my lids flying open. "Like I should be able to do something."

Gram moved away from me and slipped off her apron. She took one of her bags from the shelf and put a few jars and such inside. "We'll get this figured out. In the meantime, I need to head over to Catherine's and see that boy of hers. Did you want to come with me?"

What I needed to do was investigate the ruins I'd overheard

Father Machai and Reynaldo speak of. Perhaps there'd be more clues or something there.

"No, I think I might go into town and see Rhyne for a bit." Which wasn't a complete lie. Aware of the dangers of the woods, I did intend to see if Rhyne wanted to go with me.

When she left, I found my pack and shoved in a few things. Food, medicine, and bandages, just in case. After my last mishap on the bridge, I didn't dare leave home unprepared.

Once everything was in order, I left the cottage, headed into Dark Pines, and found the streets were clogged. Word of Peter's untimely death was the talk of the town. Numerous guards were posted at the newly erected watchtower near the western wall, while patrols lined up near the gate, getting ready to scour the woods. Again.

When I got to the Butcher's I saw Bowman behind the counter. "Brielle, how are you today?"

"Good, thanks. I wondered if Rhyne was around?"

"I'm afraid not. He's out hunting, not sure when he'll be back in."

"Thank you."

"Listen, lass, I'm sorry for how I acted yesterday. It's just that Wanderer is bad news. You know the rumors that fly about."

I fisted my hands, but pasted a smile on my face. "Thank you for watching out for me."

As another customer came in, I gave a quick wave and pushed my way back onto the street. Sometimes the townsfolk could be so ignorant. With a sigh, I stood glancing around the storefronts. Since Rhyne wasn't available, I had no idea what to do. I couldn't go by myself—Gram would wring my neck. A familiar figure sauntered toward me, and I smiled. Raul wore a crimson tunic tucked into black breeches, his hair tied at the nape of his neck.

"Brielle, my little flower, I was just thinking about you."

A blush crept up my neck and I fanned my face. Already, I heard the whispers as several people stopped to stare at us. But I ignored them and moved toward Raul.

"Then it's a good thing I came into town."

He chuckled and the warm, rich sound made chills dance across my spine. "So it is. Tell me, what plans do you have for the day?"

"Actually, I wondered if you might accompany me into the western woods. There's something I need to check on and Gram would be beside herself if I went alone."

He gave a slight bow. "I'd be honored. Would you like me to fetch my horse?"

"No, we won't go too far. I just need to find something."

"May I ask what it is we're looking for?" he inquired as we walked toward the main gate.

His arm brushed against mine. Fiery lances pierced my skin, making me all too aware of him. I shot him a quick glance to find him watching me.

I swallowed hard in an attempt to bite back the attraction. "There are supposedly ruins of the old church nearby. I wanted to explore them."

He offered me his arm, and with trembling hands, I grasped hold of him. Heat splayed across me as if a blanket had been draped over my body. Everything tingled from my toes to my hair, every pore aware of his presence.

"I think I know the place you're talking about," he said, his voice huskier. "Maybe on our way back, we can pick strawberries. There's a patch of wild ones growing nearby."

"That sounds fun. I haven't had a chance to go gather any yet and it's almost the end of the season."

We hiked along the dusty track into the woods. As soon as we stepped beneath the trees, dreariness seemed to wash over us. The temperature dropped significantly and an eerie silence overtook the woodland. There were no birds chirping or squirrels jumping from limbs. No bugs or flies buzzed about. I listened closer for the familiar sounds of the people in town, but heard nothing.

I scanned the surroundings and my stomach knotted. This felt too much like that night on the bridge. The urge to turn around made the hair on the back of my neck stand on end.

Stay calm. Raul is with you. You need answers.

"Are you all right?" Raul glanced at me.

"Yes, sorry, I'm jumpy today."

He drew me closer to him and wrapped a protective arm about my shoulders as we continued to press deeper into the foliage. Ferns and brambles thickened at our feet as if to bar our way.

At last, we came to the site of the church ruins. Moss and vines clung to toppled stones, while eerie silhouettes crept about the darkened crevices. Stone stairs led to a lower level, which looked as if it had partially caved in. Remnants of two walls stood about eight feet tall with roots and trees growing out of them.

The heavy scent of dirt surrounded us, as if something had recently dug up the ground. Wisps of fog danced between rubble, like tiny spirits out to play.

My skin broke out in gooseflesh. I glanced in the distance and went still. There, standing on the hill, was the ghostly figure of a woman. The same one I'd seen before.

"Raul," I whispered.

"Yes?"

"D-do you see her?" I gestured to the hill. "The person up there?" I didn't call the ghost by name for fear that it would make it that much more real. But I knew deep down, just like I'd told Gram, that it was Lucia.

He froze next to me. "Yes, I do. Brielle, I want you to stay here. You understand?" With that, he left my side and moved further into the trees, then disappeared within the overgrowth.

My gaze darted back up the hill, where the figure walked into the rolling waves of fog. A gust of wind billowed through, taking with it the smoky residue, and when the hill cleared the woman was gone.

My legs wobbled beneath me and I reached for a tree to steady myself. What did she want with me?

Once I got my bearings back, I trudged closer to the ruins, examining the stones. There, along the back portion of one of the walls, were claw marks. My fingers trembled as I traced them. As I examined the crimson stains almost hidden beneath vines, I realized it was blood.

I backed away from it, my palm covering my mouth. The Beast *had* been to Dark Pines before. A hand clamped down on my shoulder and I jumped.

"Sorry," Raul said as I spun to face him. "I didn't mean to scare you."

"Did you find her?"

"No, I lost her in the mist. She disappeared before I could get a close look at her. But something feels off with this place. There's a darkness that resonates here. Maybe we should move along now."

I nodded because I felt it, too. But before I left, something at the bottom of the stairs caught my eye. A pile of bones stripped of flesh. Kenrick needed to know about this place. The sooner the better. Perhaps he could piece together more clues and put a stop to the killings.

As we hurried toward the road, I caught Raul's arm. "Gram would be mad if she knew we were here today. But I have to find out what's stalking the woods. I beg you not to mention this trip to her."

His gaze softened as he stared down at me. "Your secret is safe with me. Besides, if she knew I was alone with you, she'd have my head."

With a deep breath, I said, "I've been having premonitions of the Beast's attacks. I dream about death and bones and blood. All I see are the victims' faces, but I never get there in time to stop them. Gram said I need to forget about them and not mention them. But I can't let people meet their end like that. Your grandmother told me to trust myself, and I do. I just don't know how to stop the Beast."

"My little Brielle. Shh ... don't cry." He wrapped his arms around me and I sank against his chest. "Listen, I'll help you try to figure out your visions. Perhaps we can remember something my grandmother said that might help us." He pulled back, brushing my hair from my face. He leaned closer, his breath warm upon my cheek. I tilted my head the slightest bit and our eyes met. Our lips were mere inches apart and if either of us shifted, I knew they'd touch. A repeat of our last kiss.

My blood pounded in my ears as we stood, toe to toe. "Thank you," I said.

His thumb swiped across my bottom lip and he took a step back. "I should see you home before night sets in. I still have to find Lord Kenrick and see if I can accompany him and his men on their hunt tonight."

With the moment past, I blinked and started to walk again. "I didn't realize you and Kenrick were friends."

"We're not, but I don't want the Beast hurting anyone I care about." He gave me a knowing look.

Or more likely, he wanted to keep an eye on Kenrick.

Chapter Fourteen

The next day, I helped Gram take laundry off the line. We'd strung rope between two large oak trees, and our garments waved back and forth like dead people on nooses. Not quite the image I wanted haunting me after everything I'd seen as of late.

Gram hummed an off-key tune beneath her breath as she put the last of our clothes in a large woven basket. I recognized the lullaby from my childhood. She used to sing me to sleep with it when I had a nightmare. I studied her wrinkled face. Where would I be if she hadn't taken me in after Mother and Father's ship was lost at sea?

Behind her, I noticed Father Machai coming up the path. Gram glanced in his direction. "Brielle, I need you to go to market and fetch me two bunches of laurel from the Wanderers."

"I thought you didn't want me to see them?" I quirked an eyebrow.

She snorted. "Like you listen. Now off with you, so I can tend to Father Machai."

What did Gram and Father Machai have to discuss? As of late, they seemed to be meeting more frequently. I wondered if it had to do with her research. For some reason, I was certain she was looking for information on the Beast too. With a sigh, I pulled on my cloak then grabbed a basket for the laurel.

"Good day, Brielle." Father Machai nodded as I passed him in the doorway.

"Father."

"Don't be too late," Gram called after me.

"I won't." With one last wave over my shoulder, I strode into the woods.

The wind howled, whipping through the treetops, while the branches bent beneath the unmerciful gusts. Leaves skittered at my feet as if trying to run away from the fast approaching storm. The forest darkened, plunging everything into shadows. I swallowed hard, looking behind me.

"Just focus on getting to the market," I whispered.

The breeze tugged at my cloak, wrapping it about me as I walked, while tendrils of my hair escaped their clasp. Twigs snapped and I picked up my pace, eager to get out of the woods.

Right as the gate came into view, a large raindrop spattered against my cheek, followed by several more. I pulled my hood over my head and rushed into Dark Pines.

People scattered when a rumble of thunder shook the ground. Bolts of lightning zig-zagged across the sky like barbed weapons being flung to the earth. Sheets of cold rain pelted me as I rounded the corner into the market.

Ahead of me, I noticed that the Wanderers' carriages were not parked in their normal spots. *Shite.* I'd come all this way for nothing. But as I started to walk away, I remembered Rhyne saying they'd moved to the western woods. With a sigh, I hurried back through town—puddles of muddied water splashed across my boots and dress.

I kept to the main path, not daring any shortcuts with all that

I'd witnessed lately. As I rounded the bend in the road, I heard music drifting on the wind. The scent of campfires led me through a more recent trail and into the woodland.

At last, I came upon the Wanderers. Their colorful carriages were circled up. A few younger men had sticks with fire on them and they spit in the air, causing them to flame up. Some of the women did intricate dances, sending sprays of mud on their bare feet.

My gaze shifted over the busy group. Some made food, while others worked on performances. A group of acrobats tossed a younger man into the air. He did a flip, then came back down in their arms.

After a moment's hesitation, I spotted Raul's colorful carriage. His canopies were already tied down, and he hurried to put the last of his goods away. The downpour drenched him, plastering his white tunic to his chest. He glanced at me, eyes twinkling. From beside him, I caught sight of Rhyne.

Rhyne's eyes widened when he saw me. "Bri? What are you doing here?"

"I came to get a few things for Gram."

"Raul?" Rhyne cast him a wary glance.

"Brielle, what a surprise." Raul grinned. "Quick, come in." He secured the shutters and ushered me inside away from the noise.

The crimson décor darkened the interior. Within seconds, he lit a lantern and the flicker of flames danced, illuminating the small room.

My eyes trailed down his jawline to his tunic and I gasped. "You're bleeding."

"It's just a scratch."

"He'll be fine," Rhyne said, slipping in behind us.

Raul took my drenched cloak from me and hung it over a beam of wood at the center of the carriage.

"That's more than a scratch. He's lost a lot of blood." Before Raul could stop me, I closed the short distance between us and tugged up his tunic. My gaze swept his sculpted chest to the gashes just above his heart and upper shoulder.

He cringed as I touched the tender flesh. "I'll heal, Brielle."

I scowled at him. "These wounds need to be treated before they fester."

Not waiting for him to reply, I rushed out of the makeshift home and into the steady drizzle once more. Slipping in the mud, I pulled several wooden crates from beneath Raul's carriage and rummaged through them. At last I found the camphor, which would keep the infection at bay. Once I shoved everything back in place, I ran around the carriage and in out of the rain.

"Change out of those wet clothes before you catch your death." Raul set a black tunic on one of the seats.

A blush raced to my cheeks. "Pardon me?"

He threw his hands up in the air. "For God's sake, Brielle, put on my tunic and hand me your dress."

When I still didn't move, he turned to face the opposite way. "I won't look, I promise. Rhyne, turn your head too."

My eyes widened. "But I can't—"

"Now do as I say, Loreen will slit my throat if you get sick."

"I doubt she'll end your life if I become ill. Besides, she's the one who sent me here." After long minutes of me hopping up and down, and wriggling, I finally kicked the clothing off. Self-conscious, I quickly tugged the tunic over my head. "I-I'm done now. You can turn around."

His tunic hung to my knees, making far too much of me visible. Raul's mahogany colored eyes trailed over me, a small smirk playing at his lips. "I do say you look ravishing in my clothes."

"Raul," Rhyne growled. "Don't start this. Not now."

In one quick motion, Raul bent down, picked up my wet dress, and hung it next to my cloak.

I raised an eyebrow as he stared at me. "Well?" I gestured to him. "Well what?"

"Are you going to disrobe?"

He slowly pulled his shirt over his head. I didn't miss the wince as the fabric brushed against his wound, nor did I miss the amused glance he gave me as he moved to unlace his breeches. For a second, I stood and stared before remembering my manners.

If Gram walked in now, she'd murder us all. Loud claps of thunder reverberated around us and the carriage trembled, nearly making me jump out of my skin. The shutters creaked as the wind pounded unmercifully against the wooden structure.

"You can look. I'm dressed."

Raul knelt on the floor in a pair of tan breeches, tiny drops of blood slid down his shoulder like crimson tears. He pulled out a fur rug, while Rhyne moved to stir the coals of the small woodstove in the corner.

"You need to lie down." I stepped to Raul's side, giving him a gentle push.

"Brielle, I'm fine, really."

"No, you're not. Now you can either tell me where you keep your pans and water or I'll pull this carriage apart to find them." I glared, giving him my best Gram look.

He settled onto the furs. "My, she's a bossy one, isn't she? Well, my little Brielle, the water-skin is hanging outside the door, and I have a pan stored beneath the seat."

I went to work boiling water and mixing the camphor. Once the concoction was done, I found a cloth and sat next to Raul, while Rhyne watched us. As gently as I could, I cleaned the wounds. His skin felt like fire, so hot beneath my fingers. "Shite. You're with fever. Why didn't you send for me or Gram?"

His muscles tightened and his jaw clenched. "Because I'm not sick."

"Damn it, Raul. You're being a bloody fool. You're injured and burning up." The more I studied his injury the more apparent it became that the markings upon his skin were claw marks. I went still. "Ho-how did you get these?" I daubed the camphor upon the opened gashes.

"I don't know."

Setting the medicine down, I leaned over him and clutched his jaw, forcing him to look at me. "Don't lie to me."

He sighed. "I volunteered to go with Lord Kenrick and his men last night to hunt this so-called Beast. When we got into the thicket we split up." He caught my hand in his, pressing it to his cheek. His skin was so hot. "As I stepped into a clearing, I heard a low growl from behind me. I spun to face it, but it was too dark to see anything. Then I felt the claws. I don't know what it was, but it let me get away."

My throat tightened as I examined him closer. "You must be more careful. Promise me you won't wander the woods alone," I said, bandaging the abrasions.

The Beast doesn't let its victims get away. But what reason would he have to lie to me?

"Little Brielle, don't worry for me. Besides, I wasn't alone in the woods when this happened. There were soldiers all around."

"Then there is no safe place."

"No." Raul gave me a forced smile, his fingers clasping mine tight. "But I thank you for your concern. You are my truest friend."

The carriage rattled as the storm outside strengthened. "Do you have any blankets?" I glanced around.

"Yes, in the trunk, fastened above the seats."

"Rhyne, can you help me?"

"Sure."

It took us a moment to get the trunk open, but when we did, I found an array of quilts stacked neatly inside. I pulled out two then closed the lid.

"Here, let's get you settled in." My fingers shook as I bent to cover him. I needed to get some tea in him, a medicinal one to help him sleep.

Raul clutched hold of my bare ankle. "You must stay with me."

"And what pray tell do you suppose I ought to tell Gram come morning? It's bad enough that I already stayed out once when the bridge went out."

A tired smile tugged at his lips. "The most scandalous of stories, of course. She'd believe nothing less."

"Maybe I ought to show her that book of yours while I'm at it." Raul gave me a sly wink. "If you'd like, I can pull it out."

"Raul, I swear, if you lay one hand on Brielle while we're here, I will hurt you." Rhyne glowered from the doorway.

Raul turned to me once more. "Please stay, Bri. I can't have you wandering about the woods. Night will fall soon enough. You mustn't be out there, not with all that's happened recently. Besides, Loreen would appreciate me keeping her only living relative safe."

His fevered eyes pleaded with me. I knew it wasn't a romantic invitation, in fact, he could barely hold his head up. If not for my own safety, I realized I must stay for his.

"Rhyne do you think the Wanderers would mind if I stayed on?"

"No. Probably not."

I glanced back at Raul, who was curled up under his blankets.

"My home is your home. No one will bother us."

"I can't very well leave you like this," I said. "I'll take care of you through the night."

After heating a cup of tea for him, I watched him fall fast asleep. If I hadn't come along, would the Wanderers have been able to help heal him? I stared at Rhyne.

"Worry not, Brielle, he will have a fast recovery."

I nodded. "Thank you."

We sat in silence for a while, before Rhyne spoke again. "Get some rest, I'll keep the fire stoked." He gestured to the place on the floor next to Raul, while he climbed onto a nearby bench seat and tugged a cover about his shoulders.

I stared at Raul. His long lashes touched his cheeks like angel feathers. His bronzed skin glistened with sweat. He looked so innocent, almost serene in his slumber. Moments later, I blew out the lantern and laid on the furs next to Raul, listening to his steady breathing.

Turning on my side, I touched his cheek, biting back tears. "Sometimes you can be so foolish."

A sigh escaped his lips and he reached out, drawing me closer. I went still. Bedded down next to a man like this placed me in a compromising position. What would happen if the wrong person found out? I pushed the thought from my mind. Raul's health was far more important than my reputation.

My heart skittered out of control when he shifted in his sleep, and as his arm tightened about my waist, I sucked in a deep breath, not needing these kinds of reactions to him. But I didn't dare pull away, for fear of waking him. Instead, I nestled into him. Perhaps the nightmares would stay away tonight.

Chapter Fifteen

Gram had been far more lenient on Rhyne and Raul than I thought she'd be. She sent them on their way with a scolding for letting the villagers see me come out of Raul's carriage. Other than that, she'd handed them each a loaf of bread and thanked them for keeping me out of the storm. I'm not sure who'd been more surprised, them or me.

After I dropped a salve off with Carlton Blacksmith, I caught sight of the Butcher's Shop. I was half-tempted to stop in and see Rhyne, but wasn't sure if Bowman was upset with us for being with Raul.

"There she is." I heard Sarah's voice before I saw her. "Can you believe what she did with that Wanderer? Mother said she was practically naked when she came out of his carriage."

My fists clenched at my side as I searched for another path around her and her "flock" of sheep.

"At least now I know why all the men in town sniff after her." She smirked.

I stopped abruptly and stared her down. "As opposed to faking an attack to gain attention?"

Lydia Milkmaid gasped. "How dare you accuse Sarah of such nonsense? She still has the scar on her arm."

"Oh, yes, the ever brutal self-inflicted knife wound. Although, I'm surprised you were brave enough to do even that."

Sarah's lips pursed as her face turned the color of a strawberry. "You—you will pay for such rumors. Come along, girls, we wouldn't want to be seen with this trollop."

Good riddance.

Appearing oblivious to the town gossip, Father Machai let me into the library wearing the same kind smile he always did. He left me by myself and I sat at a table rereading letters and the sheepskin book I'd found, but the more I read, the more there seemed to be missing from the puzzle.

I had a feeling both Gram and Father Machai might be able to help me, but they were becoming more secretive, while their meetings had become more frequent. Twice, I'd seen Father Machai's nephew stop by with parchments, but he only stayed long enough to deliver the scrolls then was on his way.

What bothered me most was that if Gram truly knew what was going on in Dark Pines, why didn't she try to put a stop to it? And Father Machai, how could a man of the cloth ignore the grisly murders?

"I hope I'm not intruding."

I glanced up as Kenrick entered the room, several scrolls in his hand.

"On the contrary, I could use the company." I smiled, motioning to the seat next to mine.

He sauntered to the table and slid into the chair. His leg bumped mine and my pulse quickened. I met his gaze and wondered if he understood what his presence did to me.

"I brought scrolls I found at other locations to compare with the letters and books kept here." Kenrick set several yellowed papers on the table in front of us. "I didn't realize until tonight that I have a letter from Father Gerard's successor at the Fire Ridge Monastery."

I took the parchment from him.

It is with great sorrow that I deliver the news of Father Gerard's death. The reinforcements from the Crowhurst Order arrived mere hours after his downfall. During this time of grief, I can offer a small bit of hope, in that a young knight has slain the Beast. At last, Fire Ridge Mountain will be safe.
Father Thomas
Fire Ridge Monastery

"Where did you find this?" I turned to look at him once more.

"It came from Candle Shore, although it's been addressed to Father Bertrum in Dark Pines."

"That makes no sense. How would it end up in a different village?" Had someone purposely moved the documents to keep everyone from discovering the truth and if so, why not just destroy them?

Kenrick's fingers tapped the table as he glanced down at me. "I've asked myself the same question several times since our discoveries. Either one of the priests took it with them when they moved on to another church or someone is deliberately concealing information."

Was this what Gram and Father Machai discussed in private? Or was there another involved in this cover-up?

"Perhaps, now would be a good time for me to tell you what I discovered in the woods, west of here," I said. "There is evidence there of the creature you hunt."

Once he agreed to accompany me, we hurried upstairs and he took his horse in the direction I pointed until the greenery got too thick for the animal to maneuver and we were forced to dismount. Even though this part of the forest seemed darker, it was warmer than the last time I'd come here. Like whatever had caused my unease had moved on.

"This is it," I said when we came to the rubble.

His hand rested between my shoulders, and I led him to the wall with the claw marks and blood.

His eyes darkened as he traced the deep grooves in the stone. "It looks almost like someone had locked the creature in the church. And these black colorings here make me believe that perhaps someone tried to burn it down."

Dread coiled in my gut. If the Beast survived this, how did we expect to destroy it?

"I also found something else when I was last here." I nodded to the underbelly of the church. Kenrick joined me at the top of the stairs and stared into the dark abyss.

"Bones," he said. He unsheathed his sword and descended farther into the ruins. Not that he could go very far because of the cave-in, but when he reached the bottom he knelt beside the pile, nudging some of them with his blade. "These have been here for years, but it looks like this might have been some sort of nest, or perhaps a breeding ground for the Beast."

My throat thickened. "You don't think it still uses it, do you?"

"No. But it is proof that the monster has been lurking in these woods for far longer than we first thought." He sheathed his weapon once more and joined me. "This is a great find, Brielle. Whatever this creature is, we know it likes to come back to its past hunting grounds, which means we might have a chance to set up an ambush for it. We just need to determine if it's still in Dark Pines or has moved on to the next point on the map."

Relief flooded through me. If Kenrick could track it, Dark Pines would be safe again. As we made our way back down the trail, Kenrick slowed and held out his hand to me.

I sucked in a deep breath, then slipped my fingers through his. The heat of his skin made me melt, and I ordered my legs not to buckle. He pulled me against him until we stood staring at one another.

Kenrick's fingers traced my jawline, his face intent. "I can't breathe without thinking of you. I don't understand this connection I feel when we're together. It's like I'm bound to you by a magical knot. Ever since I arrived here, I've dreamt of you. Visions of us dancing at a ball, and of me riding for you in tournament. It's as if we've met hundreds of times before. Yet, I know we couldn't have."

Had he read my thoughts? The intensity of our connection frightened me. Not because I feared him, but I was terrified of what I might lose should I give him my heart.

"Don't doubt that you have the same effect on me," I whispered.

His thumb rested beneath my chin and he tilted my head so I couldn't look away. Then, slowly, he leaned forward until his lips brushed mine. My arms encircled his neck. I tasted the sweet remnants of elderberry wine as he deepened our kiss.

I fell into his touch. Yearning twisted in my belly, making me cling tighter to him. His hand slid from my face and he wrapped me in his arms, pressing me to his chest.

Desire laced each kiss as if it would be our last. And yet, the familiarity of his embrace startled me. Breathless, I pulled back.

"You, you stole Kenrick from me!" Lucia screamed at me. "And you call yourself family."

"It wasn't like that," I said. "I never meant for this to happen, you have to believe me. Kenrick stopped to help me and Gram. How could I know it'd lead to this—to our falling in love?"

"He was supposed to ride in the tournament for me. But he didn't because of you. My father promised him my hand in marriage if he won."

"Lucia, listen to reason. It isn't Brielle's fault," Kenrick said, his arm about my waist. "I know what your father told you, but I had no intention of proposing to you. The Order is my first priority ... "

Her dark hair snapped behind her like angry snakes. "Was it your priority when you told Brielle you loved her? When you kissed her in the garden?" Her hands swiped a vase from the table. It crashed to the ground, spraying glass across the floor at our feet. "You'll pay for this, if it's the last thing I do."

She turned on her heel and raced from the room.

"I'm sorry," Kenrick said. "But we had to tell her, she was bound to find out about our engagement sooner or later."

"I know, but I never wanted to hurt her. I didn't realize how strong her infatuation with you was."

"Nor did I. But I promise, Brielle, I never had plans to marry her. That is a conjuration of her own imagination."

Oh God, what did these visions mean? Lucia had been dead for years, and I wasn't old enough for us to have fought like that.

"Brielle?" Kenrick hugged me tighter.

"I-I ... we should head back to the village now. I need to retrieve my things from the church."

Kenrick ran his fingers down my face. "I apologize if I've been too forward."

"I've no regrets." I gave him a shaky smile and wondered why I was trembling. Then my thoughts strayed to Raul. What had I done? My heart felt as if it'd been ripped in two. What pull did they have upon me?

"Nor do I." He kissed my palm, then the back of my hand. "Let me see you back to the village, then home."

Hellfire! What if Gram discovered we'd kissed? It'd only take her one look at us to realize something happened. Yet, I didn't want to be in the woods alone.

I accepted the arm he offered and followed him back to the horse.

After we'd gathered my things in the church, and had given the keys back to Father Machai, we made our way out into the night. The cool temperatures nipped at my exposed skin and I wished for my fur-lined cloak.

As we walked across the road, a commotion near the gate caught my attention. People stood in small pockets while the guards pushed them away.

When we approached, Percy Gatekeeper blocked our way. "No

one is to leave Dark Pines. Per order of the Mayor, the gate will be shut before sundown every night and will only reopen at dawn, until the Beast is captured."

I pulled away from Kenrick. "What? This is insane. I have to get home; my grandmother is alone at our cottage."

"I'm sorry, but no one leaves."

"Perhaps, I could escort her out." Kenrick stepped between us.

"Milord, I'm afraid the orders cannot be bent, even for you."

Across the way, I noticed Bowman Butcher. His brow furrowed as he gazed at the gate. Rhyne still hadn't come back, either. I squeezed my lids shut praying Gram and he would be all right.

"If anyone is in need of a place to stay this night, the church doors are open," Father Machai said as he joined our group.

"I think you best go with him." Kenrick grabbed hold of my arm, steering me toward the church.

"I know. Gram would want me safe." I fought the sob that'd lodged itself in my throat.

Kenrick drew me into his arms, hugging me tight. "Don't cry, Brielle. Your grandmother will be fine. She knows how to take care of herself."

Chapter Sixteen

The morning bells tolled, and I leapt to my feet, dashing out of the church. I maneuvered the narrow streets, dodging chickens pecking at scraps. Up and down the square, shuttered windows flung open to greet the morning as I raced to the front gates. The guards swung the wooden barriers open and a small crowd of people hurried inside.

Where is he?

As I searched for Rhyne, I clenched the fabric of my skirts—I'd never forgive myself if something happened to him.

Then I spotted him. Dark circles painted the undersides of his eyes, his shoulders slumped. He carried a string of rabbits and his bow as he trudged between the people.

His gaze met mine and he dropped his stuff to the ground. Without a second thought, I raced to him, then threw myself into his arms.

"I was worried about you." Tears streamed down my cheeks.

He clutched my face in his hands. "Worried about me? How do you think I felt when I got to your grandmother's and found you gone? I almost lost it, Bri. The thought of you stranded somewhere, by yourself."

My arms encircled his neck and I tugged him closer. "I'm glad you're all right."

"And I, you." A catch sounded in his voice. We pulled apart.

"Is no man safe from her claws?" Sarah's shrill voice snapped like the crack of a whip.

"Obviously not. You'd think being caught in the Wanderer camp would shame her enough," someone else said.

I fisted my hands at my side. Like Sarah had room to talk. How many men had she pursued?

Rhyne didn't bat an eyelash as the whispers continued around us; instead, he retrieved his things, then reached down and clasped my hand in his. Over his shoulder, I saw Gram's stooped form coming into town and I pulled away and ran into her arms.

"Thank the Lord you're safe." She patted my face. "You had me up all night worrying."

"Father Machai took me in, I was quite safe."

Gram clung to my arm as we maneuvered through the people milling about town. Her smile fell away. "Listen, I need to go see Rhyne's mother for a bit. Why don't you run along now. I'll be home shortly."

Rhyne caught her eye. "I'll go with you. I'm sure Ma has been worried about me."

Somehow I knew they were about to discuss more than Rhyne being out all night. The looks exchanged between them appeared more serious.

A loud ruckus near the gate caught my attention. Knights and other men carrying weapons came in, followed closely by Kenrick on horseback. They ushered in the cart with the cage attached to it.

"We've caught the Beast," Fredrick Mason hollered, shaking a large axe over his head.

Ladies shrieked, jerking their children back as the group paraded toward us. Men cheered, trying to get a closer look. When the processional stopped in front of us, I gasped. A grizzled man covered in blood sat in a small pile of bones, muttering incoherently to himself. On occasion, I'd catch words I understood. Flesh. Bones. Blood.

His greasy, gray-black hair lay plastered to his head, his clothing hung tattered and stained. He raised dark eyes, and looked right at me. He crawled to the bars, pressing his dirt-encrusted face against the metal, and a sneer formed on his lips, revealing rotted teeth and spittle that ran down his chin.

"You." He pointed at me with a high-pitched giggle. "You're going to be next. *She* said I could have you next."

I gasped, stumbling backward to put some distance between the crazed man and me. She? Who did he mean by "she?"

"Steady there." Raul ran up and caught hold of my arm. "He won't lay a hand on you. I promise."

My legs quaked beneath me, but he held me tight against him. His hand brushed my skirts as he drew his dagger.

"Raul. Stand down." Gram grabbed his arm before he could throw the blade.

Instead, Kenrick leapt from his horse and reached through the bars, gripping hold of the man's shirt. "Quiet, monster. If you speak to this lady again, it will be your end."

The man laughed almost maniacally then turned to me once more. "I *will* taste your flesh."

Kenrick raised the hilt of his sword and brought it down on his head. The man slumped to the floor. "Take him to the town center and have Mayor Weaver meet us there."

Raul's arms let me go as he slid his weapon back into his belt. "Keep safe, Brielle."

With that, he vanished into the crowd just as fast as he'd appeared.

"You should head home. This is no place for you to linger, Lady

Brielle," Kenrick said as he came to stand next to us. "This man was caught in a pile of bones, chewing off the flesh of his newest kill. But be assured, he will be tried for his crimes."

In the distance, I noticed the ropes being slung over the wooden scaffold. He was right. I didn't need any more nightmares. Yet, even I was aware that he looked nothing like the Beast of legends. Unless, of course, he could change forms. I shivered. What if they'd caught the wrong person? He could be nothing more than a cannibal. His nails, though blood encrusted, weren't long enough to make the claw marks we'd seen.

But with all the myths of shapeshifting people, this could very well be the man. Which brought forth another thought, would this metal cage be able to hold him? Unease swept through me. I needed to speak with Kenrick. None of this added up. Yes, they'd found in him a pile of bones, but that didn't mean he was the monster. Or maybe it did. Maybe I'd hoped that it wouldn't be for the mere fact that if it was, it meant Kenrick would soon leave.

"Lord Kenrick, might I have a word?"

He peered at me. "I'm sorry, milady, but duty calls."

Did he not see that this wasn't the true Beast? Perhaps that was the plan: make the villagers believe the threat was gone. Maybe the mayor had put him up to it. Or maybe he truly thought this was the creature, given the man's manic state and the bones surrounding him. But I couldn't help but wonder as I walked away whether I should press the issue.

Gram hummed to herself as she washed the last of the dishes. "Can you fetch me some more lavender and feverfew?"

"You need to quit making everyone soap."

"Well, would you rather have them stinking to high-heaven?" I pulled my cloak on then grabbed a basket and my dagger. "Funny."

"Don't you be gone too long, and make sure you stick to the paths. Even though they caught the Beast, it doesn't mean there aren't other dangers."

The sun shone bright through the treetops as I hurried toward the clearing on the other side of the creek. A large rabbit hopped into the bushes as I neared, while birds flitted overhead. When I got to the clearing, I set my basket down and took out my dagger, which I used to cut bunches of lavender.

A low growl sounded from the tree line. I stiffened, while my pulse raced. A slight rustle in the tall grass caught my attention and I froze as a large, gray wolf stepped through the greenery. Its yellow eyes were intent on me.

I fought to breathe, and my sweaty fingers gripped tight to the dagger. The animal bared its teeth, gave a low snarl, and circled around me.

Something crashed through the brambles behind the creature. Startled, it turned from me. Raul lunged into the clearing, his face contorted in rage.

"Brielle, stay still," he ordered, as he then shifted his attention to the wolf and said, "This isn't your territory."

The animal growled again, and the two of them circled one another like predators sizing each other up.

The wolf backed up a step, then sprang at me. I screamed, waiting for the impact, but Raul threw himself at the animal and grabbed it by the scruff.

The wolf yelped, fighting to leave his grasp. At last, it broke free, then scampered into the woods.

"Raul!" I rushed forward. "Oh dear God, you could've been killed. What the hell were you thinking?"

He took several steps away from me, his eyes glowing eerily. "Stay back."

The hell I would. I came to his side and clutched his arm—

And pulled back in pain. His skin was so unnaturally hot that it burned to touch. I inspected his arms and body for any scratches or bites, but miraculously he had no wounds. Impossible.

"Are—are you all right?"

After several moments, he raised his head to look at me, eyes back to normal. "Shite, you scared me to death. I'd never forgive myself if anything happened to you."

"H-how, did you do that? How did you make it go away?"

He sighed. "Fear. I was so worried he'd hurt you, I thought if I threatened him he'd leave you be."

"But … "

"Come, Brielle, let's get you home." He gripped hold of my arm and ushered me in the direction of the cottage.

"Raul, come on now, we're friends. You can tell me whatever it is that's going on. I won't judge you."

"I wish I could. But I don't want to share secrets that are not mine alone. Times are dangerous for all of my people. Give me time, and I promise I will explain all."

I had no idea what'd happened back there. There was something much more going on here and I needed to find out what.

However, by the time we got to the cottage, Raul was quick to disappear, giving me no chance to question him further. I had half the mind to follow after him and demand answers, but Gram called me inside to finish our preparations for tomorrow's Festival of the Stars.

Chapter Seventeen

Gram finished weaving daisies into my hair, then stood back to admire her work and teared up.

"You look like an angel. No one will be able to resist dancing with you tonight. Aren't you glad now that you decided not to accept any offers to attend festival? Now you'll be able to dance with anyone you choose."

I smiled, turning around so she could examine the back of the gown. Of course, Gram had no idea that I planned to meet up with Raul there. I knew she didn't approve of him, but for once I wanted to take the reins and decide for myself what I wanted to do with my life. "I feel like a princess."

The silk slipped across my legs like water, the blue lace overlay reminding me of the sea. Wearing my mother's dress made me feel closer to her, as if she were going to present me to the village tonight.

Gram ushered me over to the wooden rocker near the door. "Sit down while I get myself ready." She kept her back to me as she laid out her blue dress and cloak.

A few moments later, Gram hurried to my side. "Why don't we get going? Don't want to be late."

I smiled. "I'm ready."

Tonight would be the night everything fell into place for me, when my future would be revealed at the Festival of the Stars, or at least that's what I hoped. Gram and I climbed into the cart then slid onto the bench. With a slap of the reins, the horses moved forward.

Gram glanced over at me. "I meant it when I said you're beautiful tonight."

I laughed, toying with the skirt of my dress. "Yes, well let's hope others think so too."

"They'd be foolish not to notice you, Brielle. Just remember that you don't have to dance with anyone if you don't want to."

I smiled and let it go. She'd made clear that if she had her way, we'd go back to the old days where neither of us wanted to go to the festival. But I'd reminded her that the mayor's decree basically required me to be there.

That didn't mean I had to tell Gram I hoped to see Raul at the festival. Maybe even to dance with him.

I squeezed her arm as I caught snatches of music in the distance. Things were about to change and I suddenly wondered if I was ready for it.

Guards ushered us through the gates and Gram steered the cart toward the road in front of the tavern to park. She hobbled down then came around to wait for me.

When I dismounted, she caught my hand in hers. "I'll let you wander about on your own so you can find your friends. But you're to meet me back at the cart when the festival is over, you hear me?"

"Yes, Gram."

"All right, you be a good girl."

Jars with candles in them hung about the town square, a bonfire crackled and popped at the center. Musicians sat upon the small wooden stage, filling the village with saucy tunes.

Dancing couples spun around, the women's skirts creating a rainbow of colors. Men tossed back pints, joking with one another, while older ladies stood grouped together gossiping about what everyone wore. Even the Wanderers had come into town to perform. Fire eaters blew bright yellow flames from their mouths, and people cheered and gasped around them. Several others did tumbling acts, flipping and diving as they were tossed in the air.

The scent of campfire and apple pie flitted through the air, reminding me that autumn was nearly upon us.

I spotted Rhyne through the crowd, Gertie on his arm as he talked to Bowman. I smiled, then turned my attention to several people who shifted to stare at me as I walked by. For once, I felt as if I were the Belle of the Ball. Closer to the raised scaffold, the Star Pole had been erected for the festival. Already, white and silver ribbons hung from it.

My thoughts drifted to the man in the cage and I shivered. Soon the scaffold would be used for an entirely different reason. Bertha Gatekeeper staggered into me, nearly dumping ale on my dress.

"Sorry 'bout that." Her swollen eyes stared through me. "Liam and I met this night, fourteen years ago. We danced all night." She swayed back and forth as if he were leading her.

My throat thickened. I'd been the one to find Liam dead in the woods. I fought to keep the gruesome murder from my mind. With a sad smile, I patted her arm.

"I'm sorry for your loss."

She raised her glass in a toast then moved on. How many others suffered this night because of the Beast? The Mayor should've cancelled everything.

"There you are," Rhyne said. His golden hair shimmered against the setting sun. Ivy colored eyes swept over me as I took in his forest green tunic, black breeches, and new black leather boots. A smile tugged at his lips. "You look breathtaking."

A blush crept up my neck. "Thanks. You clean up nice yourself. So where's Gertie?"

"Her da is taking her for a spin about the square. So, would you like to dance?"

"Yes. But only if you don't try to do anything ridiculous."

He grinned. "I have no idea what you're talking about."

I swatted his arm. "So you don't remember your attempts to dance with me by the creek last summer?"

His eyes twinkled as he tugged me into his arms and spun me around in time with the music. "I have no recollection."

I snorted. "Well, let me jog your memory. It had something to do with tossing me in the water when you dipped me backward."

"Oh. Now I remember." His grip tightened on my waist as he dipped me back then snapped me up so my hands hit his chest. "Was that better?"

"Um—let's just stick with basic steps."

Rhyne swayed with me, and I glanced over his shoulder, searching the square. Then I saw Kenrick, standing on the outskirts of people. His dark hair caressed the sides of his chiseled jawline. I lowered my gaze taking in his attire. He wore a blue tunic, lined with silver thread, his tan breeches tucked neatly into knee high brown leather boots. A smile crept to my lips as I looked up at him once again.

A magnificent sight.

His gaze shifted, landing on me. But at that moment, Rhyne spun me, and when I came back around, Sarah stood next to Kenrick, tugging him into her arms for a dance. My grip tightened on Rhyne.

"You all right?" Rhyne leaned closer, his breath tickled my cheek.

"Yeah." I nodded. "How could I not be when I'm with the great Rhyne Butcher?"

"See, at last you admit how wonderful you think I am." His eyebrows wiggled.

"More like an arrogant, arse."

"And yet here you are in my arms. Even you can't resist me,

Brielle. Guess all the meat I gave you over the years finally won you over."

"Pardon me, may I cut in?" Raul tapped on Rhyne's shoulder.

I stared into a pair of familiar brown eyes. Tonight, Raul wore a plain white tunic and black breeches. He'd foregone the beads and settled on a simple crimson ribbon to secure his dark hair at the nape of his neck. His skin glowed golden against his shirt, opened just enough to reveal a silver medallion at his neck.

"Sure. I should probably go hunt down Gertie before someone else tries snagging her."

He handed me off to Raul, who led me in more advanced steps as we glided amongst the other dancers. His hands slid down my waist and he spun me out and back in again.

"So you decided to take part in the festival this year," I teased as he pulled me closer. "I thought you said these gatherings were for fools."

"That was before you were old enough to attend them. Now, at least, I have someone to share in the misery that this village considers a match-making ceremony."

I giggled as he swept me through a sea of gyrating bodies. "Glad I could oblige. Besides, our dancing together will give the masses something more to talk about."

As Raul regarded me, his smile disappeared. "Brielle, promise me something."

"Of course."

"Be careful with your heart."

I swallowed hard. "What do you mean?"

His fingers brushed tendrils of my hair from my face. "The knight, Kenrick, who has been paying you visits. I'm just afraid he might not live up to the type of man you need."

"I-I don't know what you're talking about."

"Bri, come now, this is me you're speaking to. I understand you better than anyone in this narrow-minded town. We're kindred spirits."

I shifted my gaze from Raul's. "Then don't lecture me. I realize Kenrick is leaving soon, I'd be foolish to give him my heart. But you know what my prospects are." What I really wanted to tell him was that although Kenrick had opened something in me, it was he who had my heart.

His fingers forced my chin upward so I looked at him. "Don't sell yourself short, these are your feelings we're talking of."

"I will be careful. You have my word."

"And if anyone should hurt you, you have *my word* that I'll hunt them down." His skin became hot beneath my fingers, as if he were with fever.

A lump lodged in my throat and, once more, the dangerous spark curled over his features. My mind drifted back to the previous day when he'd pulled a dagger, ready to kill the man in the cage. And of course, I couldn't forget how he nearly gave his life for me with the wolf.

"Do you think you can sneak away with me for a few minutes?" He drew me closer. "There's something I want to show you."

I sucked in a deep breath, my hands resting on his chest. Would anyone notice my absence? I knew Gram probably wouldn't like it, but I was curious to see what surprise Raul had for me, even if the tiny voice in the back of my head asked if this was a good idea.

After taking a deep breath, I glanced up at him. "I'd love to go with you."

We stopped dancing and he took my hand, leading me through the crowd to the outskirts of town. We slipped into the shadow-laden woods, where the blackness seemed to drown everything in its wake. It amazed me how well Raul could find his way through the brambles, for I could see very little. As I stumbled along, Raul steadied me, slowing his pace so I could keep up with him.

"Don't worry, I promise it's not much farther."

A short time later, we entered a clearing and stood on the shore of a small lake. Moonlight filtered in from above like a silver beacon, glittering and shining off rippling water. But it wasn't the lake that made me gasp, instead it was the hundreds of fireflies twinkling and flitting over it.

"Oh my—this is beautiful." My fingers brushed Raul's palm where I still clutched hold of him. "I've never seen so many fireflies in one place."

He chuckled as he turned to study me. "This is the only place in Dark Pines I've ever seen them. Most people bypass this lake because it is small and has been fished so much that there isn't much left in it. But there are other creatures and life that thrive here. I thought you might appreciate the beauty."

"It's perfect."

In the distance, music from the festival twinkled on the night air and the bugs seemed to light up in unison.

Raul released my hand and caught my chin. "Dance with me," he whispered.

My breath caught in my throat as butterflies tickled my belly. "I'd love to."

His fingers slid to my waist, and I anchored him close, as my arms wrapped about the back of his neck. We swayed on the shoreline, amongst the wildlife, lapping waters, and brilliant show the bugs put on.

For those few moments, it was just him and me. No worries of creatures in the woods or gossiping townspeople. Just us.

I watched him, the way his arms flexed as he twirled me about, the way his eyes lit up when he smiled. He leaned down so that his cheek rested against mine.

"Brielle, there is something I want to tell you."

I wet my lips. "Yes?"

We stopped dancing and I felt his breath upon my earlobe. "I-I will be leaving Dark Pines day after next."

My body tensed and I met his gaze, our lips mere inches apart. "So soon?" No, that's not what I wanted to tell him. *Come on, you have to tell him how you feel. What if he doesn't come back? And you never get the chance to admit that you love him.*

If he left, then that'd be one less person who understood what I was going through with my premonitions. One less friend in a village filled with hypocrites.

His fingers brushed tendrils of hair from my face. "Don't look so forlorn, my little Brielle. I won't be gone long, I promise."

I covered his hand with mine. "But I'll miss you."

Tenderness washed over his features. "I would take you with me if I could, Dear One. Pack you up in my carriage and never look back."

"Would you really?"

"In a heartbeat," he murmured, his nose grazing mine as he moved his mouth closer to mine.

My heart raced, pounding a rhythm so loud that I was sure he could hear it.

"Raul." His name formed on my lips as a plea, but to do what, I wasn't sure.

A twig snapped from beside us and he stepped back, the moment broken.

"Let's get you back to the dance before someone notices you're missing," Raul said.

I nodded and let him lead me back, the whole time wondering what had nearly happened between us. Maybe I ought to take him up on his offer, to let him get me away from this place.

When we arrived, the musicians had just ended the song. "I think I ought to let you dance with someone else for a bit," Raul said.

"You know, I am not opposed to being your partner again." I smiled.

"I know." He squeezed my hand. "I'll find you later."

"Thank you, for taking me to see the fireflies."

"You're most welcome. It is good to remember that even amongst the darkness there is light to be found."

My eyes met his and for a moment everything else drifted away. "Yes. It is."

He grinned and I watched as he got lost in the wave of couples readying for the next set of music. After a moment, I ambled toward the tables of food where Rhyne chatted with Gertie about the decorations. They looked so happy together and I wondered if tonight would be the night he proposed.

The music stopped once more and Mayor Weaver took his place on the raised scaffold. "May I have your attention please? As you know, it is a long-standing tradition for our eligible young ones to dance before the Star Pole during the Festival of Stars. This is the night where you can see what matches could be. Though, not the final determination, the stars do not lie."

The crowd cheered. Nervous flutters twisted in my gut and I took a deep breath. For a Christian village the people sure put a lot of stock in the old pole. I knew several couples who'd made their declarations based on who they ended up standing next to at the end of the dance.

"I ask all unmarried men and women to come forward and take your place at the pole. Girls, please take hold of the blue ribbons. Men, find your place at the white ones. At the end of the song, each row should go boy, girl, boy, girl. One match for each person."

Everyone made their way forward. I clasped hold of a piece of blue ribbon, Clare Candlemaker stood in front of me, Henry Blacksmith beside me. When the music started the people at the pole would weave with their ribbons, dancing in and out between one another. After the threads were all braided, everyone would be next to someone, and according to tradition that would be your best match.

The sound of the flute twinkled, indicating the dance started.

Clare turned to me and giggled. "This will be so fun."

We ducked beneath Henry's white ribbon and off we went. I circled round several men, then ducked down again. I laughed as

Rhyne and I twirled by one another. The music went faster and the adults stood on the outskirts, clapping their hands in time. I hopped over the next ribbon, and then ducked under another one. Slowly, I saw we were nearing the end of the roped braid. Cheers got louder. My heart pounded in time with the drum.

I closed my eyes, letting the music sweep me away. At last, it stopped and I slowly opened my lids. With a gasp, I looked to find myself between Kenrick and Raul. Somehow we'd ended up with only three people in our row.

I had no idea where Rhyne was, but from across the square Gram's face twisted in surprise. She shook her head no. *Oh God. What's wrong?*

"Does this mean I must fight Lord Kenrick to the death in order to claim you?" Raul teased from beside me.

My fingers quivered and I gave a forced laugh. "I don't think it'll have to come to that."

Kenrick chuckled. "I tell you what, I agree to share her with you for the rest of the evening."

"Sounds fine to me. You can have the first dance, since I've already had one." Raul bowed.

"So you've been keeping tabs on who she dances with?"

Raul merely smiled. "One must know their competition."

With that, he sauntered away leaving me alone with Kenrick. My stomach knotted with nervousness.

"How did this happen?" I gestured to the ribbon.

"Someone likely missed a turn somewhere along the way," Kenrick said.

I wanted to point out how odd it was we ended up together. Were the stars truly trying to tell us something? And if so, what did it have to do with Raul? My gaze shifted as I searched out Rhyne. Finally, I caught sight of him standing with the Dyers. Gertie laced her arm through his. I hoped he ended up with her, she made him happy.

"Shall we dance, milady?" Kenrick offered me his hand.

"I'd love to." I looped my fingers through his, letting him lead me forward.

His arms slipped around me, and already, I felt something simmering between us. His breath fanned across my face as he leaned down. In that moment, he became my focus. I lost sight of everyone else. A short time later, with my hand in his, he led me away from the dancing couples and over near a large oak.

When we stood alone, he glanced down at me. "I've thought often of our kiss."

I stared at him, my heart thudding so loud it drowned out the music. More than anything, I wanted to tell him I'd spent many hours daydreaming of him and our kiss. But I voiced none of these things. Because the truth was, I didn't know what to do. There was this odd connection to Kenrick, but what of my feelings for Raul?

"You're an outsider, Lord Kenrick. You came into Dark Pines to kill the Beast and now that that's done, you'll leave."

"Do you truly believe this?" He raised a hand to trace my cheek, where just minutes ago Raul had touched.

I swallowed the large lump in my throat. "Yes."

"I wouldn't leave you, not like that. You don't understand—these past weeks all I've thought about is you. When I'm with you, I feel content with life, as if we were brought together by fate."

"And what of Sarah Weaver?" Of course, I knew he didn't have feelings for her, but fear made me blurt the first thing that popped into my mind. I took a nervous step back. We bordered on talk of things far too personal.

"No. I escorted her around town only because I was trying to get more information from her father about the attacks. I figured if I showed interest in his daughter, he'd have me to his home more often. But I promise you, she means nothing to me. And I know how awful it sounds that I used her, but the urge to catch this Beast drove me to drastic measures." His eyes bored into mine. "You're the one

I've grown close to. The one I go out of my way to bump into and talk to. I cannot think of anything but you. Brielle, I think I've fallen in love with you."

Kenrick took hold of my hand, his fingers entwined with mine. Our nearness made it almost impossible to think. I took a deep breath.

"Kenrick, I—"

"There you are." Sarah stepped between us, clutching tight to Kenrick's arm. "I lost sight of you during the dance around the Star Pole."

"I'm sorry, Sarah, but I have some things I need to discuss with Lady Brielle." He started to pull away from her, but her father came over as well.

"Oh, but I do love this song." Sarah pouted.

"Not now, Sarah," Kenrick said. When he clutched my arm this time and started to lead me away, the mayor intervened.

"Ah, Lord Kenrick. Can you please join us? There is something of the utmost importance we need to discuss."

I felt him go rigid beneath my touch. He hesitated a moment, then turned to me. "I promise, we'll finish this conversation later." With that, he followed after the mayor and his daughter.

"Are you all right?" Rhyne and Gertie approached, both smiling. I laughed. "Yes, of course." But I really wasn't.

"So, I wanted you to be the first to know that Gertie has accepted my offer of marriage."

"Oh, I'm so happy for you." I reached out and hugged first Gertie, then Rhyne.

"It was a complete surprise." Gertie smiled up at him. Her freckled face shone with love. "I wondered why he seemed so nervous the other day when he came to speak to my father, but now I know why."

I laughed. "Please tell me he at least made himself presentable before talking with him."

"Yes. He was a perfect gentleman."

I shifted my eyes over their shoulders, and saw Kenrick in deep conversation with the mayor. I wondered what they spoke of?

Sarah suddenly appeared at my side, her eyes narrowed. "Well, I hope you're happy. You've ruined tonight for me. Do you realize that if you would've left Kenrick well enough alone, he would've fallen for me?"

"Not now, Sarah, I'm in no mood for you tonight." I refused to let her destroy the rest of this evening for me, like she did everything else in my life.

"Aren't you now?" She lifted her cup of raspberry wine and dumped it down the front of my mother's dress. "Oh, I'm so sorry. The cup slipped."

I gasped. The red liquid stained the front of me like blood. "H-how could you?"

She moved away from me. "Have fun dancing now."

Tears in my eyes, I turned to Rhyne and Gertie. "I'm sorry, I need to go." I backed away from them.

Rhyne gave me an apologetic glance. "That girl needs a thrashing. If you want, I'd be up for it."

"Rhyne, no. I think I'll head home."

"Then I'll take you."

"No. Stay. I can walk." Before I could rush away, I caught sight of Sarah wrapping her arms around Kenrick. Her lips pressed against his.

I gasped and turned to go.

After all he'd said to me. I suddenly wondered if I could trust anything he'd told me these last few weeks. A strange knight who haunted my dreams pursued me one minute, then abandoned me the next. Tears threatened to spill over. However, Raul had been there for me when I needed him. He was the only man I trusted. Maybe I should convince him to let me go with him when he left. But what kind of future could I have traveling with the Wanderer? And what of Gram?

I hurried toward the woods. But before I made my get away, I felt a hand on my shoulder and turned to see Raul.

"And where are you off to?"

"I-I want to go home."

"Then, come, let me escort you." He caught my fingers in his and led me toward his horse, tethered at the edge of town. The urge to cry overwhelmed me and I took several deep breaths. *Stay calm.*

From behind me, I heard Kenrick call my name but I kept going. I didn't want to turn and see the smug look on Sarah's face. Nor did I wish to see Kenrick, whose pretty words had only moments before made my knees weak.

Raul helped me into the saddle then climbed on behind me. With a quick slap of the reins, the horse trotted forward. It took all my strength not to glance back.

"Are you going to be all right?" Raul touched my arm with his free hand.

"Yes. Sorry. I just had to get out of there." I turned and gave him a forced smile.

We traveled through the twilight lit woods, the sounds from town following us into the trees. The further away we got, the darker it became. I shivered against the bleakness, glancing over my shoulder more than once.

At last, we pulled in front of the cottage. Raul hopped down first then reached back up to help me down. He walked me to the front door then wrapped an arm around my waist, tugging me closer.

I swiped his hair from his face. He bent until his lips brushed against mine. My hands slid to his chest as I deepened the kiss. More than anything, I wanted to forget about Kenrick. I was happy before he came here, and I'd be happy when he left. I didn't need him. I had all I needed in Raul and always had. I was in love with him. Now, I just needed to decide where we went from here. Kenrick had been a distraction and nothing more. I knew now, without a doubt, where my heart belonged.

Raul's hands tangled in my hair, his mouth tasting of apples and cinnamon. All I wanted to do was get closer to him. To never be separated. Breathless, we pulled apart.

He trailed his fingers down my face with tenderness. "I should probably head home now or I might do something foolish, my little Brielle."

I laughed. "Good idea. The last thing we need is for Gram to catch us in such a compromising position."

He leaned in for a peck on the lips. "I'll always take care of you."

My heart skittered out of control. "Always is a long time."

He gave me a lopsided grin. "Yes, it is. Perhaps I can convince you to run off with me. To leave Dark Pines behind and come with me when I leave tomorrow."

My stomach knotted with nervousness. Was I really going to make a drastic life-altering decision just because Kenrick angered me? But I wanted to be with Raul. I missed him something fierce whenever we were parted. The only problem was, I didn't think Gram would agree to this. I knew it'd hurt her if I left without warning.

"And what of Gram?"

"I could speak with her in the morning if you'd like. Maybe she'd come with us." He grinned, touching my face. "If she knew how much I cared about you ... "

"How much is that?" my voice squeaked.

"More than anything."

I hugged him tight, until at last he released me, climbed back onto his steed, and rode off into the woods. Tomorrow, everything would change. If I decided to go through with this, then there was no going back, but I knew that Gram needed me here in Dark Pines with her. Would I really be able to walk away from the woman who'd raised me? And then there was Kenrick; soon he'd be a memory I tried hard to forget.

Chapter Eighteen

As I closed the door behind me, I sank to the floor, confusion racing through me. Could I truly make a drastic choice and follow after Raul and see all the places he'd described to me in great detail? Was I truly going to throw away the life I'd work so hard for here in Dark Pines on the chance that he *could* be my true love?

But if I did leave, I wouldn't have to hear the mockery and whispers of the villagers any longer. I'd be free from them. Besides, hadn't Gram wanted me to travel—have new adventures? Although, I very much doubted this was what she had in mind.

Yet, my heart ached at the thought of him not being here—not being close to me …

So many thoughts bombarded me. Both good thoughts and bad ones.

But one constant remained. My feelings. The warmth I felt whenever Raul's name was mentioned.

Then another thought struck me. Had Gram seen me with Raul

tonight? The way we'd been dancing? I hoped no one told her that we'd snuck off together. I'd be in for it if she did find out. But if I decided to leave tomorrow, did I really care? *Yes. You care what she thinks. She's been a mother to you.* And I wasn't so sure I could go through with it. That I could leave Dark Pines.

As if hearing my thoughts, I heard footsteps on the stoop. I stood and opened the door to find Gram, who said, "I met Raul on the lane and he said he has some important matters to discuss with me tomorrow. Do you want to fill me in? Because the last time we spoke of him, I thought I told you I didn't want you two alone."

"You speak as if you know his heart and his intentions. Everything will be fine, Gram. I felt a little sick, so he escorted me home. And—"

"And what?" Her gaze met mine.

"He admitted to having feelings for me." My teeth grazed my lip as I searched her face. "And if I'm being honest, Gram, I have feelings for him too ... but don't worry, everything will be fine, I promise I won't get into anything over my head."

She touched my face. "I wish that were so, that everything would be fine—but I know otherwise. Don't worry child, I'll be here no matter what happens. Just stay calm and I'll help you through. Now, why don't you get changed then head for bed. You've had a long day and we've got lots of vegetables to clean tomorrow."

Tomorrow. That one word held so many possibilities. It held the promise of Raul. But also that meant, if Gram didn't agree, I might have to say goodbye. I crawled into bed, staring at the lone blinking lantern. A sharp pain exploded in my head. I cried out, gripping my face. Nausea washed over.

"Gram, I don't feel so well."

"Shh ... I'm right here, just close your eyes. I'll make you some tea." She began to hum my lullaby, her voice soothing, yet distant.

I squeezed my lids shut as dizziness swept in. What was wrong with me? I rocked back and forth, hoping whatever ailment had come over me, passed quickly. But pain shot through me as if I'd been stabbed by a blade. My head pounded so hard, like someone had taken an axe to a tree, striking over and over again.

The vision was coming—more violently—more real than it had ever been before.

Puddles of blood soaked between my toes as I knelt behind the twisted maze of thorns. Horrific screams echoed around me, pleading for my help. I leapt up, racing toward the voice.

The stench of rotten meat made me gag. Vomit burned the back of my throat.

"Someone help me!" Mary Dyer begged as she crawled toward a bed of ferns.

"Mary, take my hand," I shouted, reaching forward to grab her.

Bones crunched beneath my steps and I glanced down at the ivory colored skeletal remains. Pieces of flesh littered the pile, along with twisted yards of intestines and innards.

Mary cried in pain and held tight to her throat, the new wound overflowing with blood. As I stared in terror, claws came out in front of me, slashing at her body. My stomach clenched as the wave of nausea washed over me. I fell to my knees, retching.

"No!" I screeched. Cool air touched my cheeks, the putrid smell of spoiled meat still permeated the air around me.

"Shh … it's all right." Gram's voice soothed me.

My lids fluttered open. Confusion swirled through me as I took in the wooded surroundings. What was I doing in the forest? I shifted on my knees and something sharp jabbed into my leg.

I glanced down. My gown was drenched with blood, my skin stained crimson. Beneath me lay a nest of bones. I swallowed hard, my gaze focusing on Gram, who now stood with a pail of water, wiping me clean.

"W-what's going on? Why am I in the woods, and why am I covered in blood?"

"Bri, there's something you ought to know." Her eyes welled. "Something I've been keeping from you. I didn't want you to find out like this, but we're running out of time and I think it's time you knew the truth."

My heart hammered loudly. I swallowed hard. Did I really want her to finish this sentence? But I had to know.

"Gram?"

"It's not your fault. You have to understand that. You didn't ask for this."

"I-I'm the monster?" My gut churned as she nodded her head. Then I saw Mary Dyer's body. What remained of it. *Gertie's mother.* Her flesh was torn from the bone, her arms and legs scattered in the brush. Bile burned the back of my throat as vomit erupted from my lips. The taste of blood was fresh on my tongue as I emptied my stomach. After a few more heaves, I turned to Gram.

"*I* did this?"

Her brows furrowed and sorrow washed over her face. "Yes."

In the distance, I heard the distinct sound of horse hooves thundering closer.

"The screams came from this way," Kenrick bellowed. Armor clanked and I knew his soldiers were with him.

Gram jerked me to my feet and led me into the thicket. We dodged between trees, briars tearing at my already dirtied shift. She ushered me into the creek and the cold water stunned me.

"Come, we must hurry."

Water splashed against our legs as we pushed through the darkness, the mossy rocks slippery beneath my feet. We came out of the woods at the back of our cottage, where Gram forced me to take off my clothing. She picked up a bucket and dumped it over me, furiously scrubbing my skin.

Once she was assured most of the blood was washed off, she tugged me into the cottage, where she tossed my shift into the fireplace. The wet garment hissed as the flames licked at it. Gram gripped hold of me and escorted me to the already filled tub.

"Gram, what's going on? H-how long have I been like this?" Sobs raked through me as she cleaned my hair. No wonder she made so much soap, with all this blood …

"When your bath is done, I want you to pack a bag. We have to hide you somewhere away from Dark Pines."

Tears trailed my cheeks as I stared at her. "Gram?"

"Oh child, this isn't your fault. You're cursed."

Cursed? "I don't understand?"

Gram offered me a sheet to dry off with and went to fetch several loaves of bread, which she wrapped in cloth. As she loaded herbs into a small leather pouch, she sighed and turned to face me.

"You've carried the burden for centuries now."

"Centuries? How can that be?"

"Dark magic."

I closed my eyes, shivering as Gram came over to help me finish drying. Was this what Raul and Rhyne's grandmother meant when she'd mentioned magic?

"Whoever cursed you to become a Beast, damned Kenrick to be the knight hell bent on slaying you. It's how you got this." She pointed to the scar above my heart. "Every thirty-five to forty years you're reborn. Your parents never come back. Just you. You're delivered to my doorstep as a babe, although I'm never sure how you get there, and me, I never die. I'm the same age, year after year. The three of us, you, me, and Kenrick, bound by the same curse. And the ghost of your cousin, Lucia, shows up like an omen before your change and during the attacks as if to warn us, or perhaps others."

Lucia. I glanced at the painting of her and a sickening thought entered my mind. "H-how did she and Aunt Narcissa die?"

Gram turned away from me. "They were murdered."

My fingers trembled. "How?"

"It wasn't your fault. You didn't know it was them. I came home from visiting a sick child to find the remains ... I never blamed you." Her eyes welled.

"No. This can't be true. It can't be." I'd slaughtered my own family.

"Bri, I have no reason to lie to you. Be reasonable."

"Reasonable? I've just discovered I'm a monster and you want me to be reasonable." Sorrow clutched hold of me.

The wrinkles in her face seemed deeper as she rubbed her forehead. "Please, listen to me child. Everything I've said is the truth."

My nails dug into my palms. Deep down, I knew she didn't lie, I'd read enough in my research in the library to know she spoke the truth. But I wished she did. "Why don't I remember any of this?"

Gram handed me a brown dress, then pulled out a large leather bag. "It's part of the curse. The onset of your condition strikes when Kenrick is near. You start off killing one to two people a year. And the closer you two become, the more you hunger for blood and flesh. The more you kill. When you were twelve, Kenrick's family passed through Dark Pines. It was the first time you killed—the first time the Beast struck during this cycle. I hoped he wouldn't come back, that maybe the curse had weakened and that would be the end of it. Then he showed up this summer." Gram's voice cracked. "You never live beyond your seventeenth year. Kenrick always comes and he always slays you."

"Oh dear God. That's why you told me to stay away from him." I wrung my hands together. And here I was helping him research his beast, when all along the Beast was *me*. "Have I ever hurt you?"

"No. My powers protect me." She patted my shoulder. "We're trying to find a way to break the curse. That's why I've been doing my own research ... trying to scour things that I might've missed. I've searched for centuries to no avail. I tried everything I could to contain this affliction. At one point, I locked you in a cage; I even chained you to the metal bars, but you easily broke through them."

I let out a slow hiss of breath as I thought of all the people I'd killed. "You could've put me in a dungeon or killed me."

"You are my granddaughter, how can you suggest such a thing? I finally had to ask for outside help in Father Machai. And we did try to imprison you, but you knocked down part of the church wall."

"But there was a fire, I saw the charred wood."

"We lit the fire to burn evidence of you. We've had the good fortune of Father Machai not going to the church with this. But we have made little progress. This time things have been harder, because your transformations are more violent. It's not easy to hide your victims when they're left in pieces. Your hunger increases each time you're reborn, although I can't explain why. But both Father Machai and I know that you're a good girl. This isn't your fault."

I thought of the ruined church and the claw marks in the stone. "I was here before, in Dark Pines, wasn't I?"

"Yes."

My chest constricted as I envisioned all the people I'd killed in Dark Pines. People who'd been my friends. And what of the other villages? I didn't deserve to live. Not like this.

"We moved a lot over the years, to hide my immortality. I liked Dark Pines as it was out of the way and we didn't get many newcomers," Gram said, folding several dresses and shoving them into my pack while I hurried to grab an extra pair of boots. "You had Rhyne Butcher and Raul. There has never been anyone else over the years. I thought perhaps if I encouraged your friendship and gave you someone else to focus on, not to mention all your studies to be a healer it might break the curse. That if you had other things to concentrate on like your apprenticeship, you wouldn't get attached to Kenrick, then it wouldn't have to come to this. And then, of course, Kenrick came much earlier. I didn't expect him until closer to your birthday; he threw a bit of a snag in things."

"Gram, why didn't you tell me? Why did you let me believe I was having premonitions, when it was really my memories?"

She hugged me tight, trying not to cry. "Oh child, I wanted to save you the heartache. I thought I could protect you this way."

"But it isn't me who needs protecting." I cried against her shoulder, trying to forget the horrible things I'd done.

"Yes you do. Kenrick is destined to kill you, and he will, as he always does. Your only chance for survival is to leave at first daylight and head to Fire Ridge. We have a cabin nestled away in the woods for you to hide in."

"What of you?"

"I'll stay Dark Pines for a bit. Father Machai and I have more things to look through." She picked up her cloak then tied it about her shoulders. "Now, I must get word to Rhyne and Raul to be ready in the morning to take you away."

My mouth gaped open. "I thought you didn't like the Wanderers?"

Gram snorted. "They're dangerous, but loyal. And Raul, above anyone else, is in the best position to keep you safe. We need to keep you alive so we can find a way to break the curse. If you die, you'll be reborn again and have to go through this horrible transformation once more. We need to find a cure. To end this, once and for all."

"But will Rhyne and Raul be able to keep themselves safe from me?"

"They can take care of themselves. Tomorrow, when you leave, I'll tell everyone you and Rhyne have run off together. The village gossips won't question it, seeing as how you've been caught in his cousin's carriage with him. Not to mention the two of you spend a lot of time together."

My gaze wandered to the fireplace, the flames dancing wildly. "What of Gertie, though? She'll be hurt when she hears Rhyne has run off with me. And Bowman, he won't forgive Rhyne for going— not if his cousin is along. You know how hard he's tried to keep Rhyne from the Wanderers."

"He will recover. It's better for him to be angry than to know the truth. Besides, Rhyne's mother will handle him. She knows of our dilemma. She knows Rhyne and her people might be able to help you. Not to mention, Rhyne has his own reasons for needing to leave." Gram kissed my cheek. "Now, finish packing your sack, then get some rest. I'll be home as soon as I can."

After all the confliction the last few weeks, I was going to leave Dark Pines after all.

I had to. The longer I stayed here, the greater the chance I had of killing someone I cared about. Whatever ill feelings I had toward my neighbors, I didn't want any of them dead.

Worse, Gram said that there might be a way to break the curse. What would I do if someone found me and killed me before we find a way to beat this?

Chapter Nineteen

It was still dark out when Gram shook me awake. "Time to get up, Brielle. Rhyne and Raul should arrive any moment."

I rubbed my swollen eyes and took the dress she handed me. Once I slipped out from under my blankets, I tugged the garment over my head then pulled on a pair of boots, fighting back the tears that burned at the edges of my vision.

"Gram." My voice choked up as I hugged her.

"Oh child, don't fret. You'll see me again soon. For now, we must keep you safe. You don't know how horrible it is to watch you die every time. Things *have* to be different this cycle. We have a few leads now. We will find the blood contract for this curse." She stroked my hair then kissed my cheek. "Then we can end this for good. Now you wait outside while I fetch your pack."

Blood contract? What else didn't I know?

The cool air traced across my skin like icy fingers, causing it to pucker with goose bumps. I shivered, then turned to glance at our tiny cottage. Today, I'd say goodbye to everything I knew. There'd be no more sneaking off to the creek to meet Rhyne, or hunting in the woods. I wouldn't be able to watch Gram make her salves and soaps. A sense of loss washed over me. Soon Dark Pines would be a memory, nothing more. How many times had we gone on the run in order to keep people from discovering my secret?

In the distance, I heard the carriage, the jingle of the harness loud in the quiet of the morning. Raul reined in the horses, bringing the cart to a stop. With swift, easy movements, he hopped from the seat and came toward me. Behind him, I saw Rhyne in another carriage, accompanied by their grandmother.

Raul smiled, his hair shimmering in the early morning light. "I told you we'd run off together."

Gram snorted behind me. "Don't make me regret this Raul Tinker."

He took my pack from her and slid it into the carriage. "I'll take *good* care of her."

"That's what I'm afraid of." She stared him down.

"Don't worry, Loreen, I'll make sure that my cousin minds his manners," Rhyne said, coming up alongside us.

"Let's not forget what we discussed."

I glanced between the three of them as they communicated silently with looks and nods.

"Brielle will be safe with us. I gave you my word and my word is my honor."

When Gram seemed satisfied, she shook first Raul's hand then Rhyne's before she faced me. "You take care, dear one. Stay hidden as much as possible and stick close to Raul."

He grinned, giving me a wink.

"But not too close," Gram muttered.

I gave her a sad smile. "I'll be fine. No need to worry."

She hugged me one last time before Rhyne hefted me onto the front seat of Raul's carriage, then he hurried back to the second cart.

Gram walked back to talk with their grandmother. I saw them nodding then heard Rhyne say, "We'll take care of everything. Grandmother and I will see them passed the borders of Dark Pines and on their way. We'll part ways before Fire Ridge as to not raise any suspicions. Folks here will think she's run off with me, so if anyone decides to search for us, they'll be looking for me too. Which means, I might be able to buy Bri more time."

"I know you have your own reasons for leaving, Rhyne, things you need to take care of, but thank you for watching out for my Brielle. Thank you both, I appreciate it."

"You're very welcome. I know you would've done the same for my grandsons." The elder Tinker patted Gram's hand. "Now, Rhyne, why don't you ride with Raul and Bri for a bit. I can handle this cart on my own."

Once Rhyne, Raul, and I were settled into place, Raul grabbed the reins and gave the horses a light slap.

The cart jerked forward. I waved to Gram until we disappeared around the bend, away from Dark Pines and away from home.

I wrung my hands together, wondering if I'd ever come back or if the curse could truly be broken. My gaze shifted to Raul, who sat tall against the still dusky backdrop. Why had he agreed to come with me? And how did Gram expect him to protect himself?

With a sigh, I turned to Rhyne. "I'm sorry about you having to leave. I know how much you love Gertie," I said. "You could still change your mind, you know."

"I love her, but you're my best friend, Bri. I've known you since we were children. And I have to do what I can to help you. Besides, by aiding you, I'm going to be able to keep her safe." He sat quietly for a moment, then said, "I'm leaving just as much for me, as for you Brielle. There are things I need to take care of too. Things I'll tell you about soon."

"I'm scared," I whispered.

"I know. But I'll be here for you. So will Raul."

Raul cast me a sideways glance. "Things will work out." He caught my hand in his, entwining our fingers together. "Your gram has already devised a plan. In about a month she'll announce she's received word from you and has decided to leave Dark Pines in order to come live in our new home."

"How long have you known I'm the Beast?"

His thumb drew circles across my palm and he glanced at Rhyne. "Since you were twelve and I was seventeen. The first time Kenrick's family came through."

"But you two brought me to see your grandmother."

"I brought you to her because I'd hoped she might be able to shed some light on your affliction, or find something your gram and I missed."

"Even after everything you witnessed you wanted to be with me?" My brows knit together as I studied him.

This time he met my gaze. "Yes. You've always been a sweet, innocent girl. Back when I first came to Dark Pines, you were the only one who'd even speak to me. Everyone else avoided me, unless, of course, they wanted something."

His jaw clenched and he glowered.

"I recall your grandmother coming to my stand in the market to buy herbs from me with you in tow. And you stared at me as if I were the most interesting person in the world."

I smiled. "That's because you *are* the most interesting person I've ever met."

He chuckled as he faced the rut-filled road once more. "You surprised me that day. I never expected us to become fast friends, much to your grandmother's chagrin. She accused me of spoiling you with gifts and outlandish stories. But I could tell she approved of my actions. Then about a week after my arrival, I happened to be traveling in the woods after sunset when I spotted you wandering through the thicket. Your grandmother followed close behind, carrying a bucket. Then, right before me, I watched the transformation. The sound of your bones cracking seemed to surround me. Your skin stretched, rows upon rows of teeth filled your enlarged mouth ... claws ... "

I closed my eyes; my stomach churning with the thought of anyone seeing me in that state.

"Within minutes, you tore through the woodland and took down a drunken soldier on his way home from the tavern. I stared as Loreen cleaned you up, whispering that everything would be all right. It was then she noticed me. At first, I thought she might kill me, but instead she invited me back to your cottage, pleading with me not to tell anyone. It was there that she confronted me about my being a witch, and asked me to help find a way to break your curse. Since that night, I've traveled everywhere trying to locate not only the cure, but evidence of the blood contract."

"Why?"

"Because I care about you and you didn't ask for this, nor would you in your right mind intentionally hurt someone."

He cared about me? Suddenly, I couldn't breathe. I'd been waiting for so long for him to tell me this, but how could he truly care for me when I was a killer? He deserved better than me.

"But I'm a monster." My voice raised several octaves. "Don't you understand? I could hurt you. Just being with me is dangerous."

He squeezed my hand. "My powers protect me."

I felt a surge of energy drift up my fingers and arm. My skin warmed instantly as if someone had poured hot water over me. His body glowed against the bleakness.

My hair stood on end when his power coursed around us, tiny flames igniting the air. A low hanging branch burst into fire, showering sparks onto the road. No wonder Gram said he was dangerous.

My eyes widened as I gaped at him. "Does anyone else know about this?"

"Only you, Loreen, and my family."

"Is this how you protected me from the wolf?"

"Yes. I burned his neck when I grasped hold of him."

My eyes shifted to Rhyne. "And what about you? Do you have powers too? Is that why I saw your eyes glowing in the village that night?"

Rhyne nodded. "Yes. I wanted to tell you, but I know how badly my father felt about the Wanderers already, and I didn't want to chance him overhearing us talking or something. But that's also why I've been spending so much time with Raul and my grandmother, learning to control them. It's my main reason for leaving the village. So using you as my excuse, actually worked perfectly."

"We're quite the group, aren't we?" I said, glancing at them.

"You can say that." Raul laughed.

We rode for several hours, stopping only to let the horses rest for a bit and to relieve ourselves in the woods. We kept a steady pace until dusk, when Raul eased the carriage off the road and into the line of trees. Their grandmother followed suit, however I noticed that she'd chosen to stay further down from us. I wondered if it was because she was scared of me or if she had some other reason?

When Raul saw my watching her, he smiled. "She's trying to give you some privacy, don't take offense."

He unhooked the horses' harnesses and led them to the stream for a drink then came back to set up camp. I fetched our bedrolls from the cart while he gathered firewood.

Once he got back, Rhyne took over and arranged the dry pieces of birch and pine, then he grabbed his flint. After striking it a few times, the fire caught. It roared to life and I realized some of that was his doing.

"Oh, my—" I gasped as the flames flared higher.

"This is what Raul has been working with me on. Controlling my ability to use fire. Sometimes, I don't realize how reactive it is to me." He grinned as he dug through a leather pouch, securing dried venison, bread, and cheese for our dinner.

Wind whispered through the treetops, causing dead leaves to float to the ground. The scent of smoke and autumn tickled my nose as I inhaled deeply.

Raul handed me some food, then sat across the fire from me. He looked at home out here in the forest, as if he thrived off the earth's essence. I took a bite of the dried meat and watched the shadows shift around us.

"Should we take turns posting guard tonight?" I focused on the inky black woods.

"No. I'll set up a protective circle around the camp before we bed down," Raul said.

Wild animals howled and growled somewhere in the distance, and I cringed. I didn't know why I was so scared. The wolves might be strong, but I knew of a far more horrific creature that roamed the countryside.

Me.

I was the Beast of legends, a scary story told around campfires to frighten children. And they had every right to be terrified, the trail of bodies I'd left behind proved as much.

"Why don't you crawl into your bedroll and get some rest?" Raul gestured next to him.

"Wouldn't it be safer to sleep in the carriage?"

"You might transform in the middle of the night and it's easier if you aren't confined," Rhyne said.

"I-I don't know if I'll be able to sleep."

"In a few minutes you won't be able to stay awake." Raul brushed breadcrumbs from his breeches then stood. He took a dagger from the belt at his waist and drew a circle around us in the dirt. Under his breath, I heard him mutter a few words.

A pop sounded, followed by a *whoosh*! Fire formed within the ring he'd drawn. The magic was so thick I could almost taste it.

At last, Raul lay down beside me. "Close your eyes."

Rhyne curled into his bedding across from us. "Goodnight," he said.

"Goodnight." I tugged the blankets up to my chin and let my lids drift shut. Raul started to sing a soft lullaby, in a language I didn't understand, although if I had to guess, it was probably Romany.

The beautiful tune danced in my ears, soothing me. I felt his arm drape across my hips then fell into slumber.

I jerked awake as a hand clamped down over my mouth. Scared, I struggled to get free.

"Stay still, someone is in the woods," Raul whispered in my ear. When he seemed assured I'd comply, he released me and reached for his dagger. The magic circle dissipated.

Gertie rushed into the campsite like a rabid animal and went after Rhyne, who'd just climbed from bed. "You bloody arse! What kind of man runs off with a woman when he's engaged to another?"

Rhyne grabbed hold of her arms to keep her from swinging at his face. His lips turned up at the corners. "Your family didn't approve of me, so why would I keep trying to impress them?"

My heart hammered loud in my ears. Oh no. I didn't want this for Rhyne. I knew what he was doing, trying to make her think he didn't love her. How had she found us?

"What does it matter what my family thinks?" She stood toe-to-toe with him. "I'm the one who agreed to marry you."

Rhyne's jaw clenched. "I realized too late that you're nothing more than a friend. My da pushed me into it, he wanted to me to marry you. Don't you get it, I can't love you. Now get the hell out of here before you force me to do something I might regret."

"Please, stop fighting." I stood and pushed my way between them.

Gertie turned to me. "Brielle, this is your fault. It's your fault that he won't come back to Dark Pines."

"What is all this commotion?" Rhyne and Raul's grandmother came into our campsite, her eyes wild with fright, walking stick in her hand.

"Everything is fine, Grandmother," Raul said. "Go on back to your wagon. We'll handle this."

When she noticed Gertie, she nodded, her gaze flitting over us. "Very well." She hobbled back into the darkness of the tree line.

With a sigh, I turned back to Gertie, chewing my bottom lip. The last thing I wanted to do was hurt her. But I couldn't chance putting her in danger. "Gertie, you don't understand, Rhyne and I are in love. I chose him. You know how much I care for him; you heard the rumors about us. Well, they're all true. Now be reasonable, don't embarrass yourself—just go."

Rhyne shot me an encouraging glance that said to keep up what I was doing.

"How could you? Bri, you helped me meet up with him. Why would you do that, if you loved him? You wouldn't have helped him be with another girl." Gertie glowered.

"Wouldn't I? We needed a cover and you were it. I'm sorry, Gertie, you're really nice, but Rhyne and are together now," I said at last.

Her confused gaze met mine then she turned to Rhyne once more. "This isn't a game, Gertie. I wanted to leave, can't you accept that?"

She gripped hold of his arm, forcing him to face her. "If you can look me in the eye and tell me you don't care for me, then I'll leave."

Tears blurred my vision. Why did she have to do this now? I didn't want to be the reason they couldn't be together, but I knew this curse had to be broken and if Gertie tagged along, it meant one more person I might kill.

"I don't care about you," Rhyne said in an even voice. "Tell me what Dark Pines can offer me? A girl whose family hates me? Your friend Sarah Weaver always talking about how I'm half Wanderer and will never amount to anything? Don't you understand? I want more than that. I want to see the world. This isn't about you, Gertie. This is *my* life and I plan to spend the rest of it with Brielle. I love her and nothing you can say will change my mind. She understands me—she's always been there for me. And she didn't need to ask her gram's permission to marry me. Loreen accepted me for who I was."

Pain stabbed through me as I watched the hurt radiate on her face. I didn't want to do this. But the alternative would be worse.

"You've never mentioned wanting to see the world. And you never let on that you and Brielle had anything going on. I won't give up on you that easily."

"I'm not a possession, Gertie. I'm a person, with feelings."

"Come back home with me." She touched his cheek.

"No. I'm not going back to Dark Pines."

"Then I'm coming with you."

"I don't want you here." Rhyne jerked away from her.

My hands trembled at my side as I tried to stay composed.

"You can't stop me from following you." She reached for him once more.

"No. But I can." Raul stepped closer, dagger in hand. "Let him go, Gertie, my cousin made his choice."

Gertie looked to me as if I could change either of their minds. "I'm sorry. You need to go." I hurried to Rhyne's side and he wrapped me in his arms.

Gertie's shoulders slumped, as disbelief seemed to set in. "Then I guess this is goodbye," she said at last. "I-I should go."

My chest tightened, but I didn't move or wave farewell. I was too scared that it'd only encourage her to attempt to bring Rhyne back with her. She needed to get as far away from me as possible, even if that meant breaking her heart and ending our friendship.

She turned away and walked back into the night. When she was out of sight, I sagged against Rhyne and bawled.

"It's for the best, Brielle. We're protecting her."

"I know, but it's so hard. I never meant to cost you the love of your life. It hardly seems fair."

"Goodbyes are always the hardest. But this is my choice, Bri. I will stand by you until either this curse is broken, or we die trying to break it. I'm in this until the end, whatever that might be. Besides, with my powers out of control, I can't have her too close. What happens if I accidentally unleash fire or something?"

"You've both done the right thing. I know how hard this was for you, cousin. But perhaps when this curse is broken and you have a better handle on your magic, you can go back to Dark Pines and mend what has been torn apart," Raul said.

Rhyne nodded his understanding, but it didn't make me feel any better.

Chapter Twenty

Guilt gnawed at me as Raul, Rhyne, and I continued our travels. All I kept picturing was Gertie's eyes, and the hurt we'd caused her.

But what would've happened if she'd come along with us? I shivered, not wanting to imagine her as another one of my victims. I had enough blood on my hands. But that made me realize just how much more I had to lose this time around. Because if I didn't figure out how to break this curse, it meant I'd lose Raul. Rhyne, too. And I couldn't bear that thought. But it also meant I'd come back again—prey on more innocent victims.

"I think we'll stop here for the night." Raul interrupted my thoughts as he reined the horses in off the main road.

We climbed from the carriage and him and Rhyne went to work taking care of the horses while I found a place to lay our bedding. Their grandmother had parted ways with us the night before, making the woods seem more lonely. Rhyne was supposed to travel with her, but she thought it best if he stayed with Raul and I, so his cousin could work with him more on his control of fire.

When Raul went to fetch firewood, I busied myself with unwrapping a loaf of bread. Once I finished divvying it up, I pulled out my dagger to cut hunks of dry venison. In a couple of days, we'd have to hunt again. For once, I was thankful that Rhyne had taught me how to track, trap, and hunt game.

Soon Rhyne had a fire roaring and he sat across from me and Raul to eat his dinner. "I'll be up for a while, so why don't you go ahead and get some rest."

With a sigh, I walked over to my bedroll and plopped down. Tiredness set in as I stared at the flames, the heat making me sleepy. "Goodnight."

"Goodnight." Raul stood and dropped a woolen blanket about my shoulders then leaned down to kiss my forehead. "I meant it when I said, I care for you, Brielle Healer. Don't ever doubt that for one moment."

Tears welled in my eyes. I didn't deserve him, not in the least. But I was grateful to have him with me. "And I you."

I yawed, stretching in the back of the carriage. With a groan, I attempted to sit up. It took a few moments for my eyes to adjust to the dimness. Tiny rays of sunlight peeked through the shuttered windows as we bounced down the road.

I twisted my skirts in my hand and blinked back the wetness in my lashes. A choked sob escaped my lips. The other night I'd killed a whole herd of deer. Not something I wanted to think about. But it was better than hurting a human.

The cart slowed, then came to a stop. Within moments, Rhyne jerked the doors open, Raul looking on with worry.

Raul climbed inside then knelt beside me. "How are you feeling? That buck's antler cut you pretty good."

"Sore."

He moved the ripped fabric of my dress aside to check my wound. "It looks better. A little red is all."

"Where are we?" I asked as he helped me stand.

"We're close to Glay."

"But that's several days from Dark Pines. How did we come so far?"

"You've been asleep for a couple of days now. You needed time to heal."

I noticed the dark rings beneath his eyes. "Me? What about you? You look like you haven't slept at all."

He chuckled. "Don't worry, I got some rest. Rhyne and I have been taking shifts driving." He hopped from the back of the carriage, then turned to lift me down. In the fading light of the day, his gaze roamed over me and he reached up to wipe the remnants of tears from my face.

"Things will get better," he said.

"Is there any way you can use your magic to make me stop changing into the Beast?"

He sighed, staring off into the woodland. "Trust me, my little Brielle, I've tried everything. But my magic, it doesn't work that way. You see, I can manipulate the elements around me. Like fire or water or air. Even earth. But I have to have something to work with. If the answer was that simple, I would've already cured you. Now, let me get things in order before darkness sets in."

I watched him as he set up our camp. Soon a fire blazed and he slipped a bowl of leftover stew into my hand.

Worrisome thoughts nagged me as I stared at him over the leaping flames. "What if I hurt one of you?"

Raul looked up at me. "I told you before, you can't harm me. Did you not see how quickly I overpowered the wolf back in Dark Pines?"

"Dark Pines?" I glanced at him. "Wait, that night I came to your carriage and you had claw marks on your skin, I did that, didn't I?"

"Yes, you'd nearly wandered into one of Kenrick's patrols that night. But I found you first and was able to get you back to your grandmother's house."

"H-how did you learn to use your magic like that, I mean to make the wolf go away and keep me at bay?"

His eyes darkened and he set his bowl down. He tugged at a piece of grass then wound it around his hand. "I've had a lot of practice over the last few years."

"I don't understand."

He sighed. "I'm not a nice person, Brielle. Your grandmother was right about one thing, I'm a *very* dangerous man."

"I don't believe you. You've always been so kind to me."

"Kind? I've done things I'm not proud of. You realize I killed my first person when I was fifteen?"

My heart clamored against my ribs. "I'm sure you didn't do it on purpose."

His face, twisted into a sneer, caused me to shudder.

"Oh, I meant to do it." He seemed transfixed with the fire and suddenly the flames leapt higher. The intense heat made me scoot back.

"Raul?"

"Are you sure you want to hear about my dark side?" He watched me closely. I did all I could do to look impassive, to show him I wasn't scared.

"Yes."

He stood, pacing back and forth through the site as if full of pent-up nervous energy. "Like I said, I killed my first person when I was fifteen. You see, my parents married my thirteen-year-old sister off to our old tribe leader. They knew he was a violent man, but they preferred the treasures he exchanged for Yalena."

He closed his eyes. "She was so beautiful and innocent. She had dreams of becoming a healer like my mother. But instead, they gave her to him like she was a prized mare. God, he treated her so badly. He forced himself on her the night of their wedding. She cried and we all heard her through the thin tent walls. She'd begged him to be gentle."

My vision blurred with tears.

"Then the torment began. Her new husband found ways to torture her. Sometimes he tied her up, treating her like a slave. Other times he struck her in front of our tribe, using her as an example for anyone who thought to speak out against him."

His hands glowed and I noticed sparks jumping from his fingertips.

"Raul," I whispered, fearful. This story sounded similar to what had happened to Rhyne's mother. It sickened me.

"My parents pretended nothing happened. But I couldn't. It was the last straw the day I found her by the stream, beaten so badly she could barely move. I marched back into camp and stabbed him through the throat. After that, the tribe banished me, all for trying to save my sister's life. And you know, she came to me later that night before I was punished. Yalena actually yelled at me for killing him. She accused me of ruining her life. I risked everything to keep her safe ... "

Waves of pain washed over his features as he raised his hooded eyes, staring right through me. I wanted to go to him, to make him better, but instead, I sat entranced.

"Once they forced me to leave, I found work as a mercenary, killing for hire. I learned to be strong, to survive. There wasn't a job I turned down. I've slain lords, soldiers, women, priests. So you see, I'm the only real monster here."

Somehow, I managed to get to my feet and walk across the clearing to his side. I wanted to take the sadness and anger from him. To show him that someone cared for him.

"You could never be a monster, Raul. You've been nothing but good to me." My hand shook as I reached for his.

He jumped slightly at my touch as if I'd shocked him, then his fingers wrapped around mine.

"Besides your grandmother, have you heard from your family at all?" I said.

"No. But there are bands of banished Wanderers that I join, the ones I travel to Dark Pines with. However, to my family, I am dead."

"Not to all your family, cousin," Rhyne said, setting down another armload of wood.

My heart ached. He'd been trying to protect his sister; he hadn't asked for any of this to happen. I nestled against him, embracing him as tight as I could.

"You are very much alive to me," I whispered.

His body relaxed and he hugged me back like he craved our closeness. It was hard to imagine what he'd gone through. He had no family, no friends, save for Gram and me.

As we clung to one another, I realized perhaps he understood me better than anyone else ever would. We were both murderers. Prisoners of our pasts. And the truth was, I loved him in spite of it all.

Over the next couple of days, we traveled farther north. We passed an occasional hunter and carts filled with goods headed for nearby villages to trade. Some of the people would stop us to buy wares from Raul's carriage but for the most part, we stayed clear from the main hubs, not wanting to attract too much attention.

Most of my nights and days were spent thinking of the people I'd killed. They plagued my nightmares, haunting me in visions of their death. I imagined their final resting places on the forest floor, and the accusations on so many faces when they discovered what I was. I shivered, turning my attention back to cleaning fruit.

Raul turned the spit over the fire, the rabbit meat sizzling as the fat dripped to the flames below. The scent of it made my stomach growl and I couldn't wait for it to be done. I finished rinsing wild blackberries and put them in a bowl to go with our evening meal then leaned back against a large rock to watch Raul, while Rhyne hung a couple pairs of breeches from some nearby trees to dry.

Sensing my observations, Raul glanced up and smiled. "I'm trying to determine whether you're more interested in dinner or me?"

My face heated as I gave a forced laugh. "You're ever the flirt. I'm simply enjoying the night."

He quirked an eyebrow then went back to rotating the meat. For several nights now he'd been trying to keep things light. Sometimes he'd joke around with me, other times he'd tell me stories. Anything to keep my mind from dark thoughts. But perhaps he was doing it just as much for himself as he was for me. "We should gather more firewood to last us through the night. It's been getting colder."

I glanced at the burnt oranges and dandelion yellows that waved from the treetops above. It wouldn't be much longer before they were shed. The closer to the mountains we got, the colder it got. Smoke curled in the air as an ember popped from the fire and landed near my boot.

Rhyne came up beside me and helped me to my feet.

The three of us traipsed into the woods, picking up armloads of downed branches and dead twigs. It took only a few minutes to find what we needed then head back into camp.

"When do you think we'll reach Fire Ridge?" I asked.

"A week, maybe more depending on if the weather holds." Raul slid the rabbit from its skewer and placed it onto a wooden plate. After he cut the meat from the bones, he split the meal in half and scraped our portions into bowls.

"We should have you cook every night." Rhyne grinned. "This rabbit is better than anything I can make."

"That's because you were always too busy running around Dark Pines to learn how to cook," I said.

"Perhaps this is his ploy to make sure you and I do all the cooking on our journey." Raul chuckled, tossing a small stone at his cousin. It nearly landed in his bowl.

When we finished eating, I washed our dishes in a small basin and put them away. As I moved across camp, a branch snapped behind me. Rhyne stilled, and he scanned the woodland. The hair on the back of my neck stood on end as I listened intently for footfalls.

Raul reached for his dagger, glancing first at Rhyne, then at me.

"Well, what do we have here?" A grizzled man with dirty blond hair stepped from within the confines of the forest, followed by three others. His blue eyes were cold as they flickered over me. A sneer pulled at his lips and he raised a sword, his tattered cloak billowing behind him like a torn flag.

Rough hands gripped my arms, as another man came out behind me, tugging me back against a burly chest. I almost gagged when I caught the rancid scent of manure and sweat. I fought to free myself from the man's grasp.

"Looks like we got ourselves a fighter." The man holding me laughed.

My insides coiled with disgust as his meaty paw groped my thigh.

Raul's face flashed with hatred. "I'll give you one chance to remove yourselves from our campsite."

The blond man snorted. "I don't think you're in a position to barter with us. So this is how things are going to work. You will go over to your carriage and start handing my men your valuables. Once we've loaded them onto our steeds, I want you to go for a long walk in the woods, while your lady friend and I get acquainted. If you comply, then we'll let you live. Make one wrong move, either of you," he gestured between Raul and Rhyne, "and my companion,

Felix, here will use her as a target for his blade." He gestured to the behind me.

Panic raced through me as Raul stared at me, his eyes glowing crimson against his tanned skin. The other two men moved toward the carriage, laughing and shoving one another.

I squirmed against my captor, but he brought me tighter against him then whispered, "I'm going to enjoy you."

The flames from the fire roared to life, leaping as high as the treetops.

"What the hell's happening?" The blond backed up several steps.

I watched in horror as a fiery stream zipped across the clearing. It transformed into the shape of a blazing hand and gripped one of the intruders by the throat. His flesh blackened beneath the magical fingers.

He screamed, falling to the ground and writhing with pain. The three men by the cart stumbled toward the woods, but long ropes of fire caught their legs, dragging them back into camp. Their clothing ignited as they struggled to stand, but their fiery manacles pinned them where they were.

I wanted to plug my ears, to drown out the horrific sounds of their screams.

Raul's lips turned up at the corners as he watched them go up in flames. Then he focused on Felix, who still held me.

"Let her go." His voice cut like razors through the air.

"No. As soon as I do you'll kill me," Felix said, shielding himself with me.

"Oh, I assure you, you're going to die either way. We can make it quick or I can watch you suffer."

I felt a blade press against my throat.

This time I watched as Rhyne made the fire leap through the air like a cyclone. "I don't think you understand what you're dealing with here," he said.

"I'm leaving here and if you try to stop me, I'll slice her open."

Felix jerked me along with him as he made his way to the woods.

I didn't want this all on Raul's shoulders. I'd seen the guilt and horror in his eyes when he'd told me about killing people as a mercenary. And I didn't want to be the catalyst for Rhyne killing his first person either. Not sure how the curse worked, I wondered if I could change voluntarily. Or if it could only be triggered by Kenrick. There was only one way to find out.

If this man wanted me, he was going to get me. Just maybe not the version of me he wanted. I squeezed my eyes shut, wishing for the onset of my curse. I prayed that the Beast would take over my body.

Please. I need to change. So I thought of Kenrick—his kiss, the way he'd held me during the dance at the festival.

Then I felt the cracking of my bones, heard my body turning in on itself, changing into something terrible, something deadly—

The man behind me shrieked, stumbling to get away from me. But I spun to face him.

Hunger pangs drove me mad. My teeth ached to tear into flesh. I stared at the pulsing circle of fire surrounding me. And the man running, like prey always does. A low growl vibrated in my throat.

Sweat glistened from his brow, and I imagined what his blood would taste like. My claws elongated and I felt my fangs graze my parched lips.

He turned his head to face me as he raced further into the woodland. I wanted nothing more than to rip into his skin, to tear his limbs from his body and savor the taste.

My body needed sustenance. I was starved for human meat. He crashed through the overgrowth, until I lost sight of him. I stopped and sniffed the air.

Thump-thump-thump-thump-thump-thump. The quick heartbeat drew my attention and I scanned the woods until I saw the outline of the bandit as he tried to hide next to the river. He tripped and raised his head—fear emanating from his every pore. But I was upon him before he could flee.

My fangs sank into his back. He squealed and his legs kicked beneath him, as if he could outrun me. His life's blood trickled into my throat, quenching a thirst and hunger that seemed unfathomable. The man's struggles became less and I knew he'd soon die. I buried my teeth deeper, until I crunched down on the spine. The man went limp in my arms. I dropped him to the ground, picking up the sound of someone else nearby.

My eyes raised. There. Standing across from me was another man. His golden hair seemed to spark. His scent drove me mad. The constant thump-thump of his heart attracted me.

"Brielle," he said my name, his eyes focused on me.

He was my friend. But the cravings nearly brought me to my knees.

Stop. I won't hurt him.

I had to get away from him.

But instead, I moved closer. Ravenous pangs of hunger needed to be quenched. I needed his blood to survive. If I didn't feed again. I'd die.

No. This is Rhyne. Stop. You can't do this.

My arms swiped forward, claws gashing at his chest. The scent of his blood drove me to madness. I lunged, my teeth tearing into his flesh.

Stop. Please. Stop.

"Bri," he cried out.

Fight back. Please fight back. I latched on tighter, drawing him to me as I crunched down on his shoulder.

With a scream, I fought to gain control.

The ghostly lady, drifted from behind the trees. She stopped, staring directly at me. "He will kill youuuu … "

It was then that I knew she spoke of Kenrick. She'd been trying to tell me all along. That I was the Beast. And Kenrick was coming.

Pain erupted through my body. My bones cracked once more,

nearly bringing me to my knees. My gums throbbed as my long teeth shrunk back into place.

"No," I cried out, dropping Rhyne to the ground and stepping back. What had I done? Oh God. Please not Rhyne.

The sharp tang of blood lingered in my mouth. I gagged as I scooted away from the body and vomited on the bank of the river. Slivers of bone scraped the back of my throat, while chunks of meat caught in my teeth.

A sob raked through me as my tacky, bloodied gown clung to me. I didn't want to be like this. To kill unmercifully. To hurt my best friend.

"No. Please don't die." My vision blurred as tears streaked down my cheeks. I crawled to Rhyne's side, clutching his hand in mine. This couldn't happen. Not to him. Why?

"Brielle?" he whispered.

"Why didn't you fight back? I'm so sorry, I never meant for this to happen. Please, I beg you, don't leave me. Please."

Blood seeped through his shredded tunic, his ivy eyes welling with tears. "I-I forgive you." His fingers clutched mine.

"Don't forgive me. I don't deserve it." I turned my head to the sky. "No. Don't take him from me. Please. I'll do anything. Rhyne, don't die. You're all I have." I laid my head against his injured shoulder. The warmth of his blood slipped down my cheek like the creek whispering over rocks.

"Go, Bri. Leave me." Rhyne coughed, took a few more haggard breaths, and then his hand went limp in mine.

He'd stopped breathing. No. Damn it. He wasn't supposed to die. I shook him.

"Wake up. Don't you dare leave me. Rhyne!" My throat thickened and I couldn't breathe. Not without his light in my life. I never meant to hurt him.

I was a monster. I'd killed my best friend. He'd only been trying to protect me. Why had he agreed to come with me? Why hadn't he just used his power on me?

We'd had so many happy memories together.

Dead. He was dead because of me. Another victim. Why couldn't he have just let things be?

It was my fault he was dead. No longer would he smile upon me. Nor would he give me his flirtatious winks. There'd be no more walks in the woods or swimming in the pond. Rhyne would never get to marry Gertie and have a small cabin in the woods. My childhood friend and dreams melted away like snow beneath the springtime sun. *He's gone because of me.* I tried to forget the look of understanding he'd given me when he realized he was going to die. As if to say it was all right. Because it wasn't all right. The monster inside me had stolen away the best person that I knew.

What happened tonight would forever haunt my memory. I knew if it weren't for Rhyne and Raul we'd have died at the hands of those bandits. But perhaps, I was meant to be slain and by dodging this attack, it only secured my fate more profoundly. I was an abomination. A murderer. Cursed. And my curse would be my undoing. From now on, I needed to stay away from everyone. No one was safe from me. I had to break this affliction or I'd have more lives—more sins to answer for.

At last, I released Rhyne's hand and placed it over his chest. More than anything I wanted to bury him. But more than that, I wanted someone to find him, to let his family know of his passing. They needed to know what I'd done. It was like penance for me.

Stifling my cries, I wiped my mouth off, staining my sleeve with bits of flesh and crimson fluid.

The moonlight filtered through the trees, illuminating Rhyne's form. My eyes welled once more at his carcass torn to shreds.

I turned to see Raul in the clearing. A dark shadow passed over his face as he secured his weapon back at his side. He rushed to me and knelt down, examining first Rhyne, then me. "I'm sorry I didn't get here sooner." He touched my face, wiping away tears.

"How can you be nice to me? I just killed your kin ... Oh God, Raul, he's dead because of me. Just get away from me, I might hurt you too!" I attempted to move from him.

"Shh ... it's all right. I know you didn't mean to do this, Brielle."

"I hate being like this," I whispered, covering my face with my hands. Deep down, I knew I needed to get cleaned up and get moving again. I'd chosen to change into the beast tonight, but that didn't mean Kenrick wasn't far behind. What would I do if he caught up to me? Would I confess to him what I was? Or would I keep traveling, hoping to outrun my destiny—my curse?

"I know, love. Believe me, I know."

I sobbed as he hefted me up into his arms. "We need to get you cleaned up. Let's get you into the river. I'll leave you to bathe and go retrieve some clean clothes for you."

When Raul disappeared, I slipped the blood-soaked clothing from my body and tossed them in the grass. Shivering, I stepped into the cold depths of the river and scrubbed my skin. I dug my nails against my flesh trying to remove any remnants of my latest kill. Remnants of my now dead friend.

Mud squished between my toes while the current slapped against my already tired body. I bent down and scooped up a handful of water, which I swished around in my mouth and spat out. If only I could get rid of the taste. I squeezed my eyes shut. I could end it. Just let myself sink into the depths. It'd be so easy to let go. *But then you'll just come back again. You have to break the curse.*

A few moments later, Raul reappeared. "I've got some dry clothing and a blanket for you to dry off with."

I accepted the items from him. When I was once again dressed, I clung to Raul as we trudged back to camp, where another scene of horror washed over me: the burnt corpses of our pursuers. If they hadn't shown up tonight, none of this would've happened. I kicked at a blackened skull, sending it skittering into the side of a nearby tree. With shaking hands, I collapsed on Rhyne's bedroll, clutching his blanket tight to my chest. His familiar scent overwhelmed me and I bawled. Rhyne was gone. He was never coming back.

I only wondered what might become of me in the days to come. Would I be strong enough to stave off this curse? To find a cure and be free from it at last? I doubted I'd ever really be free, because the memories of all my victims would haunt me until the day I died.

"Come, Brielle, we need to leave this place far behind."

If only it was that easy.

Raul leaned his forehead against mine. "Now you see what kind of monster I really am. The things I'm capable of."

Wetness hung from my lashes as I touched his face. "You, you're not a monster, Raul. Here, I killed your cousin, my best friend and you call yourself horrible. If saving us makes you horrible, then what does that make me?"

He drew back and looked down at me. "You are cursed. But me, I did this on purpose. I only hope that you will not be afraid of me."

Without hesitation, I threw my arms around him, and he embraced me back, holding me tightly against him.

"I'll never let anyone else hurt you," he said.

I sobbed. "I was so scared they'd kill us, but a part of me almost wished they would have."

"Don't ever say that, my little Brielle." He rocked me back and forth until my crying settled. "Why don't you sit in the carriage while I gather our things, we'll make a new camp a couple miles north of here."

Chapter Twenty-One

Dirt caked the undersides of my fingernails as I dug the hole deeper. *Another grave.* When it was deep enough, Raul helped me drag what was left of the dead stag's body over. Nausea clawed at my stomach. I had ripped the animal's whole spine from its body. The innards were gone. I'd eaten them only to vomit the bloody mess back up when I shifted into human form. We could've just left the body in the woods, but I didn't dare leave any sort of trail. Even if it could be blamed on a wild animal killing.

In one swift movement, Raul pushed the carcass into the hole.

Fresh moisture slipped from my eyes. I couldn't keep doing this. If only finding a cure was as simple as taking one of Gram's elixirs. She could heal people in the village all the time. Perhaps Gram's gift to save people was to counter my curse to kill.

Once we finished burying the stag and swept pine needles and twigs to hide the fresh grave, we headed back to the carriage.

I rocked back and forth, staring at the trees. It'd been days since

I'd lost Rhyne. Since I'd killed him. But the pain wouldn't go away. Every time I closed my eyes, I saw his face. The blood. The way I'd ended his life. God, I couldn't breathe without him.

A sob escaped my lips and I covered my mouth to hide it.

Raul rummaged through my pack and grabbed me a fresh dress as the moonlight shone through the timbers. He came back to my side and hugged me tight to him. "We'll get through this, Brielle." He pulled back and caught sight of my torn dress. "May I?"

I gave a small nod, and he lowered the shoulder of my gown, revealing the scar above my heart. He traced it, sending tingles through my body. Without another word, he moved away from me and turned his back so I could change and get cleaned up. There was already a basin of water in camp, we'd become smarter, knowing that my condition would come on whenever it pleased, so we prepared ourselves every night. Although, I was almost scared to go to sleep for fear that I might do to Raul, what I'd done to his cousin. To my friend.

Once I finished washing, Raul laid me on my bedroll then curled up behind me. He pressed his chest to my back, his arms encircling my waist.

"I won't let him slay you this time," he whispered against my hair.

I rolled over to face him. "How can you be so good to me? I'm a monster. What I did to Rhyne—"

"Rhyne forgave you in his last moments, and I forgive you. He'd want me to. You didn't do it on purpose. Besides, I'm not exactly innocent, Bri. You've seen what I can do. Like I've said before, at least you can blame yours on a curse. Me, I'm the epitome of evil."

My fingers touched his face. "That's not true."

He chuckled and his gaze lightened. He pulled me against him, our bodies molded together.

"Then it's decided—we're both good people." He swiped the strands of hair from my face then placed a kiss on my forehead.

My pulse soared as my veins seemed to ignite with liquid fire. I couldn't deny the effect Raul had on me. He knew what I was and still he did not shrink away.

I only wondered what might become of us in the days to come.

These violent scenes were becoming too frequent. I shifted into the Beast every couple of nights, the onset of my condition worsening. And I knew it was because Kenrick trailed me. I doubted he was very far off now. But whether or not he would put two and two together, I didn't know. A part of me kind of craved death, and every night I would beg God or Raul to let it end. To let me die. But in the same breath, I found myself determined to live long enough to stop my curse. It sickened me to see the death I caused. So much blood and bones. I knew I couldn't take much more. Not after what I'd done to Rhyne.

I shivered. A light drizzle blanketed the woodland, clinging to my cloak as we turned the carriage into the Fire Ridge marketplace. Wooden stalls lined either side of the narrow dirt road, their canvases billowing in the wind, while the vendors cowered beneath to stay dry. Aged stone buildings stood beyond the market, ominous beneath the steady cascade of rain. Raul reined the horses in and tied them off on a nearby log fence then reached up and helped me down.

"We need to buy a few supplies before we get to the cabin. I'd like to make as few trips as possible into town," Raul said.

He didn't have to tell me twice. The less people noticed us, the safer we'd stay. Already, curious stares followed us and he entwined his fingers through mine. We maneuvered through the small crowds to a stand selling grain and vegetables.

"Good day," a man wearing a ragged tunic said. "You must be new to Fire Ridge."

Raul nodded, his grip on my hand tightening. "Yes. My wife and I hail from Dark Pines."

"That's quite a jaunt from here. What brings you this way?"

"My grandmother gave us a cottage and piece of land as a wedding gift." I forced a smile and moved closer to Raul.

"Whereabouts?"

"Just north of here," Raul said, stroking my hair.

The man chuckled. "Ah, young love. Well, I wish you the best. But I must warn you, I've heard tell of recent attacks in the woods. I suggest you don't wander about after dark."

"Do they know what it is?" Raul asked.

"Some say wolves, others claim it's a Beast. But who knows, anyhow, I just wanted you to be on the lookout."

"Thank you, we'll be mindful. Although, I don't think we'll be spending much time outside for a while, us just being married and all." Raul winked at the man as he squeezed my shoulder.

Embarrassed, I turned my wide eyes in his direction. He grinned down at me, the familiar playfulness in his gaze. For a moment all I pictured was the "naughty" book he had tucked away in the carriage.

The man let out a boisterous laugh. "I remember those days."

Raul chatted with him a few more minutes then got down to business, bartering for our goods. Once we paid for the supplies, they were loaded into the carriage.

In the distance, the mountain peaks pierced the sky like giant needles. The monastery sat squat amongst the rocky outcroppings, bathed in midday shadows, its barred windows more prison-like than godly. I tugged my cloak tighter. Uneasiness settled between my shoulder blades but I shook it off, not wanting my imagination to get the best of me.

Raul tucked the last barrel into the carriage then came around to lift me onto the front bench. Once he slid in beside me, I turned to him.

"So, we're wed?" I teased as we drove out of the market.

"You know you've always wanted me to steal you away and make you my wife." He laughed as he watched the blush creep up my face. "But we'll be less memorable if we're just a couple passing through. Though it was quick thinking on your end about the cabin."

"Yes, well I wasn't about to tell them we'd run off together."

Low hanging clouds drifted across the gray sky, cloaking the Fire Ridge Mountains. The weather here was colder than it had been in Dark Pines. We followed the fork in the road west to a nearly overgrown trail.

The tall, dead grass swept against the sides of our carriage like reedy hands trying to stop us. How long had it been since someone came this way? I wondered if this cabin was one that Gram and I had lived in before.

My gaze flickered over gnarled oaks, which seemed almost creature-like in their appearance. The knotted holes in the trunks reminded me of eyes, the twisted branches of bony fingers. A raven coasted in the sky above, the wind carrying it this way and that. I listened to the constant creak of the wagon wheels as I scoured the dreary landscape. The woods, the grass, even the creeping vines. Everything looked dead; the kind of dead that came right before winter.

The whole town seemed draped in eeriness and I wondered if we'd made the right choice in coming here. We looped up the steep incline, the air suddenly colder.

After a while, Raul turned the carriage once again to follow an even more overgrown road. Soon I caught sight of the cottage nearly hidden amongst the trees. The thatched roof looked as if it might need some repair; the shutters were nailed down tight giving me the idea that someone had either tried to keep something in or something out. The weathered wood had seen better days, likely a century earlier.

On the side of the house, there was a stone well along with makeshift horse stalls constructed of logs and rocks.

"Here we are." Raul tugged the horses to a stop. "Our new home."

My brow furrowed. "It can definitely use work." Gram said one of her friends from the village had been keeping an eye on it to keep looters away, but suddenly I doubted how well of a job they'd done.

"Let's hope the inside has held up."

While Raul took care of the horses, I carried my pack to the cabin. The door groaned as I pushed it open, and I slipped inside. The single room dwelling housed a large river rock hearth, which took up the entire back wall. An old cauldron hung on a hook over decades old ashes. Dust lay thick over the sheets covering the furniture, while dishes were stacked neatly on shelves, layered with dirt and grime. A large four-poster bed sat against the far wall, its drapes faded and littered with cobwebs.

With a sigh, I stepped farther in. The dank scent of mildew accosted me and I wrinkled my nose. I moved to the heavy washbasin, intent on getting the house clean as soon as possible.

Raul sauntered in behind me. "It could be worse."

I snorted. "Not likely. I'm going to draw some water."

"While you do that, I'll strip the sheets from the furniture then try and find a bucket to catch the water leaking in." He pointed at the moisture dripping down the rafters. "Once I get the firewood cut, I'll get on the roof and see about patching it."

I pulled the hood of my cloak over my head, then trudged through the weeds. When I came to the well, I noticed a wooden pail already attached to the rope. I clutched hold of the handle and lowered it down, hoping the well hadn't dried up. To my relief, I heard a splash as the bucket hit water.

I cranked the handle again, this time raising the now full pail. I carried it back to the house and got to work cleaning. For several hours, I scrubbed the floors, dishes, and furniture. My arms ached from the exertion.

My stomach let out a low growl. It'd been a long time since our last meal. After drying my hands, I fetched the loaf of bread and salted pork from a wooden barrel and cut thick slabs of both. It took me a few minutes to get a fire going, but once I did, I slapped the pork into a pan to fry. When it was done, I put it on a plate with the bread.

The steady rhythm of an axe hitting wood echoed from outside. With food in hand, I walked outdoors, where I found Raul shirtless and cutting firewood.

I swallowed hard, watching the corded muscles as he swung the heavy blade. Sweat glistened off his bronzed skin, his hair tied at the nape of his neck with a strip of leather. My heart clattered in my chest like someone pounding on a cast-iron pan.

As if sensing me watching, he glanced up. A smile tugged at his lips and he gave me a wink.

"I-I brought you dinner." I strolled to his side, trying not to watch as he used his tunic to wipe his neck.

He set the axe down and took the plate from me. "You have good timing. I just finished chopping this last log."

I glanced at the good-sized pile of wood. "I think this will last us a few days."

"I'll stack it against the house when I'm done eating."

I attempted to keep my gaze averted from him as I chomped down my food, which made him chuckle.

"Do I make you nervous?" he asked.

"N-no. Why would you think that?"

He took a couple steps toward me. "Because you're blushing something furious and refuse to meet my eye."

I touched my cheeks. "I'm just warm."

"Maybe I ought to fetch you a cool cloth then." Amusement was evident in his voice.

"No. I'm fine. Really. I'll take our dishes in and get them washed."

I grabbed the plate from him and stumbled backward as I maneuvered to the cabin.

He raised an eyebrow then went to work stacking the firewood.

Raul was going to prove to be not only a distraction, but a temptation. No wonder there were so many rumors about women throwing themselves at him. Besides being handsome, he seemed so sure of himself. And when he smiled, it made my insides dance.

Gram might have a bigger problem on her hands if she didn't meet up with us soon. But I realized deep down that I welcomed the distraction. It gave me something to focus on other than the pain of Rhyne's death.

I scrambled through the brush, the sound of soldiers close behind me. The moonlight cascaded through the woodland, leaving me nowhere to hide. I was vulnerable. And they were coming for me.

Fear gripped hold of me as I thrashed across the shallow stream.

"You can't outrun me, Beast." Kenrick stepped out from behind a boulder, his chain mail glimmering beneath the ethereal light above.

His blade flashed in the air and he brought it down, stabbing into my flesh.

"No!" I screamed, lids flying open. My breath came in gasps as I clutched tight to my blanket.

"Brielle?" Raul shoved the bed curtains aside.

"Sorry, I had a nightmare."

He sat next to me, his hands gathering me into his arms. "Do you want me to get you a cup of water?"

"No. I'm all right now."

"What frightened you so much?"

"I dreamt that Kenrick stabbed me." A part of me wished he really had. That he ended my agony. My guilt.

Raul's grip on me tightened and he pressed his lips to my hair.

"He won't succeed this time."

I nodded. But there were some things even he didn't have control over. What made him so certain things would be different this time? Gram had tried for centuries to find a way around the curse, but to no avail. It was only a matter of time before I found myself at the end of Kenrick's blade. The more time I spent around Raul, the more I realized that if I died again, I'd lose him too. And that was something I couldn't bear to let happen. I loved him, which made me all the more determined to break this curse. Not to mention, I owed it to Rhyne to find a way to make things right. I didn't want his death to be in vain.

"Lay back down, I'll hold you until you fall asleep again."

But rest would not find me this night. And as dawn blazed in on her colorful palette, I readied myself for a trip into Fire Ridge. If I was stuck here, I might as well make good use of my time. There had to be a clue to unravel my curse somewhere. If I recalled correctly, someone in Fire Ridge knew a lot about the Beast. Maybe even enough to have information stocked away somewhere. I quivered, remembering my first encounter with Father Reynaldo. He wasn't a person I wanted to spend too much time around. I also had the worry of running into Lord Kenrick again as well ... The need to find answers overruled my qualms.

Raul decided to stay back and hunt so I trudged down the trail on foot, not wanting to waste time readying the carriage. Even with the sun peeking through the clouds, the monastery sat in darkness beside the mountain. I followed a stone footpath to the entrance. The heavy wooden doors had carvings of angels and demons in them. Battles between good and evil. Ghastly stone winged creatures cowered along the archway into the church. Their bulging smiles seemed to follow my every move.

"What kind of church is this?" I muttered under my breath, making the sign of the cross.

I understood angels doing battle, but to have the gargoyle-like sculptures posing at the entrance made me think of darker things.

Cool air met me when I stepped over the threshold. Rows of pews lined the room, facing an altar with candles ablaze. A wooden crucifix hung over the pulpit.

"Good morning. May I help you?" A sickly sweet, familiar voice called to me.

I turned to find the heavyset priest I'd seen in Dark Pines standing in the doorway at the back, staring at me. His bald head gleamed in contrast to the black beard which hung from his chin in the shape of a sharpened arrow, but it was his dark, soulless eyes that drew me. I found no comfort in them. The thin smile he gave me made me uneasy.

"Hello. I wondered if I might use your library?" My hand clamped down on the back of a nearby bench. Unlike at Father Machai's church, I felt off balance here.

"Of course. If you'll follow me, I'll escort you." He grabbed a candle from a sconce on the wall and ushered me through a narrow hallway. "You look awfully familiar, have we met before?"

Play innocent. Pretend you don't remember him.

"I don't believe so, Father."

The scent of food instantly caught my attention and I glanced into a dining area where trays adorned a long oak table. Steaming pheasant, golden potatoes, carrots, mince meat pies, apple tarts, fresh bread. Did they not consider gluttony a sin?

Someone shifted at the back of the room and I stilled. There, standing in the shadows, was the woman I'd seen at the sites of the attacks. Lucia. Had Lucia's ghost followed me here? Or was she warning me against dangers to come?

My hands caught the wall as I attempted to steady myself, and I shut my eyes against the dizziness. Once I opened them again, she was gone.

When the priest glanced over his shoulder and saw me staring, he stopped to shut the dining room door then continued on.

"Here we are." He waved me into a large room. Three walls were lined floor to ceiling with shelves of books, while the final wall had floor to ceiling windows. Statues of angels and prophets stood in each of the corners. The stained glass cast bizarre, colored silhouettes on the walls. "Forgive me for my rudeness, but I seemed to have forgotten my manners. I'm Father Reynaldo."

He reached for my hand. His cold, clammy fingers clasped tight to mine as he brought my palm to his snake-like lips. I went rigid as chills crawled across my flesh.

I gave a forced smile. "Pleased to meet you. I'm Brielle He— Tinker."

His quirked a thin eyebrow. "Brielle Tinker?"

My stomach writhed with unease under his intense scrutiny. But the need to lie to him overwhelmed me. I didn't want him to know my true name or anything about me. "Sorry, I was recently wed and am still getting used to the name change."

Reynaldo released his hold on me and rubbed a hand over the front of his too tight scarlet robe. The garment reminded me far too much of blood.

"You seem so young to be married."

"I'm sixteen, nearly seventeen."

"And you don't mind traveling with your Tinker husband?" He stepped closer, and I held my breath to block out the strong, sweaty odor that emanated off of him.

"It's nice to see the countryside I've heard so many tales about." *Shite.* Did he know I lied?

"Yes, well some of the tales aren't just stories. The world is far more dangerous than people realize." He flashed me a sardonic grin, as if he knew my dark secrets. "Now, can I aid you in finding anything in particular?"

My pulse surged beneath my skin. "No. I think I'll be fine."

"Most of our texts are in Latin, so I could help translate for you." He pressed his hand to my shoulder. "And I must say, I know my way around the library quite well."

"Thank you, Father, but I'm well-versed in Latin. I spent most of my days in the library growing up."

"Ah, that's where I remember you from. Dark Pines. Aren't you one of Father Machai's pupils?"

I managed to smile. "Yes, I am. You know him?"

"I was just visiting there not too long ago. Father Machai and I are good friends."

No they weren't. I'd heard the disdain in Father Machai's voice when he spoke to Reynaldo. What games did this priest play?

Everything about his movements reminded me of serpents, which with his girth surprised me. The way he lumbered about the room. How his tongue darted from his mouth to wet his lips.

"Why don't I leave you to your research?"

The thin smile left his face and his hand slid down my arm as he edged toward the exit, where he hovered for long moments staring at me. When I didn't move, he finally slipped away.

I released my breath. Something wasn't right with him. In order to remain inconspicuous, I grabbed two books on farming and set them on the table. After that, I read through several scrolls I found stashed away in a cubby between shelves.

The scrolls described horrific deaths in town. How the bodies had been mangled almost beyond recognition. I knew at once they meant the attacks. However, none of them indicated anything about the Beast. I swallowed hard as I stared at the yellowed parchments.

I'm responsible for these deaths. Just like I'm responsible for Rhyne's.

Tears pooled in my eyes and I quickly wiped them away. I had to keep it together.

The candle flickered and cold air swept over my arms. I glanced around the dim room for its source, but found nothing out of place. The back of my neck prickled and the feeling of being watched overwhelmed me. I quickly shuffled the parchments beneath a couple of the books then stood and shoved them back onto the shelves. When I twisted around, I found Father Reynaldo standing in the doorway, fixated on me.

"I hope you've been able to find everything you need." He clasped his beefy hands in front of him.

"Yes, thank you. I think I'm finished for today." I gripped a hold of the back of a chair.

"Please, don't let me interrupt." He peeked at the table where the remainder of the books were spread out. Why was he scrutinizing me so closely?

"You aren't. I have to head home before it gets dark. Besides, I could be here all day searching for information on farms." The lie slipped easily from my lips and I made a mental note to ask for forgiveness for telling falsehoods in the church.

"Farms?"

I smiled. "My husband and I are interested in starting one."

I snatched up my cloak and pulled it on, moving to the exit. To my dismay, he followed me.

"Perhaps I can gather more information for your next visit." Father Reynaldo held open the door for me then guided me to the front entrance. He rested his hand on my back.

Not liking his touch, I moved faster. But he stayed close. When we reached the steps, I spotted Raul waiting for me outside.

A sigh of relief escaped my lips as his gaze met mine.

"I came to walk you home." He moved next to me, offering his arm.

I clutched tight to him, my eagerness to leave Fire Ridge overwhelming.

"Ah, you must be Brielle's husband." Father Reynaldo glanced between us; his focus lingered on the gold hoops in Raul's ears and his jaw clenched. It became apparent that he didn't like the Gypsy.

In turn, Raul grinned. "Yes, Father. We recently wed."

Father Reynaldo's mouth drew down into a frown, his thick sausage fingers fisted at his side. "And who performed your ceremony? Perhaps I know them."

"Father Machai," I said, leaning against Raul. All it'd take was one messenger sent home to realize our lies, however. Would Father Machai back our story?

"You must've wed not long after I left Dark Pines." He stared into the distance and I turned to see a dark-haired woman ducking into a nearby alcove. "I hope you'll both come again. God's children are always welcome."

With that, he bobbled into the church and shut the door.

Raul and I walked down the road. I'd never been so happy to leave a place in my life. Everything about Fire Ridge made me nervous; the creepy monastery and its macabre exterior, not to mention Father Reynaldo with his wandering eyes and questions. He hadn't gone to Dark Pines just to visit Father Machai. He knew something more about the darkness and the Beast, and I needed to determine what.

At last, Raul peeked down at me, a crooked smile on his face. "So, you told him we're wed?"

"This was your idea. If I recall correctly, you started this rumor yesterday in the market."

"Maybe we should exchange vows for real." His voice softened as he looked over his shoulder at the church.

Where did that come from? I was silent for a moment, listening to the thud of my heart. It pounded so hard I thought it might pierce my skin.

Was he serious?

He traced the contours of my jaw and for a brief moment, I forgot about everything else. It was just him and I. No curse. No witchlike power. No haunted pasts.

He tilted my chin upward, until we stared at one another. I saw such tenderness in his gaze. Along with a hunger I couldn't explain. He'd once said we were kindred spirits and right now I felt that connection. Need swirled through my belly and made my legs wobble beneath me as Raul pulled me into his arms, pressing me to his chest. But we could be seen, so I pushed him away and said, "We have no one to marry us. Father Reynaldo thinks we're together, and we can't go back to Dark Pines, not now."

"I suppose you're right, besides, your gram might kill me if I married you without her permission." He gave my hair a playful tug then laced his fingers through mine.

We rounded the bend of the road, putting the monastery out of sight. "Father Reynaldo is the priest I overheard talking to Father Machai in Dark Pines. I think he might've been spying on me while I did research."

Raul's brow furrowed. "I noticed how he looked at you. There was nothing holy about it. We need to be careful of him."

"I'll have to get into the library at least once more."

"Then wait until he's away. I don't trust him." Raul squeezed my hand.

Neither did I. But for now, we had little other choice but to remain in the cabin until Gram came.

Chapter Twenty-Two

Raul threw another log on the fire, sending sparks up the chimney. "Remind me later to bring more quilts in from the carriage."

I blew on my hands to warm them. We'd spent the morning outdoors stacking wood against the side of the house. Already, the dark autumn clouds threatened rain. How long had it been since we left Dark Pines? Since I'd lost Rhyne? Emptiness filled me. A coldness I couldn't seem to outrun no matter how much I tried.

Fastening his cloak, Raul strode to the door. When he flung it open, my mouth dropped open as I saw Father Reynaldo on our stoop, his hand raised, ready to knock.

"Father." Raul stepped aside, holding the door for him to come in. "How good it is to see you again. We weren't expecting any visitors."

His labored breathing sounded like a whoosh of wind as he came into the house. Sweat beaded on his upper lip and he wiped a thick paw across it. "I wanted to bring you a late wedding gift. You mentioned during your visit that you're recently married."

He handed me a wooden box with brass brackets. I glanced at Raul then slipped the clasps open. There, nestled inside was a silver platter. The type one might expect to find in a lavish castle of a nobleman.

"It's beautiful." I ran my hand along the roses carved into it. "I don't know how we can ever thank you."

Priests shouldn't have access to such treasures and I wondered where he'd gotten it. When I flipped it over, I noticed the tiny inscription.

To B, with love. K.

B and K? *Stop being foolish.* It had nothing to do with Kenrick and me.

"Ah, the only thanks I require is your presence in church." He patted my hand.

The contact made me cringe with disgust, but somehow I managed to keep the fake smile upon my lips. "Of course, Father. What time does Sabbath begin?"

"Just after sunrise." He scanned our house as if he searched for something.

My mouth went dry. I examined the floorboards, praying no blood remained—we'd been up through the night scrubbing it clean.

"Would you like a cup of tea?" I offered, crossing the cottage to set the tray on a shelf and put distance between us.

"I'm afraid I can't stay long. I merely wanted to drop the gift off for you."

Raul smiled. "We appreciate your generosity and hope you come by again."

Father Reynaldo must've realized he was being dismissed. His eyes narrowed into thin slits, his fat red lips like bloody meat chunks.

"Oh, and before I forget, I meant to ask if you've seen Morris Farmer? His wife came to the church in hysterics, claiming he's gone missing."

My hand fisted at my side. *He knows.*

Raul scratched his chin. "No. We haven't seen anyone up this way. We've spent most of our time cutting wood and getting our house in order. But if we run into him, I'll send word right away."

"Very well. Enjoy the rest of your day. I look forward to seeing more of you." His focus lingered on me and my skin crawled beneath his scrutiny.

When he left, I let out a deep sigh of relief.

"We need to stay alert where he's concerned." Raul stared out the window at his retreating form. "Especially you. He watches you as if he might like to dine on you."

I shivered then pulled down the tray to show Raul the carving in it. "Do you think this is a coincidence?"

"Perhaps, but it seems too timely."

"Do you think he knows about the curse?"

"I don't know. But we need to find out more about him."

It took a few days for me to gather my courage to head into Fire Ridge, waiting for my opportunity to get back into the church. As I watched Father Reynaldo's form wobble away from town, I knew now was my chance.

I waited several moments then gathered my skirts in my hands and raced to the monastery. A reed-thin man in long black robes knelt before the altar, candlelight dancing in the dimly lit worship area. As if sensing my presence, he glanced up then climbed to his feet.

"Welcome, is there something I might assist you with?" A smile formed on his lips.

"May I use your library?"

"Of course, come this way." He ushered me down the hall and showed me inside. "If you need any help, just ring the bell."

After he left, I scanned the shelves until I came across a book on the histories of Fire Ridge. I slid the leather bound book from its place and carried it to the table.

The pages were yellowed with age, almost brittle. I flipped through them, lifting the manuscript to get a closer look at a sketch when a piece of parchment fell to my lap.

My breath caught in my throat, as I picked it up.

Today the young knight of the Crowhurst Order has come to save us. He offers up his sword in our endeavor to rid our village of the Beast. Our hope soars.

The parchment went on to speak of more deaths at the hand of the Beast, or rather me. Then, I got to a portion that interested me greatly.

The demon has been captured. Our knight has fulfilled his duty. Lady Lucia had been right about the creature, she looks almost human. To think she has been hiding amongst us this whole time. She acts and appears so innocent. The girl is to be put to death on the morrow. We have identified her as …

The parchment ended in scorch marks. Someone had burned the end of it, keeping my identity a secret. Or perhaps prolonging this sick game we played. But there was one name that stuck out. Lucia. If she was alive when this note had been written, it meant she hadn't died by my hand at Crawford Estate. Unless others could see her ghostly form as well.

Which raised the question: what was really going on?

My heart pounded loudly. I tucked the parchment into the book and leapt to my feet. How long had people been hiding information? My teeth grazed my bottom lip as I slid the book back onto the shelf. A chill settled in the air then the candle blinked out, plunging the room into shadows.

I clutched tight to the wall and felt my way along the wood until

I reached the doorway. When I stepped into the hall, I stopped upon hearing the low murmur of voices.

"I told you, Father, I don't know what the young lady is researching."

"Very well, but from now on, I want you to keep a close eye on what items she takes from the shelves," Father Reynaldo said, his voice hard as stone.

My stomach clenched with fear. I needed to leave. Now. Ducking, I moved away from their voices and to a door that led to the remnants of a garden behind the church. I threw open the gate and raced into the thicket, leaping over downed limbs and holes.

My lungs burned as I dodged into the market, trying to lose myself in the crowd. I bent over, my hands on my knees in an attempt to catch my breath. As I turned my head, I spotted Kenrick walking toward me.

Please don't let him see me.

He stopped at vendor selling weapons and picked up several different daggers. He seemed to be examining the blades closely.

I took a step back, trying to push myself flush with the fruit stand I stood next to. When Kenrick was finished looking at the knives, he crossed the road and headed toward the tavern, not sparing me a glance, I sighed in relief. *Shite.* He'd already made it to Fire Ridge. I needed to get back to the cabin. Now.

When I arrived back to the house, Raul appeared from the woods, carrying strings of fish and hares. "Bri? Are you well?"

"Yes. But we have a problem."

"What do you mean?"

"Father Reynaldo came back while I was there. He didn't see me, but he was hassling someone about what I'd been researching. I'm almost sure he knows something. And that's not all. I've seen Kenrick in Fire Ridge. It's only a matter of time before he locates us."

"Maybe we ought to send word to your grandmother and tell her we'll meet her somewhere else. We can't chance staying here."

I nodded. "We can pack our things and head out tomorrow at first light."

"I'm not so sure we should wait," Raul said.

"We need our rest and time to get our things in order. I don't think one more night will make a difference."

"Very well, but we will be on our way in the morning. No arguments." Raul glanced at the road behind us, his brow furrowed.

Would we ever be able to settle in some place, or was this my future? Always on the run, trying to hide what I was.

Raul followed me inside, where we washed up for dinner. I poured us each a bowl of stew and we quickly ate. When we finished, Raul helped me clean up. There was a certain amount of comfort in having him here. Even though I knew the inevitable outcome of this. Tomorrow we'd be on the run again. Trying to beat a curse I wasn't sure we'd ever find the cure for. But just for tonight, I wanted to pretend we truly were a married. As if we didn't have a worry in the world. It was just him and I. Two people in love.

Once the fire was stoked for the night, Raul turned his back while I stripped down to my shift and sat on the edge of the bed. I sucked in a deep breath as I watched Raul take off his tunic. His sculpted muscles rippled with the effort. His mahogany colored eyes met mine. He was beautiful. Biting back the lump in my throat, I knew I loved him.

"Raul," I whispered his name.

He sauntered across the room until he knelt in front of me. "What is it?"

"Do you think we should part ways? To keep you safe? It's only a matter of time before Kenrick finds out the truth … I can feel it in my bones. After everything I've done. All the people I've murdered—Rhyne's demise, I-I just don't want to be responsible for your death too."

Raul kissed my brow. "We've been over this, dear one. I will not part ways with you."

My gaze shifted as his thumb brushed against my lips. I knew I should pull away from him, yet I didn't. I wanted to feel him against me. To feel the security of his arms. To know, even if for one day, how it felt to be loved by someone.

Raul bent down until his lips captured mine. Fire blazed through my veins, his mouth crushing mine. My fingers weaved into his hair, drawing him closer. He deepened the kiss and I breathed him in. He was in my essence. My very soul. We were bound together. Behind my eyes, I saw a circle of flames surrounding us, connecting us for all eternity. My heart belonged to him. And if only for tonight, I'd be his.

As he pulled back, it astounded me how our skin glowed where we touched. I still felt his lips, even though we no longer kissed.

"You are mine," he whispered.

"Always."

He laid me back in the bed, then hovered over me, his mouth trailing down my neck. He pushed the collar of my shift to the side, revealing my scar. But this time, it wasn't a blade that touched my skin, it was his lips.

My hands drifted along his muscled chest, to his shoulders, pulling him down to me. His fingers slid over my thigh to my abdomen. Gently caressing me.

"Bri?" His eyes darkened with passion. A fire I knew only I could put out. "If you want me to stop, just say the words."

Emotion made it hard to speak, but I knew tonight might be all we had. And I wanted to give Raul every part of me. To show him how much I loved him. How much I desired him. That this flame, which we shared, couldn't be put out.

"Please, don't stop," I whispered, letting my mouth cover his.

And so, I gave myself over to him. Our bodies melding, becoming one. I clung to him until at last we both collapsed with exhaustion. When we finished, he held tight to me and nestled my head against his bare chest. His fingers stroked my shoulder as my lids drifted shut.

Wrapped in his arms, he said, "I plan to make you my wife, Brielle. Tonight was only the beginning for us."

Or the end.

"Raul, you don't understand, I-I might not be able to marry you ... "

"If this is about your gram, I already told you I'd talk to her. Let's not fight about this tonight." He kissed me once more. "You need your rest. We have a long journey ahead of us tomorrow."

My grip on him tightened, knowing that tonight the Beast would come. Kenrick was in town—and knowing what I did about the curse, I would be punished, again.

Chapter Twenty-Three

I *ran into the woods, shoving aside branches as I charged into the night. The crunch of my heavy footsteps sent small animals scurrying for safety. But it wasn't them I was after. I tilted my head, catching the scent of humans. Like a predator, I followed the trail. I inhaled whiffs of lavender and alcohol.*

I burst from the forest onto a road. There, ahead of me, stood a bar wench with her bosoms barely hidden beneath her low-cut bodice.

She spun to face me, her eyes widening. Fear rolled off her in waves I could taste it in the air. "No, please."

She hefted her skirts and started to run. But I was too quick. My claws ripped at her back. Screams filled the night, echoing around me. I gripped tight to her hair and dragged her into the trees.

She kicked out, fighting my every step but I held tight. Her hair tore from her skull, blood seeping into her face. I bent over her, my tongue catching the fluid before it could hit the ground.

I needed more. My fangs sank into her throat, silencing her blood curdling yells to nothing more than a gurgled plea. The warm, human meat was the only thing to satisfy my hunger. With strong hands, I pulled her arm off much like a turkey leg and chewed the flesh from the bone.

Snap.

My head whipped around, eyes scanning the wilderness. A faint glow moved along the tree line, headed in my direction. But I turned my attention back to my meal and crunched down on the arm bone, swallowing. It turned to dust on my tongue.

"At last, Beast, you're mine."

A man stepped from the shadows, his face highlighted by the dancing flames of the torch.

Kenrick.

His sword flashed beneath the warm glow of firelight. I stumbled away from him.

Please. *I needed to change back.*

Panic burned in my veins as I spun to flee him. Briars scratched my skin and I pushed into the overgrowth. But before I made my getaway, something pierced my shoulder.

My head snapped around to find an arrow stuck in my flesh. A high-pitched growl erupted from my lips. It quickly turned to a scream.

"Ahhh … " My shoulder throbbed as I fell to my knees. My claws sank back into my fingers and toes like splinters of wood being shoved beneath my skin.

More torches moved into the area, circling round. I was surrounded.

"Please, don't kill me!" I screamed right as the sword came toward me.

Kenrick stopped mid-swing, his eyes flashing in surprise. He dropped his weapon then staggered back. Disbelief painted his features.

"You? You're the beast? It can't be. What kind of dark magic is this?" His face seemed stricken, almost disgusted.

I wiped the blood from my mouth, then tugged my sleeves down to hide the gobbets of flesh still trapped beneath my nails. "Please, it's not my fault."

But that wasn't really true, was it? I'd held back. And it didn't matter that I'd done so to spare him pain, because I'd also done so out of fear of what he'd do if he found out what I was.

Now I'd find out.

"Father Reynaldo came to the door of my room this night," Kenrick said. "He told me you were a monster. I didn't want to believe him, but he brought me to the church and showed me the parchment that named you. And still I gave you the benefit of the doubt."

"I didn't mean to betray you."

Pain flashed in his eyes. "But you did. And now you leave me little choice. What else am I to do?"

One of the soldiers stepped between us, his sword raised above his head. "I'll tell you what we do. We kill the Beast. That's always been the plan."

But Kenrick twisted and grabbed him by the wrist. "No. No one is to kill her. We'll bring her to the dungeons until we can get to the bottom of this. That goes for all of you. Lower your weapons."

"But, milord," the soldier said.

"Do as I say. Are we not men of honor? This woman at least deserves a trial." He dragged me to my feet, and he gave me a gentle shove forward. "Get the irons."

Soldiers marched in, carrying rope, weapons, and shackles.

Tears trailed down my cheeks. "Kenrick, I beg you, give me a chance to explain myself."

He stopped, eyes swirling with confusion. "You'll have time to explain when we've reached the church." He stared at the arrow protruding from my shoulder. With gentle, but sure hands, he tugged the tip from my shoulder. I cried out in agony as blood oozed to the surface. My stomach churned and I stumbled on my legs.

"Kenrick, please."

"Don't speak to me. Not now. You have twisted everything beautiful between us. I don't know what to think."

"But it's a curse. I didn't ask for—"

An explosion of fire whooshed through the trees, setting the branches ablaze.

"Look out," one of the soldiers shouted, diving to the ground.

Raul and his grandmother stepped from the foliage, both armed with daggers. When had she arrived? Did she know about Rhyne?

I watched as Raul used the fire from the torches, causing it to strike like lightning. "Unhand her."

Kenrick pulled me closer, shielding me. "Stand your ground, men. This is what we've trained for."

"I'm warning you. You don't want to stand between me and the girl I love. If you release her, we'll let you live."

"They're the demon's accomplices," a soldier to our left shouted.

"She's no demon. Brielle has been cursed. And after all these years, you should be smart to figure out who did this and why," Raul snapped, moving in front of his grandmother and staring at Kenrick.

"Stop where you are," Kenrick warned as he took another step closer.

"Raul, please, get out of here. You and your grandmother aren't a part of this. Go while you can."

"I won't leave you," he said. "I gave you my promise. That I'd be with you until the end."

"You are not bound to me. Please. Go." I didn't want his death on my hands too. I couldn't bare it. Hellfire, I could barely handle what I'd done to Rhyne. At some point, I felt as if I should be punished for what I'd done. And maybe that was this moment.

Three soldiers ran toward him, swords drawn. With a flick of a hand, he sent a wave of fire at them. Their screams pierced the night, as their uniforms went up in flames.

Kenrick shoved me to the side, out of the way of the battle.

The soldier beside us grabbed his bow and shot an arrow. This time, Raul didn't have time to react. I watched in horror as the wooden shaft hit him in the shoulder, dropping him to the ground. All at once, soldiers were upon him.

"Raul, no!" I attempted to go to him, but Kenrick held me tight.

Raul's grandmother knelt beside him. She sprinkled some herbs on his wound from the pouch that was secured at her neck.

"Look out," I screeched. But it was too late. One of the men raised the hilt of his sword and brought it down against the back of her head, knocking her out. They bound both Raul's and his grandmother's hands, then secured them atop horses.

"Chain her," Kenrick ordered one of his men. I realized that with the other men here, he didn't have a choice but to take command and have us imprisoned. But for now it was better than death or so I thought.

My body shook, and I found it hard to breathe as one of the men brought over heavy iron shackles and clamped my ankles then my wrists. I struggled against my captor, trying to break free from his hold. He raised his hand and struck me across the face. I staggered backward, my cheek stinging.

"Do not hit her." Kenrick grabbed him by the back of his tunic, jerking him to the ground, where he held a blade to his throat. "You will not harm her; she has a right to a trial. Do you understand me? That goes for all of you. These people will not be beaten or battered by our hand. That is not who we are. We need to get to the truth. Now hold her still," Kenrick ordered as he wrapped a rope around my wrists as well then tied it to one of the horses. With a glance, he said, "I will stay my hand, and let the church determine your guilt. I will at least give you that courtesy." When he made sure I was secured he turned to his men and shouted, "Move out."

The horse wrenched forward, tugging me along with it. Twigs, rocks, and rough terrain tore at the soles of my bare feet. I sobbed. Why did things always end this way? I stumbled to the ground, and the steed dragged me several feet before Kenrick and another one of the soldiers rushed to get me to my feet. I glanced at Raul, who was slumped in an awkward position over the horse. From here, I couldn't tell if he was breathing. His grandmother was also limp, her body hanging haphazardly over her mount.

I prayed that they would wake up and get away, that they wouldn't do anything foolish.

If only things could've been different.

Kenrick walked ahead of me, making sure that his men didn't drag me again. But as I stared at Kenrick's back a sense of betrayal washed over me. How could he claim to love me one moment and in the next be ready to kill me, century after century after century?

Our caravan rolled into town, kicking up a cloud of dust. The horses led me to the monastery. *Oh God.* My stomach knotted as terror wrapped around me like a heavy cloak. Gram's words swam through my mind—Kenrick was truly handing me over to the church.

We approached the front stairs and Father Reynaldo appeared in the entryway. His mouth twisted into a sneer, a pleased look upon his face. He clapped his hands together as his rotund frame maneuvered the stone steps.

"You caught the demon and the Wanderers, just as I knew you would."

"I'm not a demon. You've got to believe me." Tremors raked through my body.

Kenrick moved forward and stood beside Father Reynaldo.

"By the end she'll admit her guilt." The priest patted his arm. "You've done a godly deed bringing her here."

Kenrick cut the rope loose from the horse then placed a hand on my lower back. "Where do you want her, Father?"

"Just follow me. I have a special room where I deal with witches and demons."

"You promised Brielle would get a trial."

"And she will, my young friend. But first we need to ask her some questions."

"And what of her companions?"

"I think it's best we keep them contained, don't you?"

We're going to die. But if I did, I'd come back and kill more innocents. I had to stop this now. No one believed more than I did that I deserved death. I yearned for it. But I couldn't go yet.

Kenrick had asked for them to give me a trial. But I didn't doubt that he would follow through on his mission to slay the Beast. Could I fault him for wanting to do the right thing? For wanting to protect the people? If I was wrong and I couldn't break the curse, he couldn't let me live, and I wouldn't stop him.

The decorative gargoyles seemed to mock me as I trudged under the arch. The stones were swathed in bleakness, ghostly silhouettes plunging the hall into darkness.

Torchlight bounced off the walls as we descended into the bowels of the church. My skin prickled as if someone had dowsed the lower levels in magic. Moisture dripped from the ceiling and down my cheek like cool teardrops. We passed several cells, the scent of mildew and urine heavy in the air. Uneven stones beneath my feet made me trip, but Kenrick righted me with a gentle tug to my arm.

At last, we came to the end of the corridor and stood in front of an archaic, heavy wooden door. Father Reynaldo produced a ring of keys and the barrier groaned open. Nausea bubbled in my gut as my gaze flickered across the room.

My breathing came in gasps. Shackles hung from the far wall. In the corner loomed a rack used to stretch people. At the center of the room stood an iron coffin, and next to that a table with arm and leg restraints.

Kenrick released his hold on me and I heard him gasp. Under his breath, I heard him utter the word, "No."

I stopped moving as I took in all the horrific devices. Then my eyes fell to Father Reynaldo who wore a wide grin. *Evil. He's completely evil.*

"Bring her here." Father Reynaldo stood next to a chair attached to a large wooden arm. Below it was a deep stone tub built right into the floor, filled with water. "We can forego this whole process if you confess right now. Admit that you're a witch or a demon."

"I'm neither. Let me explain."

One of Kenrick's men gripped hold of me, dragging me forward. I tried to fight.

"I thought you said she'd get a trial?" Kenrick attempted to intervene.

"Patience, Lord Kenrick. I have to question her, these proceedings are delicate in nature—You don't think I like doing this, do you?"

Yes, that's exactly what I thought. No matter what I said, I knew he'd find me guilty or twist my words to suit him.

Even as I fought, the soldier shoved me into the chair. Heavy clamps fell across me as they restrained my chest, my legs, and then my arms. I couldn't move. Sobs erupted from my throat as Father Reynaldo lifted the lever, lowering me to the water.

Ice cold water took my breath away as he dunked me under. I struggled beneath the sloshing waves, panic erupting as darkness surrounded me. I heard nothing but the thrashing of my heart against my ribs. My lungs burned. I needed air. Bubbles rose above my head and wisps of my hair floated around my head, like strands of seaweed.

I struggled to keep my mouth shut. To not breathe in the water. I tried to rock back and forth, but I couldn't move. He was going to kill me, but perhaps it was better this way. I could let go, let the water claim me. Death is what I wanted, what I begged for, was it not? The image of Raul and his grandmother saving me pulsed through my mind. Memories of Rhyne, whose life I'd ended. They'd all sacrificed themselves for me.

No. I had to fight. If not for me, then for all my future victims. For the people I'd already killed—I needed to end this for good, not just for the time being. I had to stay strong. They deserved an end to this curse just as much as I did. This burden was mine to bear. My atonement for all I'd done. I'd have to survive it.

At last, the chair lifted and I gasped for air like a hungry babe at her mother's breast.

My skin broke out in gooseflesh as the frigid air touched me. My hair clung to my face, my clothes heavy.

"When did you pledge your soul to the devil?"

"Never. My soul belongs to God."

"Liar!" Father Reynaldo shouted. "You've used dark magic to hide amongst us, murdering villagers and feasting upon their flesh. Confess, demon."

"I'm not a demon. I've been cursed."

"I see you want to make this hard. Very well. But in the end, you will tell us the truth."

"Perhaps she's telling the truth," Kenrick said, his face pale as his gaze met mine. A spark of tenderness enveloped him. Did he believe me?

"And perhaps she's bewitched you with her power." Father Reynaldo glowered.

I sucked in a deep breath. Once again he dunked me into the tub. My jaw clenched as I attempted to keep from sucking in the water. I squeezed my eyes tight against the pain in my chest. Moments ticked slowly. My body pled for air as dizziness washed over me. This was my punishment for falling in love. My trial for wrongs that had not been my choice.

God. Please make it stop. Let me live.

Father Reynaldo swung me from the depths, hoisting me above the water and I gulped for air. Droplets ran along my forehead, down my nose, and off my chin to the stone floor beneath me.

"Let's try this again." Father Reynaldo secured the lever then moved to my side. "What witch do you serve?"

"None," I croaked.

His gaze fell to the bare flesh below my shoulder, where my dress had come down.

"What is this?" He pulled it back to reveal the scar above my heart. "The mark of the devil?"

I turned to look at Kenrick. He reached for the back wall as if to steady himself when he saw the scar, as if now he remembered something. "I'm sorry, Father, but I think you're mistaken. That is a sword wound," he said.

"I know the mark of the devil when I see it, Lord Kenrick. Maybe I should have you escorted out of the room until we've finished questioning her."

Father Reynaldo's fat fingers pressed against my body, grazing my breast. I whimpered, trying to jerk away from him. The pleased look on his face made me sick. He moved away, then grasped for the wooden handle once more.

I dropped into the sloshing water, and this time my feet touched the stone floor of the tub. Something brushed my leg. A bloated, distorted face came into view. A corpse, chained beneath the water. I opened my mouth to scream, letting water seep down my throat.

I'm going to die.

The chair jerked and I felt myself being lifted up once more. I sputtered, vomiting water down the front of me. My throat felt raw.

"Tell me why you've come to Fire Ridge, monster."

"I. Have. Been. Cursed." My teeth chattered. A part of me wanted to tell him it was so I could kill him. So I could tear his fat fingers from his obese body. But I didn't dare taunt him. Not if I wanted to leave this room alive. To be able to fight one more day.

"The demon is strong. Let us move her to the dungeon. We will try to extract more information tomorrow."

They loosened my restraints and I fell to the floor in a heap.

Kenrick dropped to my side and gripped hold of my arm, helping me to my feet. His fingers loosened as his gaze riveted on the blood seeping through my clothing from my earlier wound. Father Reynaldo ushered us from the torture chamber and to a cell. He unlocked the door and Kenrick led me inside.

"I'm sorry," Kenrick whispered.

Did he finally understand that I'd really been researching to find a way to break the curse?

When he released me, I was so weak that I fell. My knees hit the rocky floor and I cried out in pain. The door slammed shut behind me. Coldness nipped at me as I sat shivering in my wet clothing. Lines of moonlight filtered in through the small barred window above, which were nothing but mere slits. It teased me with glimpses of freedom I'd never find. I stood and crossed the small confine and peered into the cell next to mine. Empty, as was the one next to that. I was alone.

At last, I cowered against the wall, pulling my knees to my chest. My body ached, my wound still trickling blood. The skittering of tiny feet sounded across the cell and I cringed. Rats. My fingers gripped my damp skirts. All I envisioned was their teeth piercing my skin.

Sobs shook me. My life hinged upon the crazed priest, and the man destined to forsake me. For the second time this night, I prayed Raul and his grandmother would survive, because they'd try them as witches.

From down the hall, I heard voices, followed by female screams. I rocked back and forth, plugging my ears. But I couldn't muffle the shrieks. I could only imagine what kinds of tortures were being dealt.

I hefted myself to my feet, and leaned against the wall. If I called on the Beast now, I could break out of this place. Like I had when I was confined in the church in Dark Pines. But if I did, I knew I'd only kill more people. But to lose a few now and be able to finally put an end to it might be worth the risk. Yet, visions of Rhyne's last breaths sobered me. Could I truly do this again? Force the change? Tears blurred my vision. Shite. I didn't know what to do. *Yes you do.*

Taking a deep breath, I squeezed my eyes shut and focused on changing into the Beast. Nothing happened. No urges to rip out flesh. No hunger for human bones and blood. I tried again. But to no avail. Why couldn't I change? Something was wrong. Something stopped me.

As more screams echoed through the prison, I sank back to my knees.

I'd find no sleep this night.

Chapter Twenty-Four

I sat propped against the stone wall. The hard surface did little to help the tenderness of my bruised flesh. My shoulder pulsed with pain, but it'd stopped bleeding. I glanced at the barred window as beams of daylight penetrated the drab cell.

Two rats scurried through a crack in the wall.

Father Reynaldo pressed his face against the iron bars in the door, his sadistic smile made me shiver. "I see you're awake bright and early."

I scooted farther away as the bolts slid back. The hinges gave a high-pitched groan.

"I'd think your duties to the church would take precedence. It is Sabbath." I glared. No matter how scared I was, I wouldn't let him think me weak.

His robust form filled the entryway. "I'll have plenty of time for the sermon, when I've finished questioning you. Lord Kenrick, would you be so kind as to bring our prisoner along?"

Kenrick appeared from behind him. His jaw clenched as he stepped inside. Even from here, I sensed his distaste for Father Reynaldo. Did that mean he might help me?

I cowered in the corner wondering what I'd be forced to endure today. "God please give me strength," I whispered.

Strong hands gripped my arms and I yelped as they squeezed my wound. Kenrick loosened his grasp "Sorry, I didn't know he'd do all this," he whispered then ushered me toward the door and down the hall.

"This isn't what a Knight of the Crowhurst Order represents. Please, Kenrick, you have to stop this." I glanced at him over my shoulder. "The curse is real. I really was researching for a cure here in Fire Ridge."

"I believe that you're trying to break the curse, but you murdered innocents, Brielle. I-I had no choice but to hand you over." Regret filled his eyes.

"I know, and I have to live with the nightmares every day. Don't think that I don't know that I deserve to be punished, but not in this manner." It was hard to fathom that such a short time ago, he'd pledged his love for me. I twisted so I could talk to him. "If you'd just give me a chance to explain what I know of the curse. Don't you see, if you kill me, I'll come back again—I'll kill more people. If we can find a cure, we might be able to end this now. Please—I haven't lied to you, Kenrick."

Father Reynaldo put a heavy hand on his shoulder, his voice urgent. "Do not listen to her, Lord Kenrick, lest she put you under her spell."

"Under my spell? Don't you think if I was a demon or a witch I would've broken out of your dungeon? Why would I lend myself to your tortures?"

Father Reynaldo spun to face me, his beady eyes lingering on my ripped dress. I wanted nothing more than to cover my bared flesh, but Kenrick held tight to me. However, his hand snaked around to pull my dress back into place for me, as if that would deter Father Reynaldo in anyway.

"You cannot use witchcraft because you're in the House of the Lord. Our building blocks are constructed of God's magic—so you cannot use yours."

He unlocked the torture chamber and my body stiffened.

Be strong. Do not show them weakness.

Two other soldiers took me from Kenrick.

But I threw my body backward, struggling to get free of my captors as tears streamed down my face.

"Secure her here." Father Reynaldo gestured to the long wooden table. "Perhaps today, she'll give us the answers we seek."

"No. Please. Don't do this!" I screamed, shaking my head back and forth.

Two more men caught hold of my legs and lifted me onto the slab. The coldness seeped through my thin dress as my body pressed against the table. Metal clamps tightened around my ankles, while my arms were lifted above my head and belted into place.

Father Reynaldo waddled to the fireplace, to adjust the iron pokers in the flames, pushing their tips further into the coals.

"Have you ever been burned? Heard the sizzle of flesh as it's melted from the bone?" A malicious grin pulled at his lips. "The smell is wretched."

My pulse pounded in my ears as he picked an iron rod from the fire. The sharpened end glowed crimson. He brought it eye-level. I whimpered.

"There are so many places we can put this. Like here, for instance." He touched the smoldering rod against the pad of my foot.

My body jerked and I yelped in agony. The skin on my sole burned but I couldn't move away from him. I couldn't get away from the pain.

"Why have you manifested yourself, demon?"

"Please, I'm not a demon."

"What witch have you given your allegiance to?"

"I told you, I'm not associated with anyone."

"Such a shame. You could end this all here, if you'd just be honest with me." Father Reynaldo raised the blazing sharp poker.

I thrashed against the table as he brought it to my leg, pressing it against my thigh. A shriek bellowed from my throat. My skin seared, causing black dots to dance in front of my eyes. Pain spread across my skin, until it traveled my whole leg. He pressed hard, digging the sharp pole into my body. The stench of my flesh burning made me gag.

"Let's try this again. Who called you into being, demon?"

My chest constricted as I gasped for air. "Someone cursed me. I told you this yesterday."

"Again with the lies. Why is the truth so hard for you to speak? Are you protecting the Wanderer scum?" This time he pressed the fiery rod to my other leg. The dagger-like point stabbed into me, torching my flesh from the inside out.

Agony clutched hold of me; I squeezed my lids shut, refusing to give him the answers he hoped to pry from my lips. I wouldn't falsely accuse anyone, no matter how much he tortured me. Tears trickled down my cheeks and I gritted my teeth against the torment. Hatred spun through my veins like a spider creating a web. I wished I could turn into the Beast upon command and rip off his thick head. My eyes fluttered open, and I pictured his blood gushing from his throat.

"Enough." Kenrick grabbed hold of Father Reynaldo's arm. "Stay your hand, Priest. She does not deserve to be tortured in such a manner. It is not your right to judge her."

"Oh, but it is. I am the right hand of God, and you, Lord Kenrick, are on the verge of blasphemy. Guards, see our young knight out of the room so I might finish questioning our prisoner."

"I'll report you for this," Kenrick said.

"And I'll tell them that she's bound you with her spells. I advise you to stay out of this and let me do my job."

Kenrick struggled against the men. "But what if she's right? What if by killing her, we're only allowing her to respawn and start anew? Think this through." They shoved him from the chamber, the door slamming shut with a loud clang.

"Now, where were we? Oh, yes." Father Reynaldo jabbed another poker to my abdomen, the hot metal scorched through the fabric of my dirtied dress. I clenched my teeth, trying not to scream. But the pain was too much.

"Name the witch." He put his sweaty face in mine.

"No."

As he branded me once more, I focused my thoughts on Raul. I imagined his smiling face, the way his gaze melted me. I remembered the contours of his muscles when he chopped firewood and how his skin glittered like a bronze statue. I focused on the memories from the night he'd made love to me and promised that we'd wed. If I was to die, then I wanted him to be my last thought. I closed my eyes as my head flopped to the side. How I wished we would've really run off together.

"Oh, Reynaldo, you don't want to kill her too soon, where's the fun in that?" a familiar, feminine voice said. "I want to see her turn into the monster and watch her true love murder her again. Such tragedy. If only she'd learned her place back then, we wouldn't have to go through this."

My lids opened and through blurred vision, I swore I saw Lucia standing by the door, her dark hair swept atop her head.

Was this another vision?

A hand connected with my face, the sting pulsing hot. I peered at Father Reynaldo, who leaned over me. But there was no sign of Lucia. Had I been hallucinating?

"Don't think I'll let you slip into death so easily." He set the poker down in a pail of water and it hissed, sending steam billowing up. "I've sent for the magister. He will be here in a couple of days to determine your punishment."

I swallowed hard. The magister's gruesome reputation preceded him. He was the law of the country and dealt out punishment to the accused. I'd heard plenty tales of how he extracted confessions from his victims.

A guard undid my clasps, and my gaze drifted to the doorway where a woman in a velvet cloak stood watching my ordeal. Though the hood kept her identity a secret, it didn't hide the wicked smile on her lips. I knew that face. And she was no ghost. After all these centuries, Lucia was still alive, which meant she was somehow bound by this curse, and I was going to find out how.

For two nights straight, I refused food, allowing myself only small sips of water. I didn't want to die by Father Reynaldo's hand or the magister's. If I had to choose, I would rather waste away. My body hurt all over, my skin still tender. There was no relief from the pain. Inky blackness swathed the cell, the air chilly. I crawled to the corner furthest from me and hefted up my skirts to relieve myself. Hot urine splashed against the stones and against my legs. It sickened me, but I had no other means. When I finished, I limped across the uneven rock floor.

My cell door clanked open and a guard slid a tray inside. All it contained was a stale piece of bread and a small mug of water. I sat down, wrapped my arms about myself, and glared at the meager meal.

"You should eat and drink," a female voice called from the chamber next to mine. "You'll need your strength if you are to defeat him."

With weak arms, I pushed myself to my feet once more and edged to the thin window that separated us. I saw a dark haired girl hunched in the moonlight. Her torn gown clung to her in rags. Dirt and blood streaked her thin face. She looked no older than me.

"Who are you?"

"Maria Farmer."

I gripped the metal bars and leaned closer. "Where did you come from? You weren't in here before."

She took a ragged breath and trembled. "They've had me locked away in the hole for weeks. No light. No people."

How could he get away with this? Did no one question his authority? "Why are you in here?"

A cold laugh echoed off the stones. "Blasphemy—I spoke out against Father Reynaldo for stealing from the poor and for his gluttonous ways. For his sins against women."

"Then our fates are the same."

A soft sigh came from her lips. "Yes, but if we give up then he wins. He might've conquered my body, but he shan't have my mind or my heart." She kneaded her hands together, then repeated over and over, "He can't have my heart. He can't have my heart."

Oh God. What had she endured at his hand? The thought of the sweaty priest touching her made me sick. I closed my eyes, fighting back images of him staring upon my own bared flesh.

"I'm sorry. If there's anything I can do … " Not that I was in a position to help her, seeing as how we were cellmates. Damn. If only I could turn into the Beast. I was certain that the cell was spelled. But what kind of magic could keep me from changing when Gram, Raul, and Rhyne had searched for years for such a tool? If I could get Kenrick alone, perhaps I could persuade him to help me. I knew that he didn't want to see me tortured. Deep down, I wondered if he might still love me? If I could use that to my advantage?

"Thank you." Maria stood and came to the window; her fingers squeezed mine through the small slits. "My family no longer comes to me. I do not know if it is because they believe the charges brought against me or if he threatens them." She swayed back and forth her sights focused on the door to my cell. "He can't have my heart. He can't."

I patted her frail hand. Father Reynaldo was breaking her. "We'll lend each other strength."

"I can use all the strength I can get. It has been so long since I've had anyone to speak with. Besides him." She spat. Her knuckles turned white as she gripped tighter to the bars. She released the iron rods and scraped at her face with her hands as if to wipe away the nightmare of his touch. "I want him to stop. To leave me be."

"Shhh ... he's not here. It's just you and me." I lowered my voice to a soft whisper, hoping to calm her.

Maria shrieked, picked up her cup of water and dumped it on herself. She then took the hem of her dirtied dress and used it to wash her arms and hands. She sat down and cradled her head in her hands, rocking herself.

I plopped on the floor to give her privacy. There was so much I wanted to ask, but didn't dare breech the subject, not with her in this state. So I waited until her cries faded away then stood once more, peering into her cell.

"Tell me, what more do you know of Father Reynaldo?"

She snarled at the mention of his name. "I saw him steal from the coffers. I knew I must report him, so I talked to one of the visiting priests who'd stopped in Fire Ridge on his way to Brightway. He seemed to believe me and promised to send word to the head of the church. However, when I went to visit him the following day, he was missing. Within the night, Reynaldo sent soldiers to retrieve me from my farm, claiming I'd blasphemed against the church. Once he got me back here, he tortured me, claiming to do it in the name of God." Her lip quivered. "He just kept hurting me, and the pain, it never goes away."

More than anything, I wanted to transform into the Beast and kill this man for his crimes. He deserved to die. And yet, I had no means to do so while in this prison.

"He's nothing but a monster," I said. "In the end, we must believe he'll get his just punishment."

She sniffled, wiping a hand across her face. "And what of you? How did you end up in this hellish place?"

I lowered my head and stared at my feet. There was no point in lying, seeing as how the truth had already come out. "Because I am cursed. I am the Beast."

"Did he tell you that?"

"No. It's a fact." I swallowed hard then went on to tell her of my affliction and how it came to be. She listened intently as I described the horrific things I'd done.

"It isn't your fault. How dare they keep you locked away when they should be trying to find a means to end this." Renewed courage sounded in her words, and in that instant I was glad I shared my story with her.

I gave her a weak smile. "Perhaps, but I have paid the price for centuries. This time doesn't appear as if it will turn out any different."

"What is the name of the person who cursed you?"

My nails dug into the cold, hard wall. "I don't know." But I would find out.

Chapter Twenty-Five

Several days later, a ruckus came from outside the cell. A crowd cheered as the sound of horse harnesses jangled. I stood, walked to the barred window and gasped.

There, parked in front of the church, was an ebony carriage. The magister's carriage. First one long spindly leg appeared, then another, reminding me of a black widow spider. His pale skin stood out against his dark clothing, black hair tied back with a red ribbon. Pock marks scarred his face, making him look more severe.

He strode to the front steps of the church, where he turned to address the villagers.

"Dear people of Fire Ridge, I've come to deal with your prisoners according to the law. They will no longer threaten you or your families."

His raspy voice sounded like a knife being sharpened on stone, and every word stabbed straight into my heart. Cheers rang through the square, and my stomach knotted. This would be a blood bath.

The people wanted to see our deaths, this was nothing but a show for them.

I edged away from the window and slumped down, my knees drawn to my chest. How long did I have before they killed me?

A part of me wished they'd get on with it because my mind conjured too many horrific things and I'd rather know what I faced. But at the same time, it terrified me to consider the painful methods they'd use to try and extract information. And once again, I was faced with my future—of my coming back and having to start all over again. The killings. The curse. Dying.

After a few hours, the scrape of the heavy wooden door sounded from down the hall. The wait was over. My fists clenched at my side as I climbed to my feet, ready to fight. My mouth went dry, my legs trembling beneath me.

"Come, Maria Farmer. Time to finally get to the truth." Father Reynaldo jerked her cell door opened.

I froze in place. The pleasure in his tone sickened me and I wrapped my arms around my chest.

"I am innocent," Maria answered.

As they dragged her away, struggling and fighting, I leapt to my feet and hammered on the wooden barrier.

"Let her go! She's done nothing wrong."

My breathing came faster as anger welled inside. Why couldn't I change into the Beast when I needed to? The idea of ripping out the priest's throat swirled around me as the torture chamber door slammed shut. Not too long later, Maria's screams echoed through the prison.

I covered my ears, trying to drown out the terror and pain she endured. I bit back tears, and rocked back and forth. Hadn't she been through enough?

"Please, make them stop," I whispered.

They called us monsters, yet, their methods against innocent people made them worse than us. Even when I closed my eyes all I saw was Father Reynaldo's smug look. The enjoyment he got from torturing people, how could no one call it into question?

More shrieks reverberated off the walls and no matter how tight I clutched my hands over my ears, I still heard everything.

"Only a few more days and it's your turn." Father Reynaldo peered into my cell, his pig face trickling with sweat.

"Go to hell," I spat.

His mouth twisted. He fumbled to get his key ring, when the magister called for him.

"We'll finish this later." He backed away.

I dug my nails into my palms. He better hope we never found ourselves alone together, because if we did, I'd do whatever it took to see him suffer.

Unable to sit still, I paced the small room. With every moment that ticked by, I worried for my new friend. When a commotion sounded in the hall, I glanced up to see guards coming into my cell with Maria. They dropped her at my feet as if to make a point.

I stared at the bloody mess that used to be her back. Her skin was torn, as if she'd received thousands of lashes from a whip. Once the soldiers disappeared, I rushed to her side. She whimpered, her face pressed to the cold stone floor.

"Oh God, what have they done to you?" I regarded the horrific state she was in, and nearly vomited when I noticed they'd hacked off her pointer finger. "Those sick bastards."

I ripped a strip of fabric from my dress, grabbed the small metal cup of water, and washed her hand as best I could, before bandaging it. There wasn't anything I could do for her back, not without salve and clean bandages.

Maria raised her head and her gaze met mine. "Thank you," she whispered. Within seconds, she fell into unconsciousness.

Please God. Help her.

I brushed the hair out of her face and touched her cheek. She was so young and would have had her whole life ahead of her.

"Somehow, we have to make this right. You can't die, not like this."

Maria didn't stir, but her chest rose and fell with each staggered breath. A reminder that she still fought to live.

Daylight faded, plunging the prison into shadow, and I shivered against the chill in the air, wishing for a blanket. My teeth chattered, but all I could do was hug myself, and try to conserve body heat.

"I brought you a present." Father Reynaldo unlocked the cell once more, a sneer pulling at his lips. He waved some men forward. They dragged Raul and his grandmother into the cell and tossed them to the floor. "I thought you might want to spend your husband's last nights with him. Come day after tomorrow all three of them will be tried for their crimes." He gestured to Maria, Raul, and his grandmother.

I rushed to Raul's side. "Their crimes? Maria has done nothing but suffered at your hand. And Raul, he just got to town, he couldn't have possibly done anything. You have no proof." But even as I said the words, I knew that several soldiers had witnessed Raul use his power when they tried to capture me.

"He practices witchcraft, and will be tried as an accomplice to the devil. And his grandmother, she delves into the same things as him. We will try them all."

"You're sick, and in the end you'll pay for this."

He smirked. "Is that a threat?"

"No. It's a promise."

"You heard that, didn't you?" Father Reynaldo glanced around at his small retinue. "The demon threatened my life. Me. A man of God."

I lunged at him, but he and his guards quickly stepped into the hallway and slammed the door shut. I trembled with hatred. I wanted him dead.

At last, I turned my attention to Raul and stared at his bruised, swollen body. My throat constricted. Blood caked his tunic, the sleeve ripped to reveal a large gash across his arm.

"Raul?" I knelt beside him. My fingers touched his head. He was burning up.

His eyes opened a crack. "I have failed you."

"No. That's not true. You and your grandmother didn't desert me." And I loved him. When everyone else turned their backs on me, he'd stayed, or rather they'd stayed, even after I'd been responsible for Rhyne's death. They knew I was the Beast, but still fought to keep me safe. My hands cradled his face. "Don't you dare give up, do you hear me? We're going to get through this." The cycle had to end now. It had to. I could not lose him. I would honor Rhyne's memory by trying to save his family.

He gave a weak grin. "Little Brielle."

His head lolled to the side and my heart clenched as I felt for his pulse. A sigh of relief escaped my lips. He'd passed out, same as Maria. Perhaps it was better this way. If they slept, then they didn't suffer the pain.

I sat beside him and stroked his hair. Thoughts of what was to come consumed me. This was all my fault. If I hadn't been the Beast, they wouldn't have come here. Rhyne wouldn't have died. *God forgive me.*

"We don't blame you, you know," Raul's grandmother whispered. "For Rhyne's death."

"You should."

"But the curse was not your doing. You've bared it for far too long on your own. You and your gram. Come, sit next to Nadenka." She patted the spot beside her.

I released Raul and moved to her side. She wrapped her arm about my shoulders. "You know, Rhyne considered you his closest companion in Dark Pines. He spoke very highly of you—how you never batted an eye about his being part Wanderer. You helped him without even knowing it." She patted my cheek.

"But he's dead because of me—how can you be so kind?"

"No—he's dead because of the curse. There's a difference, Brielle

Healer. You are not your curse. You are a good person, hampered by something awful. Something you're trying to rid yourself of." She put her hand on my shoulder. "If you give up now, you'll doom yourself to repeat the cycle again. Stay strong. Not just for you, but for my Raul. He loves you."

But sometimes staying strong was easier said than done.

Morning dawned, rain spattering against the stones outside. A rumble of thunder shook the foundation, followed by a bolt of lightning, which lit up the dungeon. Rats twittered their disdain as they scurried under the door.

Maria stirred.

"How are you?" I crawled to her side, my fingers brushing her arm.

She shifted her position, attempting to sit up, but cringed. "I hurt all over."

"Your wounds look better today, but likely won't heal for a long time."

Something clanged against the bars of the window, and I glanced up to see Gram hunched down beside it.

I rushed to the window. "Gram, what are you doing here? I thought I'd never see you again."

She hugged me through the bars, stroking my hair and back. "My child, I've been so worried. I should never have sent you here."

"You didn't know. We all thought I'd be safe."

"All is not lost. Just keep fighting. We'll find a way out of this. I'm to meet Father Machai day after next, he's trying to garner proof of Reynaldo's crimes."

She scanned the cell. The stench of urine, rotten food, and blood hung heavy in the air. Her gaze traveled to where Raul and Nadenka still slept. "He looks as if he's with fever. Let's hope it's his power healing him and not sickness setting in. Judging from his wounds, he'll likely be unconscious for several hours. Nadenka doesn't look like she's fared much better."

"Gram, is there anything you can do for them?"

"No. They need to rest in order to regain their strength. In the coming days, they'll need every ounce of magic they can call on."

"What do you mean?"

"Their punishments have been announced this morning." Her face paled.

My lip trembled. "What kind of punishments?"

She shook her head. "I'd rather not say. You have enough nightmares to contend with."

"No. Please tell me it isn't so! Their only crime has been protecting me. I can't let them destroy them. To destroy Raul, I-I lo … "

"I know." Through the bars, Gram drew me into her arms once more. "Lord knows, I see the way you two are around one another. Even when I tell you to stay away from him, you always manage to find your way to him." She sniffled. "He promised he would protect you or die trying. Believe me when I say I'm sorry it's come to this. We must pray that help comes in time."

She pulled away, her gaze landing on Maria and her mouth tightened when she stared at the lash-marks on her back. Gram reached into the pocket sewed in her skirt and pulled out a small vial. She handed it to me, but motioned at Maria, who'd managed to move herself closer to us. I bent down and placed it in her hand.

"This means death. One sip and you'll fall asleep. Forever," Gram said.

Maria gave her a startled glance, but tucked it away. "Thank you."

I met Gram's eye. Poison. Dear God. She knew what tortures were to come. It'd be something long and drawn out, a production for the villagers to enjoy if Maria didn't take an easier way out.

"Gram, there's something else I need to tell you."

Her gaze met mine. "What is it?"

"Lucia. I've seen her again. And I heard her in the torture chamber with me when she thought I was unconscious ... I think she's alive. I'm not sure what she has to do with all this."

"We shouldn't jump to conclusions until we know for sure whether she's alive or dead. She's blood. I know that she was devastated when Kenrick declared his love for you. But your Aunt Narcissa sent her to their country home for several months, hoping that the time away would do her some good. It was not too long after that, that we found their bodies in the house and the Beast was born."

"Wait, what did you just say?"

"That the Beast was born the day the bodies were discovered at Crawford. It's where it began. It's why we left there."

And I knew that's why I had to go back. Raul's grandmother had told me that I had to go to the place it began. If I ever managed to escape, I would head there.

A cell door down the hall slammed shut. Gram's brow furrowed. "I best be going, child. I'll try to figure more out about your curse."

"I love you."

She bent and kissed my forehead. "Goodbye dear one. Remember, be strong."

Then she drew back and I watched her disappear, wondering if I'd ever see her again. In this lifetime.

Once more, I slumped against the wall. Coldness from the roughhewn blocks seeped into my bones and tears flowed freely like rainwater. Thunder cracked and I jumped.

Shadows lengthened on the floor as night drifted in.

"Kill the demons!" Shouts came from outdoors.

"Make 'em pay!"

I climbed to my feet and trudged to the window. Already, people gathered in front of the church, their torches blazing like fiery swords, even in the downpour.

The rain failed to muffle the carpenters' hammers as beam by beam, the scaffolding rose in the courtyard before the church. I swallowed hard. Tomorrow it'd be the stage for everything. The crowd pushed in closer to have a better look. Their faces twisted in glee, as if they were readying for a festival. I saw the bloodlust on their faces, heard the gruesome words of their hatred for us.

"Come away from there," Maria said. "No sense letting them get inside your head."

"I don't understand how they can act like this."

"Because Reynaldo has fed their fears. They're victims of his stories and his preachings." Maria gestured for me to sit beside her.

Gathering my skirts, I made my way over to her. "This isn't fair."

She gave me a sad smile. "I know. Will you pray with me?"

"Of course."

Clutching my hands in hers, she bowed her head. "Dear Father, I ask that you give me strength to face whatever might come my way. That you'd allow me a place beside you in heaven. But most of all I ask that you protect my friends and my family. Spare them pain. I ask this in your name. Amen."

"Amen."

When she let go of my fingers, a tear fell from her chin and splash to the stone floor.

"I'm scared," she whispered.

The lump in my throat thickened, but I tried to keep the fear from my face. "You are brave."

She managed to give me a wobbly smile. "I'm trying to be, but inside, terror grips tight."

The bolt on the door twisted and we both jumped. A guard set our food trays on the floor. I contemplated that this could be our last supper together. At least we'd been given more than bread and water. There was chicken, soup, and a pastry. I attempted to wake Raul and Nadenka to eat, but they didn't stir.

So, Maria and I cleaned our trays and set them at the door for when the guard came back in. Stomach full, she laid down, and fell fast asleep.

Why did evil get to determine our fates? No matter how much good we did in life, we still had to answer for the sins of others. For their mistakes and their choices. I killed, but not because I wanted to. Maria, she was about to be put to death for speaking out against evil. Where was the justice in that?

Once more the bolt on the door turned, but this time it was Kenrick who stepped in. His gaze met mine. "I wanted to check to make sure you were doing all right."

I shrugged. "Given the circumstances? I'm alive. That's about all I can say."

"I do not agree with Reynaldo's methods. They're not just. I didn't mean for you to be turned over to this. I thought you'd receive a fair trial."

"Kenrick, when I spoke of the curse, I spoke the truth. I need more time to figure it out." My fingers trembled as I resisted the temptation to take his hand in mine. I knew I should be mad at him for handing me over to the church. But I wasn't. Kenrick was bound by his duty as a Knight of the Crowhurst Order. He'd been trying to protect people. And if it came down to it, I'd submit to death by his hand. But not until we knew if we could break the curse.

If we could find a way to end this once and for all, that was worth the risk.

"I feel that Reynaldo knows more about your affliction, Brielle. I fear that he is lost in darkness. I've sent word to Father Machai in Dark Pines, but I'm not sure if my message will reach him in time. For that, I am sorry. I will do what I can to keep you alive. Believe me when I tell you, I'm truly sorry."

Footsteps sounded down the hall.

"I must return to my post. I just needed to see for myself that you still lived."

With that, he closed the door. I closed my eyes. If he truly hated me, would he have come to see me? My heart ached for him. I still cared for him, even after all of this.

From across the room, Raul shifted. His eyes opened and he looked right at me.

"How are you?" I scooted closer to him.

"Better than I was when they brought me in." He grunted as he propped himself up on his elbow.

"They brought us dinner. It's likely cold now, but you should eat."

"I'm not hungry."

"You need your strength."

He gave a soft chuckle. "I don't think it'll matter after tomorrow."

"Don't talk like that—"

"Brielle, there's no need to sweeten our fates with encouraging words."

I sniffled, trying not to think about the punishments that'd be dealt. He didn't understand how much his and Nadenka's help and devotion meant to me. How much his death would scar me. Raul wouldn't be here if it wasn't for me and I'd never forgive myself for that. Not only had I failed them, but I'd failed Rhyne too.

"Kama Sutra," he said.

"What?"

"That's the name of the book. The one you saw in my carriage that day. The one Rhyne yelled at me for showing you."

I shook my head at him as I laughed, moisture streaking down my cool skin.

"You'll be surprised to know Reynaldo confiscated it."

"How can you joke?"

He offered me a smile. "They cannot truly defeat us, if we don't allow them to break our spirit."

He touched my cheek, tracing the line to my jaw, then he opened his arms to me. I went to him, pressing myself against the length of his body, the warmth already like a blanket against the chill.

"Where were you and Nadenka the last few days?"

His arm clutched me closer. "They kept us bound and unconscious in a dark room. Whenever I started to awaken, Reynaldo would have me beaten until I collapsed. He's managed to keep me weak enough so I couldn't use my powers. But you'll be glad to know that your knight, Kenrick, had no part in my tortures. In fact, he attempted to stop them before being escorted out."

"Then maybe there is still hope for us," I said.

"Maybe."

I touched his arm then whispered into the side of his neck, "Are you scared?"

"Terrified." His voice softened. "But I have you here to comfort me."

I shifted so that I stared at him. My fingers trembled as I stroked his face. "Back in the woods, when you tried to rescue me, did you mean what you said, I mean do you really—"

"Love you?" He finished for me. "Yes, I've always loved you, Brielle. Why do you think I come back to Dark Pines so frequently? It wasn't just for Rhyne. When I said I loved you before, I meant it. Every word I've uttered to you has been from my heart. The day we shared our first kiss, I wanted so much to tell you then."

"You've known from the start what I was, and yet you still loved me?"

He smiled, drawing me closer so his breath fanned across my skin. "The curse wasn't your fault. I saw the girl beneath it all. The perfect, beautiful, kind woman who'd do anything for anyone. You cared for me when no others would."

I wet my lips, realization thundering in my mind. "You've never forsaken me. When all others turned their backs on me, you remained. In spite of my curse, you've risked everything. How could I not return your love?"

His eyebrows raised. "Bri?"

Without a doubt, I knew it was true. Over the centuries, the one man I thought I loved always betrayed me. Killed me for something I had no control over. A curse that in reality, he'd caused. Yet, Raul understood me. He fought not just for me, but to free me. "I love you, Raul. Please forgive me for taking so long to tell you."

He cupped my chin. "There's nothing to forgive."

Raul bent down until his lips captured mine. Fire blazed through my veins, his mouth branding me as his. My fingers weaved into his hair, drawing him closer.

"If only we had more time." He cradled me in his arms. "But death shall soon part us."

I cried against his chest.

He rubbed my back, as if to calm me. "Shh … it is inevitable. But we've got tonight. And just knowing you love me is enough for me to believe my life wasn't a complete failure. Let's not think about tomorrow or what it will bring. We need to focus on the now. For it's all we have."

He rolled on his side then unhooked the crystal necklace that hung at his throat. With one hand, he pulled my hair out of the way then reached behind me to fasten the jewelry to my neck.

I fingered it. "Why have you given me this?"

"Because it is all I have to give."

My lips brushed his cheek. "You're wrong. You've already given me this." My hand rested on his chest, over his heart. "That is all I need."

"And you are all I need." He entwined me in his embrace once more, pulling me to his chest. "No matter what happens tomorrow, remember that."

My body molded against his as we curled together. Here I'd found the man I wanted to give my heart to and in mere hours we'd be parted.

Please, God, if you're listening. Spare him. And Nadenka and Maria.

Chapter Twenty-Six

The low drone of bells tolling woke me from my slumber. I lay there, tucked in Raul's arms, lines of sunlight filtered through the bars like golden lances piercing the gloom.

I shifted position so I could sit up. Maria was already awake, staring out the tiny window. As if sensing my gaze, she turned to me.

"This will be my last day." Her brows furrowed, but she remained still, breathing evenly, her hands clasped in her lap as if she'd accepted this fate.

"You don't know that." I stood. My eyes welled and I reached out to touch her shoulder.

"Oh, dear friend—don't cry for me. I will hold true. I will not admit to a crime that is not mine. My soul will be clean."

"But you're only sixteen."

Raul's hand brushed my ankle and I shifted my focus to him. My heart clenched in my chest. I was going to lose all of them.

"We are all called upon for different purposes. In the end, my

God will welcome me, where others have turned me away." Maria limped to my side, her arm wrapped around my shoulders.

Her courage didn't waver. She knew she'd meet her end, and still she held strong. I only hoped when it was my turn, I'd be able to do the same. The echo of footsteps sounding in the hall made my stomach churn. It couldn't be time already.

Maria reached for my hand. She slipped the vial of poison into my palm, then wrapped my fingers around it.

"Maria?"

"If I'm to see my God, I cannot go that way. Not by my own hand."

Raul stood. "Our time grows short."

He helped his grandmother to her feet as well. He then clutched me tight, pressing me against him. His lips crushed mine as we heard the door open behind us. He pulled back, hands cupping my face. "I love you, Brielle Healer. Never doubt that. May we meet again in the next life."

Nadenka peered at me. "Do not fear the darkness—you are the light. It must yield to you."

Guards poured inside. A sob raked through me as they reached out for Raul, and I clung to his waist, not wanting to let them take him. "I love you. I always will." I didn't want to be reborn again, not if he wouldn't be with me. *He* was my true love.

They tore us apart.

"Please. Don't do this." I tried desperately to reach out for them, but they ushered the three of them from the cell. "No!" I pounded on the door. "Please!"

"Bri, stay strong," Raul's voice sounded down the hall.

Why didn't he use his power? He could stop them. I collapsed to the floor; my body quaking as I buried my head in my arms and cried.

"Ah, no need to cry." Father Reynaldo tugged the door open, his rolls of fat jiggling beneath his crimson robe. "I've decided to let you watch your friends die. Maybe then you'll confess your sins."

"You're horrible, everything about you speaks of perversion," I screamed and rushed at him with my fists drawn. He swatted me aside like a fly.

He laughed. "I like to think of myself as a warrior of God. Cleansing the earth of filth." His thick hand gripped hold of me, pulling me to my feet. "Guards, escort our prisoner to the front of the scaffold."

Bright light blinded me as I stepped outside. My vision took long moments to adjust, having been in the dungeon for so long. Crowds parted as we came through.

A child pointed at me. "It's the demon."

Something hit me in the forehead, and I realized he'd thrown a rock.

"Killer!"

"Monster." A woman shook her fist at me.

All around me people shouted obscene things. But I wasn't the main attraction, not today. As I came to stand at the front of the wooden stage, I watched guards lead Maria, Nadenka, and Raul out. Their clothes had been changed. They were now adorned in white garments. Maria wore a plain ivory gown that brushed the ground as she walked, as did Nadenka. Raul had on a billowy white tunic and pair of white breeches. They looked so pure, almost angelic.

The magister and Father Reynaldo stepped onto the scaffold. Behind them, I caught sight of a large, iron torture device. Oh God. The maiden. Vomit burned the back of my throat as my gut wrenched. I'd heard of this device. It was horrific. The doors on it were already open and I saw the pointed iron spikes protruding from it. Spikes that'd go through both the front and back of a person, through flesh and bone. They'd pierce a victim's head, chest, and their arms and legs.

A slow death, meant to bleed a person out.

Next to the scaffold, I saw two stakes surrounded by wood and hay. I clenched my eyes shut against the sight, but soon opened them again when the magister cleared his throat

The magister read from a parchment, excitement evident in his voice. "We have gathered here today in order to carry out the punishments for crimes committed against not only the church, but against the village of Fire Ridge. I bring before you the first accused. Maria Farmer. She has blasphemed against our church and has been caught enjoying pleasures of the flesh while practicing witchcraft."

"We ask at this time for any witnesses to these crimes." Father Reynaldo stepped to the front of the crowd, his hands clasped in front of him as if he was about to pray.

The first was a girl not much older than me. "I saw Maria Farmer curse Madelyn Barmaid's infant child. Two days later it died."

"Thank you, Beatrice Milkmaid."

Several more people stepped forward blaming the ruin of their crops on her, as well as illnesses and any deaths in the village. Did the people have no conscience? They were sealing her fate.

"If that is all the accusations, then I'd like to now sentence Maria Farmer to death. Let us hope her soul will be set free." The magister looked about the square for any more witnesses.

I glanced behind me at the gathered crowd. This was a fixed trial.

"Kill her, kill her, kill her … " The chants rang out.

My focus returned to the scaffold, where Father Reynaldo grabbed hold of Maria and led her to the Maiden. I couldn't breathe. The magister opened the doors wider. Panic flared on Maria's face, but the fear disappeared as she stared at the sky, toward the heavens. Horror cloaked me as they shoved her inside the crude contraption. The doors swung shut with a wicked groan. Maria's screams filled the square, drowning out even the sound of the chanting and shouting of the crowd.

Blood trickled from the bottom of the Maiden, staining the scaffold crimson. I turned away, crying

I jerked free from the guards and hauled myself up onto the

platform. My foot kicked out as a soldier attempted to grab my waist.

"You're a murderer!" I screamed at Father Reynaldo. "You tortured her because she spoke out against your evils."

"Foul beast, don't speak to me." His face reddened, his beady eyes almost lost beneath the wrinkles of flab on his brow.

I lashed out at him, my fingernails digging into his chunky face.

"Secure the prisoner," he ordered.

"She was a child!" More guards poured toward me, but I kicked out my legs once more, struggling against them. Their hands gripped hold of my arms, pinning me down.

"Bring the next prisoners forth." Father Reynaldo gestured to Raul and Nadenka.

"No!" I cried before they shoved a dirty cloth into my mouth, muffling me, as I continued to thrash and scream.

Raul stood there, the sun beaming down on his bronzed face. He looked at me and I went still. It wasn't supposed to end like this. He was supposed to be invincible. Rhyne's cousin who always came to our village to perform fire eating acts. Who had let me and Rhyne roam around his carriage and pick out trinkets we liked from his travels. My soul mate.

"Remember, Brielle, Amor vincit mortem," he said in Latin. *Love conquers death.*

Why did I need to remember them? Did it mean if I loved someone enough, they could conquer death?

Tears streamed down my face. With the rag in my mouth, I couldn't even tell him I loved him. The last words he'd hear would be uttered from Father Reynaldo's thick, evil mouth.

Father Reynaldo smiled at me then stared into the mob. "These Wanderers are witches. It has been witnessed by me, in this very church. This one," he pointed to Raul. "He tried to set our crucifix on fire and burn down the house of the Lord. And we have caught him trying to conjure demons in the woods. For this crime, Raul Tinker shall be burned at the stake. His grandmother, who trained him, taught him these dark arts. In the woods she tried to unleash the Beast upon our soldiers. For these crimes, she shall burn."

Fight. Please just fight.

They dragged Raul and Nadenka down the stairs to the wooden poles constructed on the other side of the scaffold. They secured them to them, and I watched with terror as three soldiers came forward carrying torches. They lit the straw. The dry material leapt up quickly, igniting the logs.

Raul squirmed against the ropes, then leaned back. He screamed as smoke filled the air between us, blurring him. I wanted so badly to plug my ears against his cries, but I couldn't move. My legs buckled beneath me and I fell to the ground.

Pain constricted my chest. I couldn't breathe.

I love him. He can't die. Not like this. Within seconds, there was a great burst of fire; flames shot high, black smoke billowing into the whole square. And still his cries filled my head.

Kenrick burst into the courtyard, frantic as his gaze swept the crowd. Once he spotted me he rushed toward me, and when he got to my side, he dropped to his knees, ignoring the other guards. "Brielle, oh God, forgive me. My room was locked, I couldn't get out here in time. They didn't deserve this. You don't deserve this. I can't believe God wants to see anyone, even sinners, tortured in this manner," he whispered. Sorrow etched his face and I saw the regret in his eyes.

Even though it was too little too late, I clutched his hand and squeezed. If I wasn't gagged, I would've told him I'd forgiven him, for he was just as much a part of this curse as me. He could no more ignore the pull than I could.

Father Reynaldo's men forced me to my feet, hauling me past Kenrick, and back to the prison. Once inside, they undid the gag and threw me to the floor. Grief overwhelmed as I lay there. Deep sobs shook my body.

Raul was gone. I'd never see his smile again. I'd never listen to his laugh or have him bring me another gift. There'd be no more blushes for him. My chest heaved as pain overcame me. His necklace brushed against my neck and I clutched the crystal in my hand. It was all I had left of him.

Oh God, he's gone. He's not coming back.

How could he have left me? He promised to be here. He *promised.*

I couldn't breathe without him.

Somehow, I'd make Father Reynaldo pay for this.

I crawled to the place where Raul had held me the night before, where he'd kissed me and comforted me. I wrapped my arms around myself and cried until no more tears would fall.

For two days, Father Reynaldo left me be. I had no idea why he delayed the inevitable, but I forced myself to eat, even though all I wanted to do was die. What did the curse matter now, if everything would be taken from me anyway? There was no more Raul. No more Rhyne. No more Dark Pines.

But you don't want to have to go through another cycle. To have more innocent blood on your hands. You have to fight this. Don't give in. He'll win if you do.

On the third day, he sent for me.

His robes swished as he led me up the uneven steps of the church. "Today, we'll give you your trial. Let the magister hear what crimes are being brought against you."

My lips pursed together as he leaned his head closer, his breath smelled of garlic and wine.

"And because I'm a godly man, I'll postpone your punishment for another day in order to give you a chance to repent."

"Go to hell." I spat on his face.

He drew his hand back and slapped me. My cheek stung, as my vision blurred. I ground my teeth together, wanting nothing more than to hurt him. My hatred for him far surpassed my fear.

The crowd crossed themselves when Father Reynaldo brought me to the scaffold, as if to ward me off. Father Reynaldo gripped tighter to my arm as he pushed me to the front of the raised stage. "Good people of Fire Ridge and visitors from Dark Pines. I bring forth our beast. She has killed our companions and relatives for years."

My breath caught in my throat as I recognized villagers who'd traveled from Dark Pines. Sarah Weaver stood with a triumphant smile upon her lips. Next to her were Lady Weaver, Bowman Butcher, Henry Blacksmith, along with Gertie, her father, and several others. Oh God. I searched the mob for Gram, but I didn't see her. I wondered if she and Father Machai would make it back in time.

"See now, the mark of the Devil upon her flesh." Father Reynaldo ripped down the shoulder of my gown, revealing my scar. The one caused by Kenrick's blade over the centuries.

I reached up to cover it, but he jerked my hands away. He paraded me around the scaffold as if I was on display.

"Now, I'd ask for witness accounts of her actions. Or if there is one who'd speak in her defense, let us hear from you." The magister stood beside Father Reynaldo as if to create a united front, but all I sensed was their darkness.

They were the real monsters.

Sarah Weaver pushed through the crowd. Her eyes gleamed, perfect curls bouncing around her face like coiled serpents ready to strike. She glanced at me and I knew then, I was in trouble.

"I would like to bring charges against Brielle Healer."

"And who are you?"

"My name is Sarah Weaver, I am the daughter of the Mayor of Dark Pines." Her voice quivered as she managed to produce fake tears.

"Very well. Please, tell us your story."

"She attacked me in the woods, wounding my arm. Then, not too long after that incident she destroyed our shop because she couldn't handle the fact that Lord Kenrick asked me to the festival." She wiped her face with a handkerchief.

My hands fisted. I pictured tearing her to pieces, starting with her face and then her throat. If only I could change.

"The night of the Festival of the Stars, I came across her in the woods, naked and chanting to the devil."

"No! That's not true!"

"Everything Sarah says is true." Bowman Butcher joined her. He wouldn't meet my gaze.

No. This wasn't fair. He always liked me.

"My name is Bowman Butcher and I've known Brielle since she was a child. For a while, I believed her normal, that is until recently. She cast a spell on my son, Rhyne, and made him go with her when she left Dark Pines. His mutilated body was recently found between Dark Pines and Fire Ridge. He died because of her. Because of the Beast. Not to mention the innocent man who was hung in our village for her crimes!"

I staggered back. How could he say this?

Henry Blacksmith came forward next. "Sh-she sacrificed people in the woods and used their bones to make potions. Rhyne suspected as much and planned on killing her, but she got to him first."

"Lies! All of this is lies."

"Silence, demon!" Father Reynaldo shouted.

Would no one speak up for me? How many lives had Gram and I helped save over the years? Now, people accused me of killing infants and sacrificing animals during full moons. But wasn't I truly a murderer? Didn't I deserve to die? Rhyne, Raul, and their grandmother hadn't thought so. Yet, I knew the horrific things I'd done and no amount of repenting would change that.

The madness spread through the crowd and people who didn't even know me claimed to have witnessed strange happenings.

"But I was cursed." I struggled to break free from the soldier who grasped my shoulders.

"Take her back to the cell. I promise, her punishment will be dealt soon."

Sarah smirked at me.

"You better hope they kill me," I said to her. "Because if I get free, I'm coming for you!"

Her eyes widened. She clutched hold of her mother and cried hysterically.

The guard dragged me away, his fingers digging into my arms. I looked up to see Kenrick being held back by a couple other soldiers. Would he have fought for me if they hadn't held him back? Or maybe Gram had been right. Duty first. After all, he'd handed me over to them, and now I'd pay with my life. Again. And again. And again.

Chapter Twenty-Seven

When the prison door clanged shut, I let out a sob. I didn't understand why I hadn't been able to change into the Beast since being captured. Perhaps what Father Reynaldo said was true, maybe the dungeons were spelled? Or was it because I was in a church? Had the shock of my capture made it dormant?

I sat staring at the gray stones, empty water cups, and several days' worth of waste. Moisture dripped from the ceiling, splashing in tiny pools. Then, I reached across the way and touched the spot where Raul had last lain. I needed his strength.

I'd come back again, and maybe next time I'd remember everything. My head drooped to the floor. *But when you come back, Raul won't be here. Nor will any of the others you murdered.* My mind conjured memories of Rhyne's smile when we'd play in the creek. Thoughts of Raul bringing me gifts and teasing me. Never again would I have those things.

The fight slowly faded from me. I was tired. Tired of killing.

Tired of betrayal and of hurt. My seventeenth birthday was only a couple days away, and I wouldn't see it. I closed my eyes until I dozed off.

A while later the prison door squeaked open. My lids fluttered open and I braced myself for the worst. A cloaked figure pushed its way in, grabbed hold of me, then shoved me out into the hallway.

"Lucia? What are you doing?"

She put her finger to her lips, glanced around, then quickly shut the cell door behind her and tugged me along.

"Come along," she said to me.

"Wh-where are we going?" My heart pounded like wagon wheels hitting ruts.

"Someone has bought your freedom this night. Now hurry."

I gasped. "Wait, I don't understand. I thought you cursed me."

"Dear cousin, Kenrick and I have made a deal with the guards to get you out of here. Now you must hurry. I've only ever wanted your safety. For you to go home to Crawford."

"Then you don't want me dead?" Had she been the one truly warning me all these years? "Quickly, while Reynaldo is at dinner. I'm already going to be in enough trouble should someone find out my part in all this. But I plan to lead you out of town, at least as far as I can."

Lucia handed me a black cloak, which I tied about my shoulders then lifted the hood to cover my head. We stuck to the shadows, taking the steps two at a time. The church was swathed in darkness as we snuck through the back door. Cold air blasted us when we made our way outside and I shivered, tugging my garment closer.

"A man waits in the wood line for us. He has a horse ready for your escape."

"Thank you."

She nodded then led me toward the forest.

With a deep breath, I edged across the dirt road. Then I saw a familiar figure heading up the stoop of the church. Father Reynaldo.

My blood burned in my veins, my hands quivered. I could kill him. Sneak into his chambers while he slept and end him the same way he'd ended so many other lives. But I had no weapon, nor did I have time.

I turned away, dashing to the woods. It took me only a moment to find the horse tethered to a nearby tree. Father Machai's nephew stepped from behind the oak.

"Brielle Healer." He nodded, glancing at my cousin who was already climbing atop her steed. He leaned closer and whispered in my ear, "My uncle has sent word that he should be here within a few days, with orders from the head of the church. In the meantime, you are to go into hiding until the details can be sorted and your name cleared."

"I don't know how to thank you."

He came closer and helped me mount the horse, then he untied it from the tree. "Be safe, Brielle. I wish you God's speed. I have packed a few days' worth of supplies in the saddlebags. Stay away from the villages, and if you must venture close to the road, keep your cloak about you."

With a gentle tug to the reins, I pointed the horse east toward Crawford Estate. It was time to face my destiny. Time to go to the place it all began.

My shoulders slumped as I tried to adjust myself on the horse's back. Blood stained the front of my gown, remnants from my kill earlier. At least it was only a cow. Although, it'd surely lead hunters straight to me.

"We should stop so you can get cleaned up," Lucia said, riding up alongside me. "There's a creek, just passed the next clearing."

I nodded. "Thank you."

She'd comforted me after I'd taken it down. But we didn't have time to bury the animal, because we weren't sure how far behind the soldiers would be. It depended on whether or not they discovered me missing the night I'd left, or the morning after.

We'd been riding for a couple of days, trying to put as much distance between us and Fire Ridge as possible. Each night, we stopped long enough to let our horses rest, eat, and drink, but we didn't dare dally for too long.

My gaze shifted to Lucia, her jaw clenched as she held tight to her reins. A look of determination on her face. We still hadn't talked about how she was here—other than her stating she was trying to warn me. Maybe while we bathed, I could ask her.

We led our horses to a small bank along the creek. "We must make this quick," Lucia said. "But we'll be less suspicious if we aren't both covered in blood."

I retrieved a change of clothing from the saddlebags, then swiftly stripped out of my dirtied garments. The creek water was cold when I dipped my feet in. But there wasn't time to contemplate it. I needed to get washed.

Sucking in a deep breath, I went into the water up to my thighs, then lowered myself to my knees. Gooseflesh broke out across my skin, but I scrubbed my body vigorously. I dipped my head back, letting the currents sweep over me as I attempted to wash my hair.

When I opened my eyes, I saw Lucia sliding into the water as well. In the moonlight, I caught sight of something strange on her arms. As I drifted closer to her, I noticed the words tattooed upon her skin. She tried to keep them hidden as she rinsed off her body.

Tattoos? I thought to myself. When had she gotten those? My mind flicked back to what Raul's grandmother had said when she'd spoken to me at the fire. She'd mentioned a tattooed girl. They had to be one in the same.

Whatever was marked on her arm was written in Latin. Swallowing hard, I picked up on several words, *fortunam*, and *maledictionem*. As I started to piece them together, I gasped. The rough translation: *He must love her, even after she is revealed as the beast. If he is true the curse shall break, if not, then he shall kill her, such is her fate.*

I had to give it to Lucia, she'd been smart. She'd had the blood contract tattooed onto her so she wouldn't have to worry about us finding it. Suddenly everything made sense. The visions I'd been having of Lucia and Kenrick weren't visions at all. They were memories. They were pictures of our pasts.

Anger blazed through me as I clenched my fists. Lucia had cursed Kenrick and me for falling in love. He'd chosen me, and she'd made us pay. And we'd keep paying because I doubted that Kenrick, a Knight of the Crowhurst Order, could ever love me in spite of what I'd become.

So why had she let me go? Fear raced through me. I had to get out of here. I needed to get to Crawford before she did. I didn't want to hurt anyone, but I knew I needed time. My foot bumped against a good sized rock. I bent over and picked it up.

"Do you need help washing your hair?" I asked as I moved up alongside her.

"No, thank you." She wrapped her arms about her body as if to shield the traitorous etchings from me.

Without a second thought, I raised the stone and brought it down against her head. She fell into the creek, face first. Not wanting her to drown, I pulled her to shore, then threw on my dry clothes, climbed back onto my horse, and rode as fast as I could.

My fingers ran over the steed's neck; already sweat lathered it again.

"C'mon, boy, just a little further." I clicked my tongue at the horse.

At last, I came to a stone gate.

A large house loomed against the night sky; vines and ivy covered the walls. Thorn bushes parted as I climbed from my horse, as if they expected me and I shivered, wondering if this place was enchanted. A great, stone archway led to a heavy wooden door with wrought iron hinges and decorations.

My hand shook, but I reached out to push it open. The scent of roses overwhelmed me when I walked inside, where moonlight filtered in through the stained glass windows. Stone tiles led into the great hall, which had staircases at either side of it. A large, wrought-iron chandelier hung from the ceiling, which had painted lovers and cherubs upon it.

White sheets covering the furniture like deflated ghosts, fluttered as a glass door blew open and wind scattered leaves across the floor. I closed my eyes and images flooded my mind. Images of Kenrick stopping in the woods to aid Gram and me after the wagon wheel had broken on our way to the tournament. A tournament he'd promised to ride in for Lady Lucia. Instead, he rode for me.

A vision of Kenrick and I walking in a rose garden, then another of us dancing at a ball. I reached out and grasped hold of the marble banister at the foot of the stairs. I recalled the first time I brought him here, to Crawford.

"Come, sit on the bench with me." He smiled, holding tight to my hand.

"But I wanted to show you the maze."

He eased me down beside him, then turned to stare at me. "These past months have been the best of my life, Brielle. And I cannot imagine spending one moment without you ... "

My pulse soared, our knees pressed together. He leaned closer, his fingers tracing the contours of my face.

"Brielle, I love you ... "

I steadied myself. How could someone have put us through this? We'd been on the brink of marriage, yet we'd been robbed of our lives and of our love. I wandered through the lower level of the house, each item bringing forth a lost memory. The dining room table, the fireplace, the ballroom.

Marble pillars led me into a narrow hallway that stretched on forever. Sculptures posed on both sides of the hall depicted lovers, God, and angels. At the end of the corridor, I came to a large oak door, with roses burned into it, and pushed it open.

"Oh my … " The library had floor to ceiling shelves filled with books. Chairs upholstered in blue satin sat in each corner of the room on a floor made of white and black marble shaped in the form of stars. I twirled around in a circle, staring at the mural above of a couple rowing across a lake.

I trailed my fingers over a cherry table, which had a leather bound book sitting at the center as if waiting for its reader to return. Beside that was a bone-handled dagger. My hand closed around it and I picked it up.

Then my gaze fell upon the painting that hung above the fireplace. The breath left my lungs and I strode toward it. Gram had commissioned the picture of Kenrick and me, sitting on a bench and smiling at each other, as an engagement gift.

How could it still be here? After all this time, how could everything be as it used to be?

Wisps of fog danced about the room, swirling upward like lines of ribbon. The painting shook as a glowing light encompassed it. Its wooden frame slammed violently against the wall.

Icy fingers brushed my neck and I spun around. "Who's there?"

I scanned the room, but it was empty save for me. *Just my imagination.* Once more, I faced the picture above the fireplace and a cold pressure jabbed between my shoulder blades, urging me forward. Taking a deep breath, I glanced behind me. Again, there was no one in the room but me.

Something wanted me to take a closer look at the painting.

It wasn't the painting that caught my eye, but rather the stone face in the pillar that looked just like Aunt Narcissa. Then Raul's grandmother's words hit me again. *"Go to the place it began and offer blood."* Without a second thought, I drew the dagger blade across my palm. The cut stung, quickly beading up with blood. I let the crimson drops hit the floor.

Dizziness washed over me.

"*How can you side with her, Mother?*" Lucia screamed at Aunt Narcissa. "*You chose Brielle's happiness over mine.*"

"*You know that's not true. You've been practicing the black arts; you tried to use a love potion on Kenrick, when you know they're forbidden. You cannot force another to do your bidding; it's a part of our laws.*"

"*And what of loyalty to our family? Brielle stole him from me.*"

"*Kenrick never loved you. He only said he'd ride in the tournament for you to honor the friendship between his father and yours. You cannot blame him for falling in love.*"

"*No, but I can blame Brielle. She seduced him away from me. But I tell you now, if I can't have him, she never will.*" Lucia shoved up her sleeves, revealing the tattoos.

"*What have you done?*" Aunt Narcissa's eyes widened.

Lucia took out a dagger, and traced the blade over the last word in her arm. Fate. "*I've made a deal. Brielle's happiness for mine. Let's see if Kenrick still loves her after this …*"

Her tattoo glowed bright red, the words emblazoned on her skin.

He must love her, even after she is revealed as the beast. If he is true the curse shall break, if not, then he shall kill her, such is her fate.

"*No, I won't let you do this …*" Aunt Narcissa lunged at her, but it was too late.

A Beast stalked into the library, claws and teeth sharp as knife points. Aunt Narcissa was the first to fall, followed by one of her ladies in waiting. The image faded into a river of crimson.

My cousin had called forth the Beast and forsaken us all. Then why had she set me free? It didn't make sense.

Other than this time, Kenrick had always slain me before he knew of my identity, making the curse impossible to break. There was nothing I could do. It lay in his hands, not mine.

"And so I find you," Kenrick said from behind me.

"What are you doing here?" I backed away, eyes wide. Then I realized just what my cousin had done. She'd let me go, so Kenrick could kill me.

"Lady Lucia and I paid the guard to let us free you."

"But why?" My mouth went dry. Did he truly love me?

"Because I could not bear to see you tortured by Reynaldo. His methods are evil. No matter your crimes, you didn't deserve to be subjected to his punishments."

"And what will you do with me?" My voice faltered.

"You've killed innocents, Brielle. And I know not if this curse can be broken or by what means it was put in place, or even if it is real—but I've seen what you can do with my own eyes. No matter what my previous feelings were for you, I took an oath to defend people against evil. I-I must do my duty, no matter how much it hurts." Sorrow seemed to fill his features.

"Kenrick, we have to break this, it's the only way to keep the Beast at bay forever."

"We don't have time for that now, there are too many soldiers. They would never let us leave and you'll end up back at the church, with Reynaldo. What more can we do?"

Kenrick was right, there was nowhere else to run, I'd die as I always did. Of course, he'd be the one to kill me, or so it was written.

"What is this place you've led me to?" His gaze took in our lavish surroundings.

"My home. The place I dwelled with my aunt and grandmother before Lady Lucia cursed me. Cursed us."

He went still as he glanced at the painting. He stifled a breath, then shot me a startled look. "Where did this come from?"

"It's been here for almost three centuries."

Kenrick moved closer to examine it, sidestepping me in the process. His mouth fell agape as he reached out to touch it. Then he glanced at me.

"This is a trick. It cannot be ... I—Brielle?"

"No. I do not lie." *Please let him believe me.*

He unsheathed his sword, pointing the blade at me.

My hands moved slowly as I drew my dress down my shoulder. "You always stab me here. Through my heart," I whispered.

We stood still, staring at one another. For a moment, I swore I saw tears welling in his eyes. His weapon wavered and he lowered it once more. A crash sounded in the doorway and people burst into the room.

One of whom was Lady Lucia. Come to watch the end of yet another tragic play on my life.

Chapter Twenty-Eight

Lucia's laugh echoed off the marble as she saw Kenrick semi-poised to stab me.

"Well, well, well, if it isn't beauty and the Beast. I must say, you two put on a better show every time." Her eyes glittered with menace, while her twisted features betold of madness and hatred. "Star-crossed lovers doomed to spend eternity apart. So sad."

Dark hair hung loose at her shoulders, snapping like Medusa's snakes. Reddened lips the color of blood, sneered. She'd changed into dry clothes, but I could still see the faint tracing of where I'd hit her in the head.

"You! This is your fault." I lunged forward, but Kenrick raised his blade then gripped tight to the back of my gown, bringing me to a stop.

Lucia's guards poured into the room, surrounding me. Their crimson uniforms reflected off the metal of their drawn swords like hellish flames ready to devour me.

"On the contrary, wench, it's all yours. Your theft. Your debt."

"And you call me a monster?" I asked.

"Says the girl who has slaughtered entire villages over the last three hundred years. The same girl who ripped her so-called friend limb from limb to slake her thirst for blood."

"Because of you and your jealousy. And if we want to talk about murderers, maybe we should speak of you killing your mother."

Lucia's gaze skewered me as she circled like a predator ready to pounce. "You call it jealousy. I call it justice. You took everything from me. Kenrick. My happiness. My life. Kenrick promised to ride in the tournament for me. He promised to ask my father's permission to call on me. Then you came along and he forgot I existed. A stupid barn-whelped bitch. Nice enough on the outside, but no more than an animal on the inside. And if not for you, Kenrick would've chosen me."

Stunned, I stared at her. "How can you do this? It was his choice to make. And because of you, innocent people have been killed. You've kept us apart. When will it be enough?"

She glared. "Never. Because the debt you owe can never be repaid." She shook as she stepped closer to us. "At least you made it so much more fun this time. You figured out the curse, and then got yourself imprisoned in Fire Ridge. Tell me, did you appreciate Father Reynaldo's methods? I have to say I've enjoyed the way everything's turned out thus far. And now, there's only one more act to this play."

Kenrick glanced between us, a horrified look upon his face. "Then you're the one who inflicted this curse upon her?"

Lucia examined her fingernails then shifted her attention to him. "Of course. And Brielle will die as she always does. A beast, slain by your hand."

My pulse thundered in my ears. A low growl settled in my throat, the urge to turn into the monster she created, nearly overwhelmed me. She'd ruined our family, and I wanted her to dead.

Kenrick lowered his weapon once more, his knuckles white

against the hilt. "You damned her for loving me?"

"No! I damned you both for loving each other. For the pain you caused me. If I can't have you, then she certainly never will." She brought her fists down on the cherry table and shrieked, as if madness finally consumed her.

Something in Kenrick's face changed as he looked once more at the painting of us, then all at once he gasped as if he remembered everything.

"I won't kill her. Not this time. I love her, even if she is the Beast." He threw his sword. The metal clanged as it bounced.

"I order you to pick up your sword," she said. "It is your duty to slay her."

Kenrick stood tall. "I refuse to be a pawn in your game any longer. I love her. I will not destroy her again."

She dived across the marble floor, lunging for Kenrick's sword. In one swift movement, she clasped the weapon in both hands. "Oh, I've planned for every eventuality. I want you dead and if I've got to be the one to deliver the blow, I will!" Frozen in place, I watched as she lunged forward, every muscle taut and propelling the blade at me.

Kenrick shoved me aside. Pain radiated through me as I struck the wall. He used his body to shield me, keeping Lucia from advancing. The weapon pierced his skin. He cried out in agony as the blade sliced his chest then jutted through his back. Blood seeped through his tunic, dyeing the fabric deep crimson, and he staggered toward a nearby wall. He attempted to hold himself erect, but within seconds, he slipped to the floor, his hand leaving behind a bloodied print.

"No! What have you done?" I shrieked.

Lucia rushed to his side. "Kenrick. I didn't mean for this to happen. I've always loved you." She pushed sweaty strands of hair from his face. "Please don't die. We can still make things right between us. We can still be together. Just you and me."

"I'd never choose a monster like you." He winced as the blade inside him shifted.

Lucia froze, a look of disbelief on her face. "No. You don't mean that. She's put a spell on you, don't you see? We're supposed to be together."

Kenrick wheezed. "We. Will. Never. Be."

With a strangled shriek, Lucia leapt to her feet and screamed at me. "*You* made me do this. This is all your fault."

She launched herself forward and her hands clamped around my throat, cutting off my air. I flailed back and forth, trying to free her fingers. Possessed by rage, she shook me, slamming my head into the floor.

"You will die."

Spots danced before my eyes. It couldn't end like this. Not at her hands. At least this time Kenrick had refused to slay me. But did that mean we wouldn't come back again? Pain erupted as my head struck the floor again. I dug my nails into her arms, scratching at her flesh.

An explosion of light erupted in the room, and I watched Lucia's body as it was flung through the air. I turned to see Raul standing at the center of the library, his power coursing from his fingers like a storm of lightning bolts hailing from the sky. I took in the scattered guards, who were pinned throughout the room—weaponless and at our mercy.

"Are you all right?" Raul asked.

I gasped for air. "I-I think so. I don't understand, I saw you die."

He grinned, giving me a wink. "An illusion. My element is fire; I merely drew upon it to shield myself and Grandmother. Something, Reynaldo didn't account for."

Slowly, I sat up, then crawled to Kenrick's side. I touched his chest and my hands came away coated with red, sticky fluid. Sobs erupted from me.

Kenrick reached for me, his fingers trembled. "I-I'm sorry, I didn't trust you." He sputtered, coughing up blood. "Please forgive me ... "

"Don't give up. You've got to fight. I beg you. You can't leave, not like this."

"Forgive me," he whispered again.

"I will always forgive you."

A tear leaked from the corner of his eye. "I-I love you Brielle, always … have." He shuddered, then went limp in my arms. I kissed his forehead, crying as I drew his lids shut. Lucia screamed. I glanced up to see her body convulsing. Her skin wrinkled, while hair fell from her head in clumps. Slowly, her flesh peeled away, drifting to the floor like strips of meat on a butcher's block. The shrieks died out as the tissue of her lips fell off, then her cheeks, tongue, and jaw. Soon, only a skeleton stared back at me, then her body exploded into a cloud of dust.

Glass blew out of the windows, spraying shards in every direction. As the winds whirled around us like a cyclone, the sharpened pieces cut at my arms. The stone walls crumbled, large chunks of rock and marble crashing to the floor as the house fell to ruin. I tried to stand, but pain shot through my body. My skin felt as if it was tearing apart. I screamed. My bones cracked and broke, and I fell to the ground once more. Spasms wracked my body and I flailed. My back arched in an impossible position, until I thought I might be cut in half.

A guttural noise sounded at the back of my throat. Claws seemed to tear me from the inside out. Then *it* ripped free of my body like a child forced from the womb. The scent of rotten flesh and death gagged me as I watched the shadowy beast materialize beside me.

Raul grabbed my arm and jerked me to him as he poured salt from a leather pouch tethered at his throat, creating a circle around us. The inky black creature hissed, staring at me through crimson eyes.

"*Mine …* " its raspy voice called, trying to reach for me.

A ring of fire blazed around us. The heat scorched my skin, and sweat dripped down my forehead, running down into my lashes.

The floor bent, dimpling as it tore open, leaving a large hole at the center of the room, a swirling mass of blackness and horror. The marble slabs came apart and tumbled into the abyss. Furniture and books were sucked inside, as the gusts picked up. The scent of sulfur hung in the air. Lucia's ashes skittered across the tiles, swirling like a sandstorm before they, too, disappeared into the deep chasm.

An invisible force dragged Kenrick's body with little regard over broken glass and furniture.

Kenrick!

A trail of blood wound behind him like a gruesome road as he spun faster, coloring everything he touched scarlet, and I knew there was no way to stop him. I covered my mouth and watched him vanish into the blackness of the pit.

The nefarious creature hovered closer, wings as dark as night unfolding behind it. *"Give me the girl."*

"No. You will not have her." Raul clutched me tight as the magical storm tried to tug me from the circle. My feet stumbled over each other as I gripped hold of him. The fabric of my dress stretched, and I was pulled to the edge of the fiery abyss. The hair on my arms singed when I drew closer to the flames and I wondered how much longer we could we hang on. Beneath my grasp, Raul's muscles flexed with the effort to hold onto me. "I won't let you go. I promise!" he shouted, his fingers bruising my arms.

The Beast's claws dug into the marble, leaving behind deep grooves as it tried to keep from being pulled into the hellish portal. A high-pitched howl shook the walls to the ground and the hole began to close.

A bluish light shone above us, and I glanced up to see Kenrick's ghost floating. I could see the ruined building through his transparency. He gave me a sad smile, then turned to Raul. "Take good care of her."

"I will."

He floated toward me and I felt the touch of cold wind upon my cheek as he stroked my face. "I'm sorry for failing you in our previous lives. I should've seen you for who you really were, and sensed that dark magic was at work. But you are free now and it's time for you to live your life, Brielle. Find your happiness and embrace it."

Then he was jerked away, back into the chasm as it vanished. The winds died down and silence enveloped the ruins of my aunt's estate. I swallowed hard, tears blurring my vision. He was gone. And this time, I knew he wouldn't be coming back. I wasn't sure how to feel. On the one hand, I was happy because for the first time since the curse was placed, I had a real chance at having a life. But on the other hand, I realized that without Kenrick's sacrifice I wouldn't be standing here. A part of me would always love him—after all, he was my first. However, I felt that at last, I could move on.

Raul's arms tightened about me and I spun to face him. "How are you alive? I thought I'd lost you forever."

He caressed my face, wiping back the wetness from my cheeks. "My element is fire, so during the stake-burning I used it to shield me and my grandmother and sneak us away in the smoke. We got back to the cottage, where we hid. But it left us drained for days, I couldn't move, eat, all I did was sleep. Grandmother is still there now, recovering. I'm sorry it took me so long to come for you."

"I missed you so much." I clung to him and cried.

He bent down so his forehead rested against mine. "Your curse is broken, now. You can live a normal life."

"At last."

His lips brushed mine and heat seared through me. His power surged around us, wrapping us together. We were bound. And nothing, not even death, could keep us apart.

The sound of horse hooves echoed around us.

"Stay here." He took his dagger from its sheath as he crept through the rubble.

My heart clamored as I stood in the darkness, waiting for him. Long minutes ticked away. Then I heard the crunch of footsteps approaching.

Raul maneuvered around the fallen rock, followed closely by Father Machai.

"Brielle," the priest said

Choked up, I rushed to him and let him hug me.

"Child, I feared I might not make it in time."

"I got to her right as Lucia showed up," Raul said. "The curse has been broken."

Father Machai smiled. "At last. Now, let's make haste to Fire Ridge. The Pope has given his orders for me to see Reynaldo punished. I've sent your grandmother ahead of us, just in case you were still imprisoned."

Oh God. Had she disappeared like the others who were bound by the curse?

We took the main road into Fire Ridge, which cut a day off our travels. When we arrived, the scaffold still stood at the center of town. Reynaldo and the magister stood at the front of it with a new prisoner.

My throat thickened. Where was Gram?

Father Machai climbed from the back of his horse and pushed through the crowd, with Raul and I close behind.

"This trial is hereby over," Father Machai's voice carried. With his robes swishing, he climbed the stairs until he stood front and center. "By order of the Pope, I, Father Machai of Dark Pines, servant of God, am here to hand out punishment against Reynaldo de Louwvre for his crimes."

Guards swiftly flocked to the stage, keeping Father Reynaldo and the magister from running.

"Reynaldo, you are being charged with blasphemy against the church. For the torture of Maria Farmer. For stealing from the coffers. For the murders of dozens of innocent people. Not only have you committed crimes within Fire Ridge, but you have left a trail of your sins from your home village of Dossier. Here, you entered into adulterous affairs and used the church to hide behind. The penalty for these crimes is death. And magister, since you have aided in the carrying out of many of these atrocities, your fate shall be the same as his."

"This is absurd. I'm a man of God," Father Reynaldo screeched as he attempted to step away from us.

Father Machai ignored his pleas. Gasps and whispers went through the crowd as they crossed themselves.

"Brielle Healer, I would ask that you name the punishment for these men."

I walked to the scaffold and stood before Father Reynaldo. My eyes bore into his as a look of disbelief passed over his features. "He should suffer the same death that Maria Farmer did. The Maiden."

Father Reynaldo blanched. He struggled to break free from his captors, sweat glistening off his rolls of fat. He screamed as they stuffed him inside the device. Justice had been served. Too bad, it wouldn't bring Maria or any of the countless others back. But it gave me satisfaction to finally see this evil man put to death. I turned and walked away, ignoring his shrieks for help.

I continued to search the crowd for Gram. But no one had seen her. A lump lodged in my throat. She was gone. Wherever she was, I hoped Gram found peace. I wiped my face with my dirtied sleeve. She'd spent so many years protecting me and hiding me. And to what avail?

"So you're still alive?" Sarah Weaver said from behind me. "Pity."

I spun on my heel, pulled my arm back, and punched her. Blood gushed out of her nose, and she cried in pain, holding her face.

"Better feel lucky, because if my curse wasn't broken, I would've torn out your throat with my teeth."

She stumbled, falling in a pile of horse manure that seeped into her dress. She shrieked, pulled herself to her feet, and rushed away sobbing.

"What took you so long to do that?" a familiar voice said.

I whipped around. "Gram? You're still alive … "

She wrapped me in her embrace and kissed my head. "Brielle, oh child. I've been worried."

"H-how are you still here? When the curse broke everyone disappeared."

"Raul." She smiled. "He once told me that a circle would protect me against dark magic. I guess he was right."

"So am I finally worthy of Brielle?" Raul appeared next to us. His dark hair brushed against his forehead, bronze skin glistening beneath the midday sun. A smile played at his lips as he hugged Gram.

She rolled her eyes. "Even if I tell you no, you two will still find a way to bend the rules."

"Gram." I laughed.

She pulled away from Raul, placing a hand on each of our arms. "You've always been worthy of Brielle in my eyes. You only needed to realize it yourself."

"Then I have your permission to marry her?"

My breath caught in my throat as I stared at Raul.

"Yes." She patted my hand, then went to join Father Machai who stood with his nephew.

Raul reached for me, tugging me into his arm. "I love you, Brielle Healer. I'll likely never be worthy of you and I know I'm not a knight or a lord, but I promise to always take care of you. Will you marry me?"

I cupped his face in my hands. "There has never been anyone more worthy. You saw me when no one else did. My heart belongs to you."

"Is that a yes?" He teased.

"Yes."

The church bells chimed in the distance and he leaned down, his lips capturing mine. "Happy birthday, Brielle."

The sun warmed my face and my heart soared. I'd finally made it to my seventeenth birthday. "Thank you."

"So I was thinking Father Machai could marry us tonight," Raul said, brushing strands of hair out of my face.

I smiled. "Why, afraid I'll change my mind?"

He chuckled. "No, but I've been waiting for this moment forever."

I caressed his face. "So have I."

"Then tonight?"

"Yes."

He squeezed my hand. "See, I told you we'd run off together and get married. You should always trust me."

"I wouldn't go that far," Gram snorted as she, Father Machai, and his nephew joined us.

I laughed with joy.

The curse was finally broken and I was free to live my life. In the end, Kenrick loved me enough to give his life. And Raul loved me enough to beat death.

Someday, people would sit around their campfires at night and tell stories about the Beast. The curse. And the legend of me.

Acknowledgements

First of all, I have to thank my lovely agent, Fran, for her undying support. I still remember the tearful phone calls over this book and how you championed me as a writer and my story. Thank you for helping to make the tough decision of finding this book a new home. Thank you for believing in me and my stories. There are no words to express my gratitude enough.

To Georgia, who has been so amazing to work with. Thank you from the bottom of my heart for allowing me to write the stories I love and for being a part of my writing journey. Working with you and your company is like being surrounded by family.

Cameron, thank you for all your editorial help as well. Thanks for catching all my crazy mistakes and making the story shine.

To my crit group YAFF, you amazing ladies read like 9 million versions of this book. Thank you for always giving your insight. Penny and Traci, I don't know how many emails and messages you two answered when I was freaking out about this book, but I'm guessing it was in the hundreds. LOL. Thank you for always being there for me, supporting me, and being voices of reason when my writerly madness takes over.

Rachel. What can I say? You're not only a great sister, but a great sounding board for me as well. Thank you for letting me bounce things off you and for telling me when something wasn't working. And thank you for encouraging me when I had to make tough decisions on this book and assuring me it was the right thing to do. Brainstorming sessions with you always spark my creativity.

To my amazing cover artist. This cover is just WOW. Thanks so much for making my book pretty.

And a shout out to my amazing coworkers who listen to all my story ideas and cover for me when I need to take time off for a book deadline—you ladies are amazing. Your encouragement always keeps me going. Love you guys—Heather, Tricia, Danie, Rachel, Wendy, and Cholle.

To my readers who have stuck with me through it all, thank you for your kind words, emails, and friendships.

Also a big shout out to my favorite kpop group 갓세븐(GOT7) for providing hours of music for my playlists. Thank you for making great music that helped inspire me to write.

Finally, to my husband and kids, as always you are my rock, my heart, and my loves. Thank you for always supporting me, always hyping me, and always having my back so I can do what I love.

REBEKAH L. PURDY

Rebekah L. Purdy was born and raised in Michigan where she spent many late nights armed with a good book and a flashlight. She's lived in Michigan most of her life other than the few years she spent in the U.S. Army. At which time she got a chance to experience Missouri, Kansas, South Carolina, and California. Rebekah has a business degree from University of Phoenix and currently works full time for the court system. In her free time she writes YA stories, anything from YA Fantasy to YA Contemporary Romance. Rebekah also has a big family (6 kids) she likes to consider her family as the modern day Brady Bunch complete with crazy road trips and game nights. When not hiding at her computer, Rebekah enjoys reading, singing, soccer, swimming, football, camping, playing video games, traveling, and hanging out with her family and gazillion pets.

OTHER MONTH9BOOKS TITLES YOU MIGHT LIKE

MAD MAGIC
STANLEY AND HAZEL
OF THE TREES
PRAEFATIO
YELLOW LOCUST

Find more books like this at http://www.Month9Books.com

Connect with Month9Books online:
Facebook: www.Facebook.com/Month9Books
Twitter: https://twitter.com/Month9Books
You Tube: www.youtube.com/user/Month9Books
Tumblr: http://month9books.tumblr.com/

NICOLE CONWAY

AUTHOR OF THE BESTSELLING
DRAGONRIDER CHRONICLES SERIES

1

MAD
MAGIC

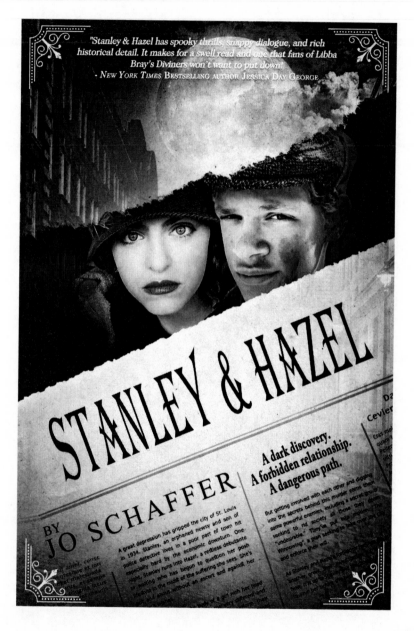

"Stanley & Hazel has spooky thrills, snappy dialogue, and rich historical detail. It makes for a swell read and one that fans of Libba Bray's Diviners won't want to put down."
- NEW YORK TIMES BESTSELLING AUTHOR JESSICA DAY GEORGE

STANLEY & HAZEL

BY JO SCHAFFER

A dark discovery.
A forbidden relationship.
A dangerous path.

A great depression has gripped the city of St. Louis in 1934. Stanley, an orphaned newsy and son of police detective lives in a poor part of town hit especially hard by the economic downturn. One night, Stanley runs into Hazel, a restless debutante whose posh world has begun to question her posh world in the midst of the suffering she sees. She's strong-willed, going without an escort and against her

But getting involved with each other and digging into the secrets behind this murder earns them some powerful enemies, including a secret brotherhood seeking to rid society of those they deem "undesirable." They've got the power, money, and winnowing a path before them, using their money and extort their way.

E. M. FITCH

ONLY SHE CAN HEAR
THE DEADLY WHISPER
OF THE TREES.

of the
TREES

BOOK 1 IN THE PRAEFATIO SERIES

PRAEFATIO

A NOVEL

*"This is teen fantasy at its most entertaining,
most heartbreaking, most compelling. Highly recommended."* -Jonathan Maberry,
New York Times bestselling author of ROT & RUIN and FIRE & ASH

GEORGIA McBRIDE

Neither quick fists nor nimble feet can save Selene Flood, a fighter of preternatural talent, from the forces of New Canaan, the most ruthless and powerful of the despotic kingdoms around.

YELLOW LOCUST

JUSTIN JO

CPSIA information can be obtained
at www.ICGtesting.com
Printed in the USA
FFOW02n0815210618
47150030-49734FF